You're a knockout, CHARLIE BROWN

by Charles M. Schulz

Selected Cartoons from
BY SUPPER POSSESSED

FAWCETT CREST • NEW YORK

A Fawcett Crest Book
Published by Ballantine Books
Copyright © 1988 by United Feature Syndicate, Inc.
PEANUTS Comic Strips: © 1986 by United Feature Syndicate, Inc.

All rights reserved under International and Pan-American Copyright Conventions. Published in the United States by Ballantine Books, a division of Random House, Inc., New York, and simultaneously in Canada by Random House of Canada Limited, Toronto

No part of this book may be reproduced in any form or by any means without permission of the publisher.

Library of Congress Catalog Card Number: 89-91123

ISBN 0-449-21730-2

This book comprises selected cartoons of BY SUPPER POSSESSED and is reprinted by arrangement with Pharos Books.

Manufactured in the United States of America

First Ballantine Books Edition: July 1989

You're a knockout, CHARLIE BROWN

PEANUTS© 1986 United Feature Syndicate, Inc.

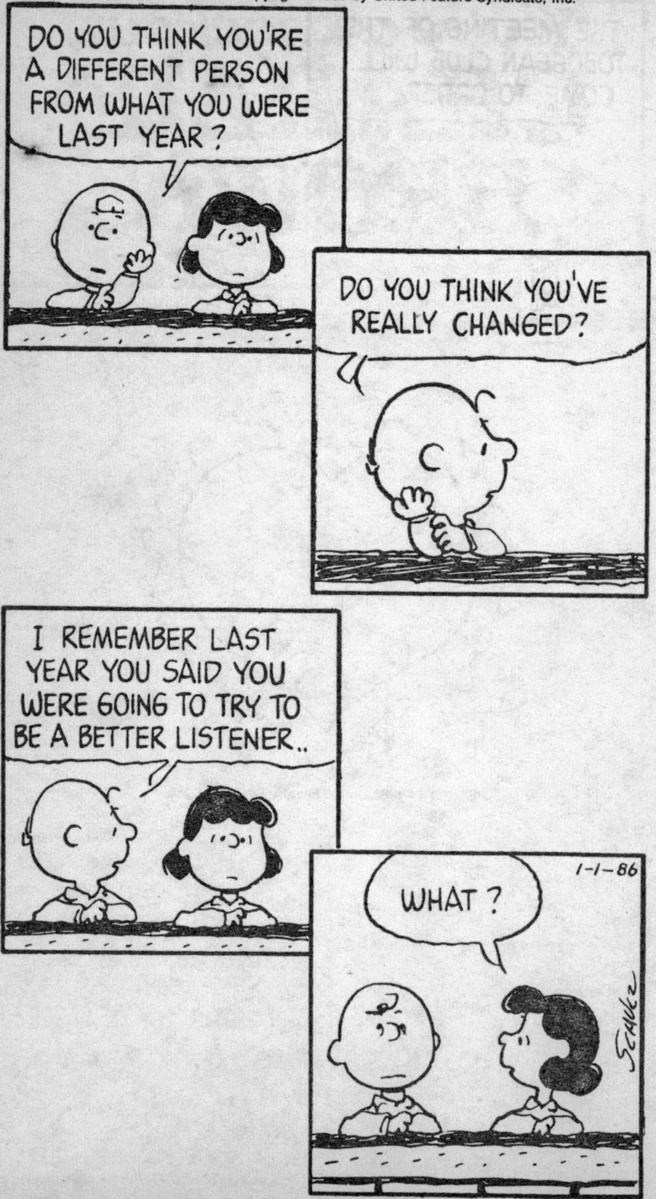
DO YOU THINK YOU'RE A DIFFERENT PERSON FROM WHAT YOU WERE LAST YEAR ?
DO YOU THINK YOU'VE REALLY CHANGED?
I REMEMBER LAST YEAR YOU SAID YOU WERE GOING TO TRY TO BE A BETTER LISTENER..
1-1-86
WHAT ?
SCHULZ

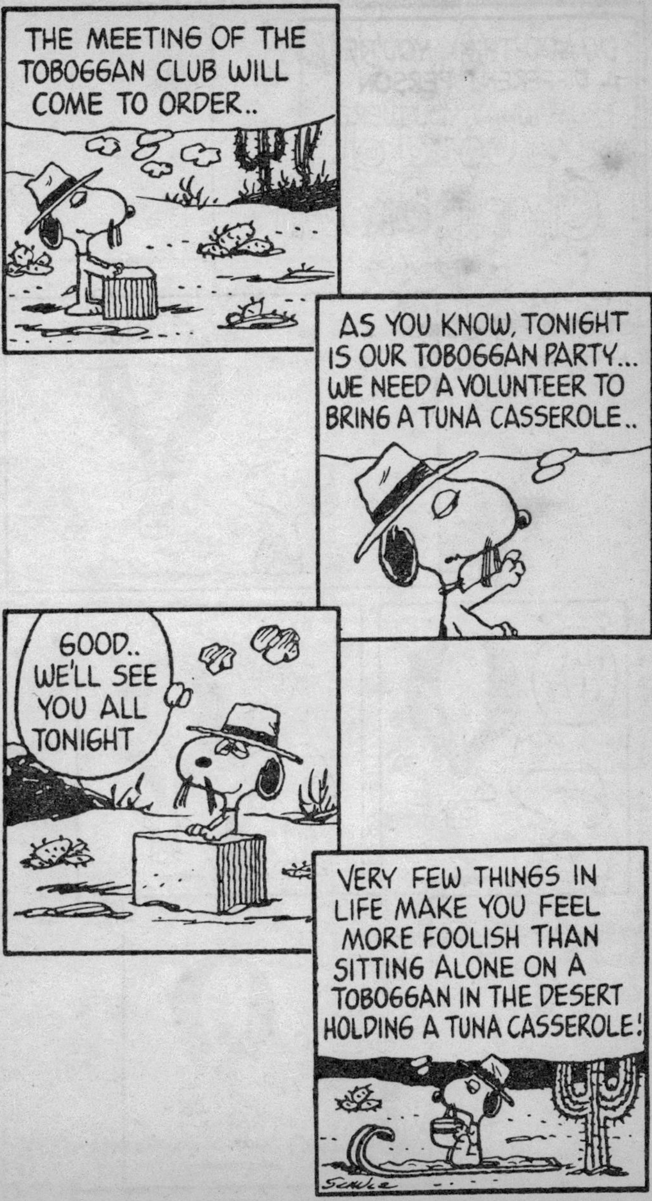
THE MEETING OF THE TOBOGGAN CLUB WILL COME TO ORDER..
AS YOU KNOW, TONIGHT IS OUR TOBOGGAN PARTY... WE NEED A VOLUNTEER TO BRING A TUNA CASSEROLE..
GOOD.. WE'LL SEE YOU ALL TONIGHT
VERY FEW THINGS IN LIFE MAKE YOU FEEL MORE FOOLISH THAN SITTING ALONE ON A TOBOGGAN IN THE DESERT HOLDING A TUNA CASSEROLE!
SCHULZ

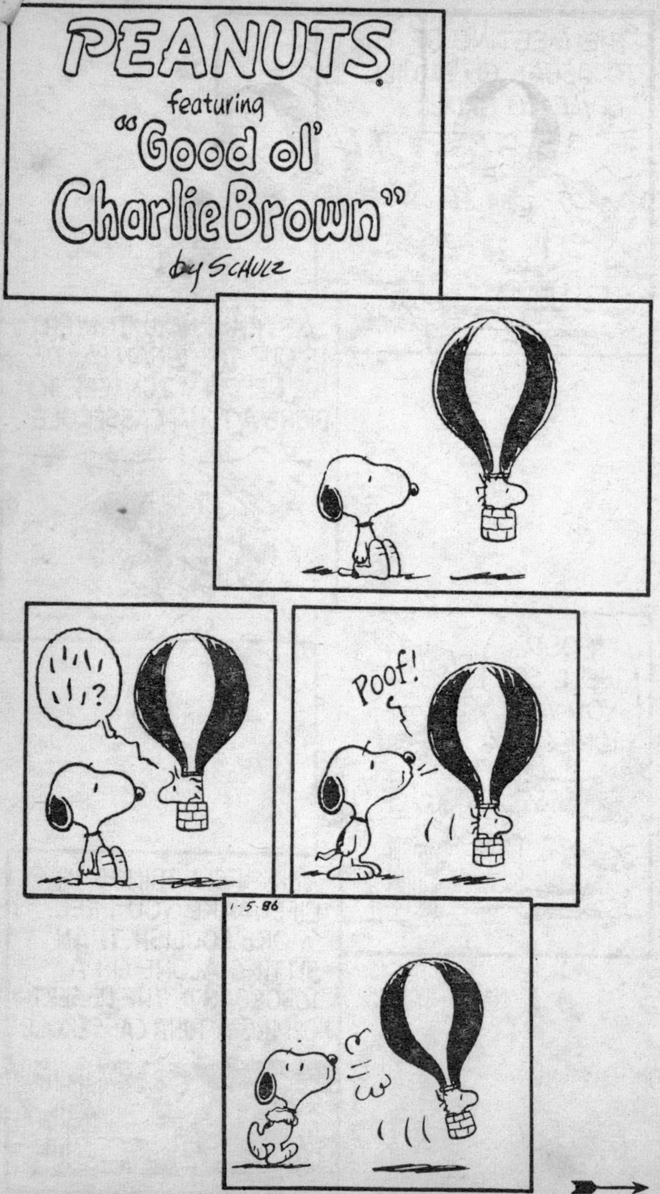
PEANUTS
featuring
"Good ol' Charlie Brown"
by SCHULZ
POOF!
1-5-86

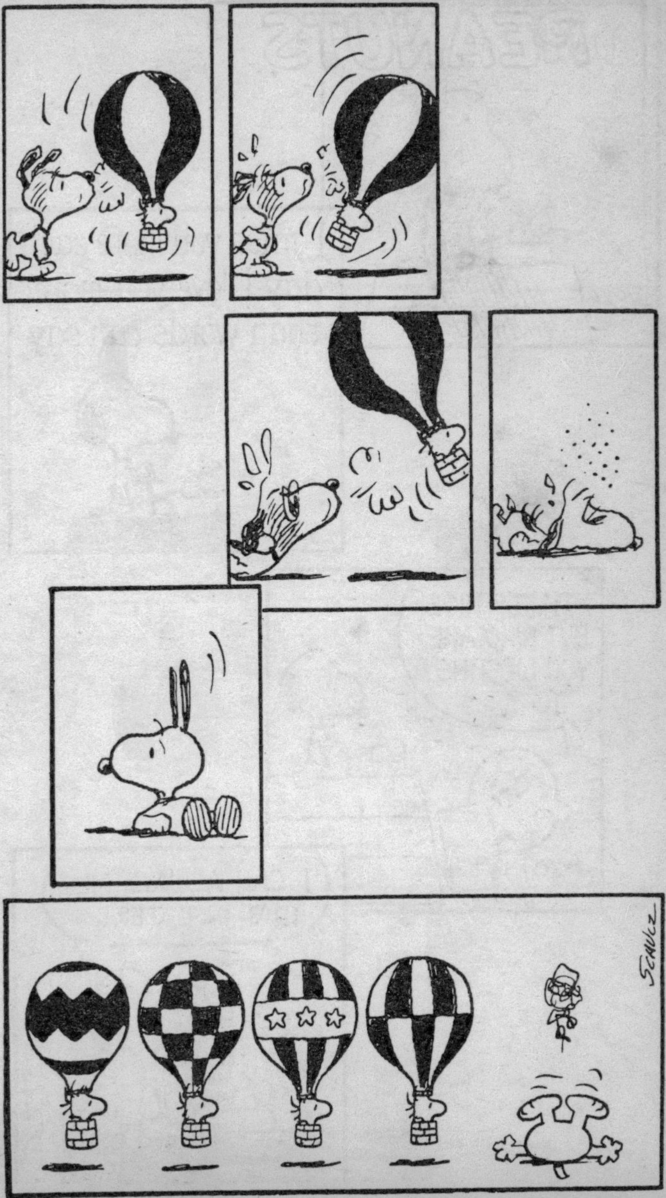
SCHULZ

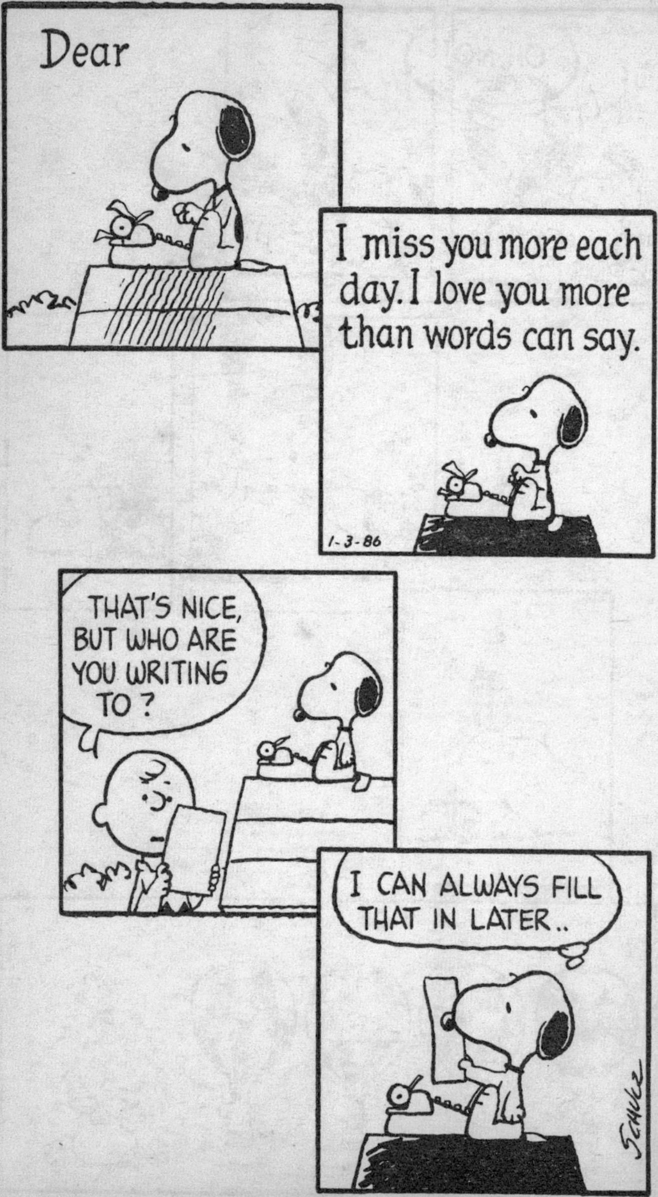
Dear
I miss you more each day. I love you more than words can say.
1-3-86
THAT'S NICE, BUT WHO ARE YOU WRITING TO?
I CAN ALWAYS FILL THAT IN LATER..
SCHULZ

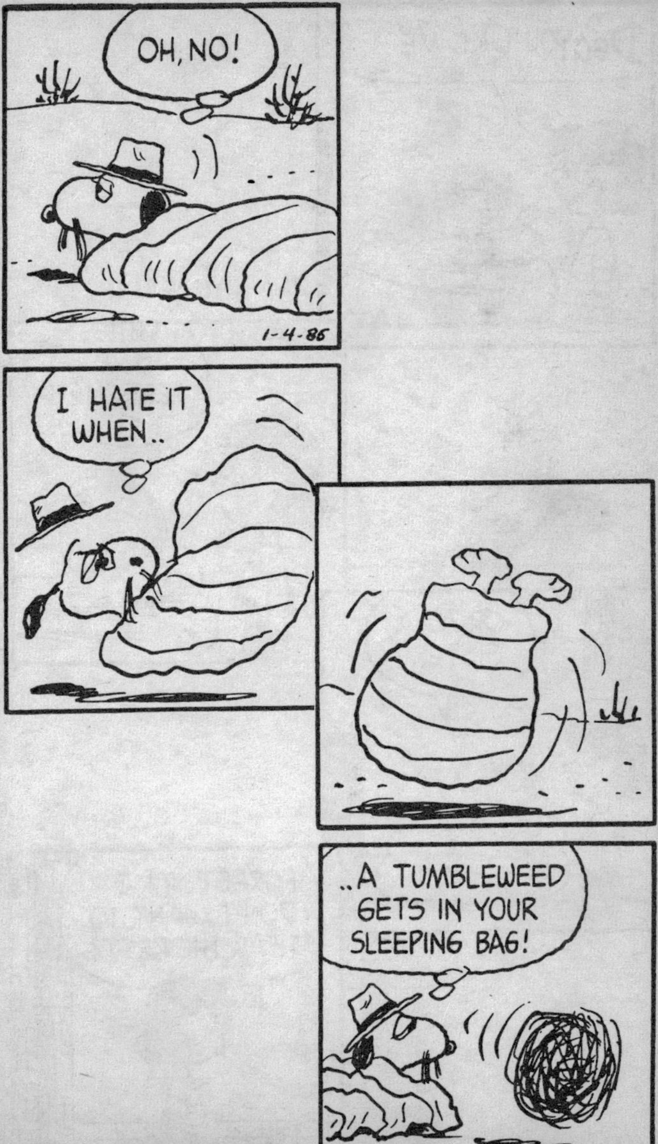
OH, NO!
1-4-86
I HATE IT WHEN..
..A TUMBLEWEED GETS IN YOUR SLEEPING BAG!
SCHULZ

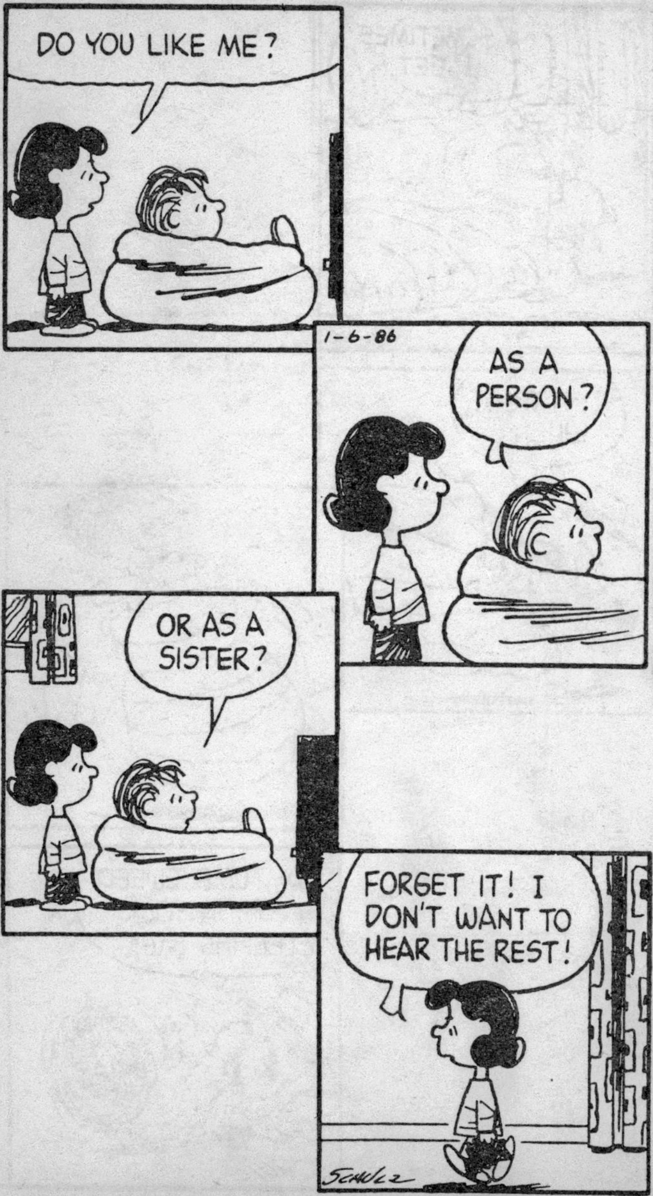
DO YOU LIKE ME?
1-6-86
AS A PERSON?
OR AS A SISTER?
FORGET IT! I DON'T WANT TO HEAR THE REST!
SCHULZ

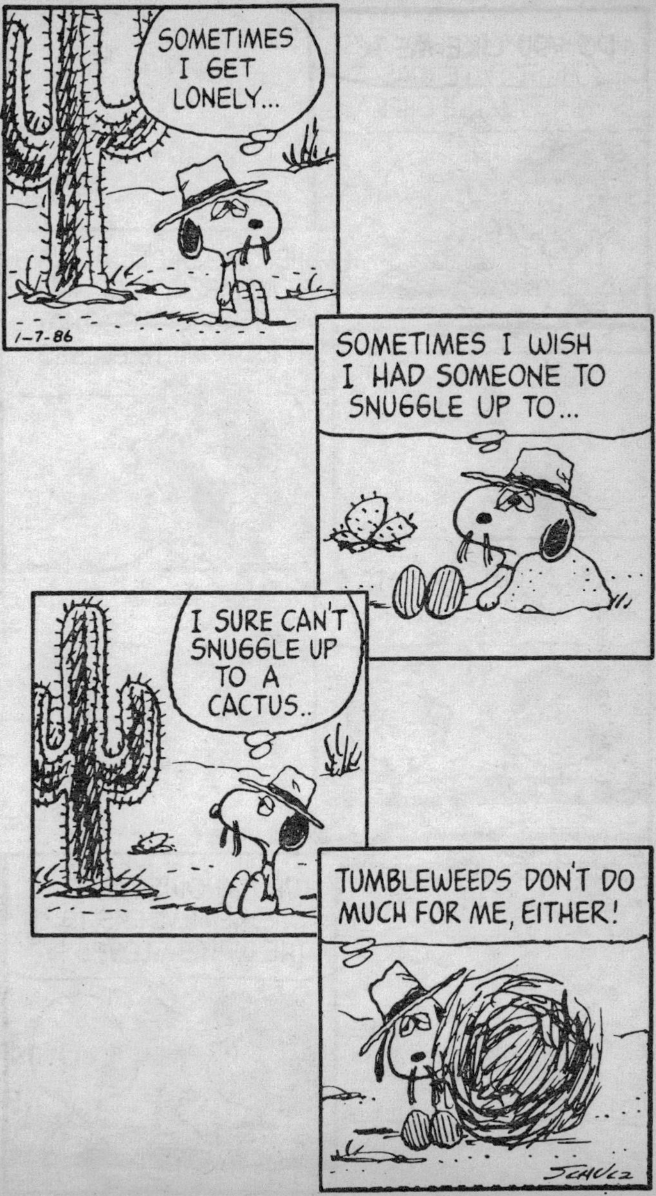
SOMETIMES I GET LONELY...
1-7-86
SOMETIMES I WISH I HAD SOMEONE TO SNUGGLE UP TO...
I SURE CAN'T SNUGGLE UP TO A CACTUS..
TUMBLEWEEDS DON'T DO MUCH FOR ME, EITHER!
SCHULZ

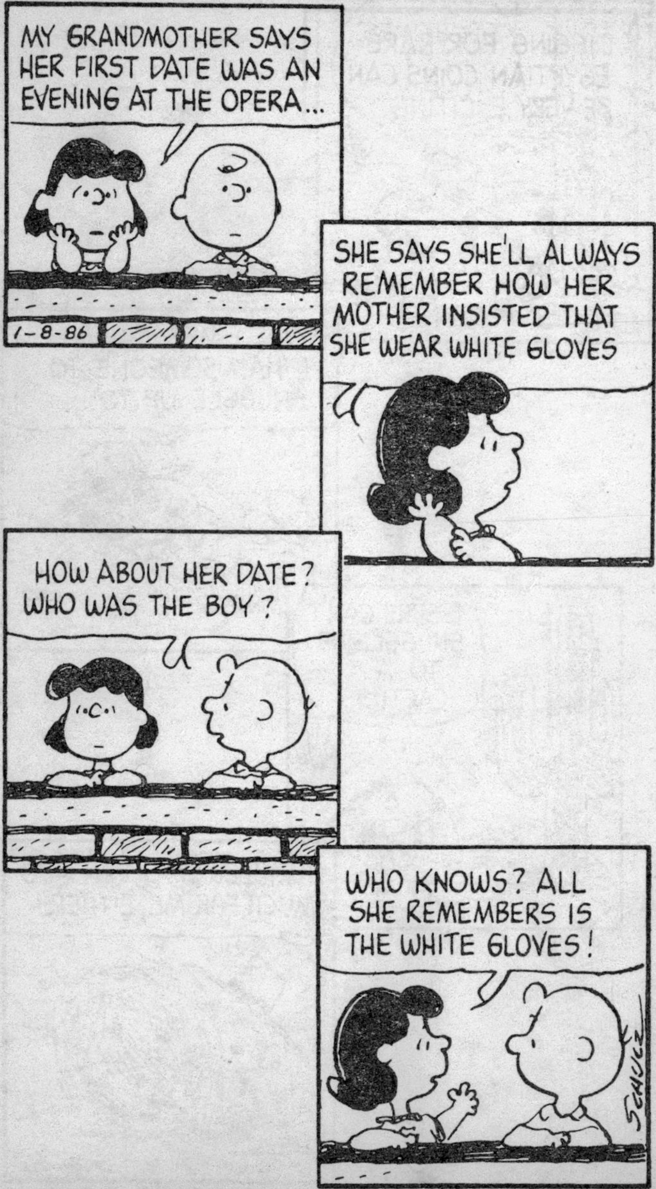
MY GRANDMOTHER SAYS HER FIRST DATE WAS AN EVENING AT THE OPERA...
1-8-86
SHE SAYS SHE'LL ALWAYS REMEMBER HOW HER MOTHER INSISTED THAT SHE WEAR WHITE GLOVES
HOW ABOUT HER DATE? WHO WAS THE BOY?
WHO KNOWS? ALL SHE REMEMBERS IS THE WHITE GLOVES!
SCHULZ

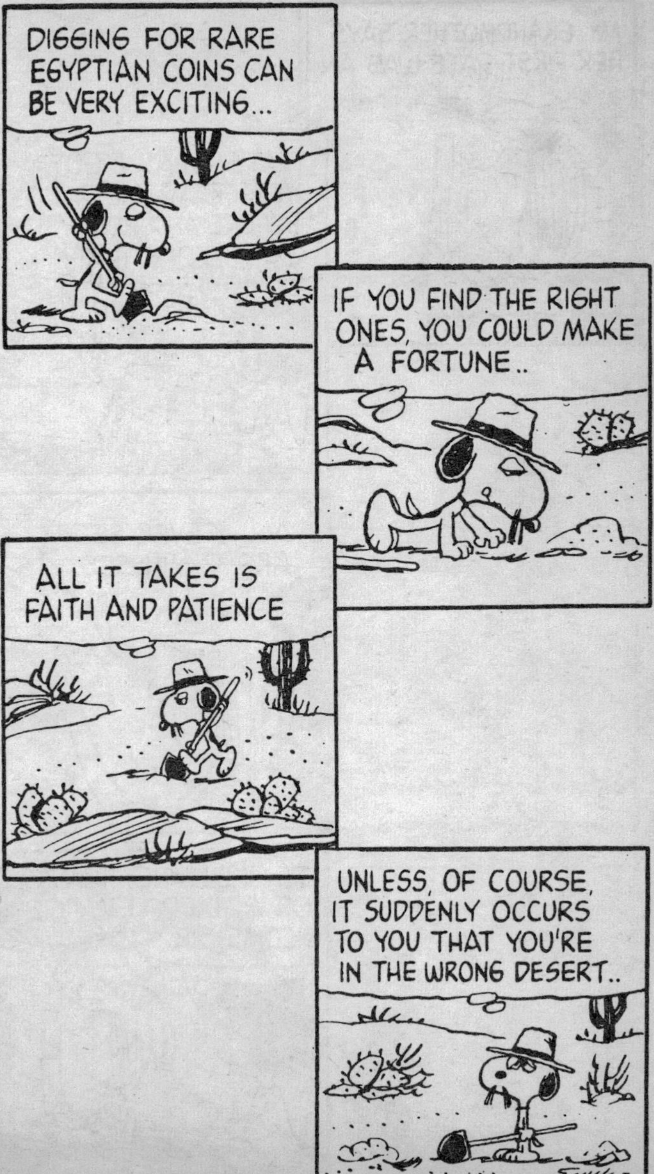
DIGGING FOR RARE EGYPTIAN COINS CAN BE VERY EXCITING...
IF YOU FIND THE RIGHT ONES, YOU COULD MAKE A FORTUNE..
ALL IT TAKES IS FAITH AND PATIENCE
UNLESS, OF COURSE, IT SUDDENLY OCCURS TO YOU THAT YOU'RE IN THE WRONG DESERT..
SCHULZ

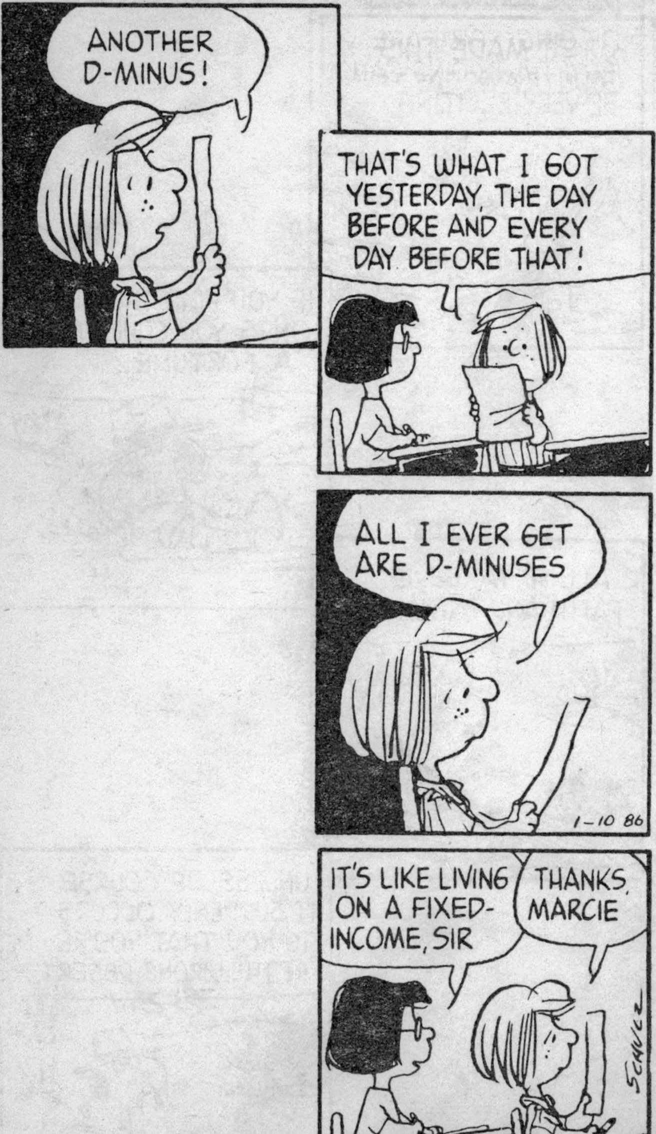
ANOTHER D-MINUS!
THAT'S WHAT I GOT YESTERDAY, THE DAY BEFORE AND EVERY DAY BEFORE THAT!
ALL I EVER GET ARE D-MINUSES
1-10 86
IT'S LIKE LIVING ON A FIXED-INCOME, SIR
THANKS, MARCIE
SCHULZ

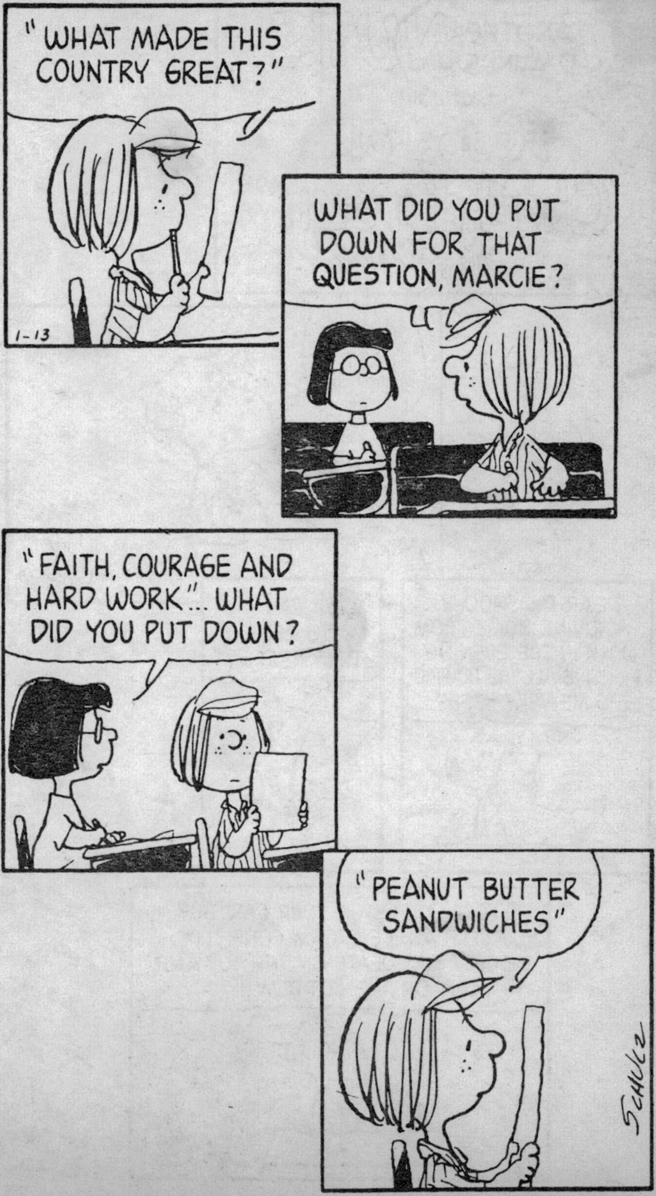
"WHAT MADE THIS COUNTRY GREAT?"
1-13
WHAT DID YOU PUT DOWN FOR THAT QUESTION, MARCIE?
"FAITH, COURAGE AND HARD WORK"... WHAT DID YOU PUT DOWN?
"PEANUT BUTTER SANDWICHES"
SCHULZ

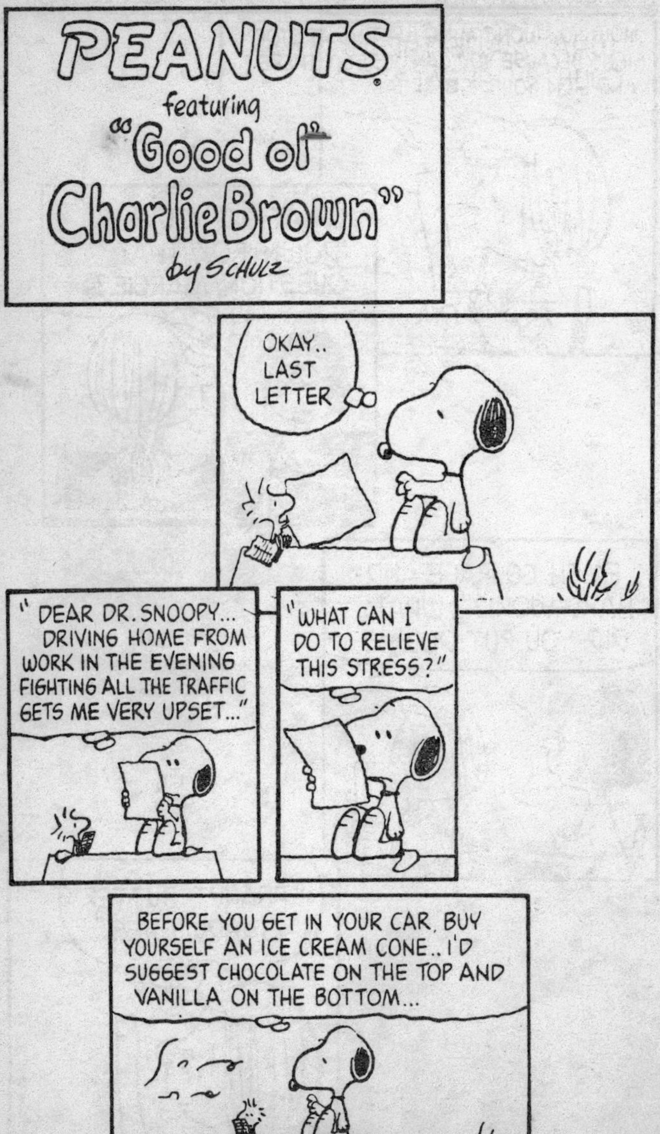
PEANUTS
featuring
"Good ol' Charlie Brown"
by SCHULZ
OKAY.. LAST LETTER
"DEAR DR. SNOOPY... DRIVING HOME FROM WORK IN THE EVENING FIGHTING ALL THE TRAFFIC GETS ME VERY UPSET..."
"WHAT CAN I DO TO RELIEVE THIS STRESS?"
BEFORE YOU GET IN YOUR CAR, BUY YOURSELF AN ICE CREAM CONE.. I'D SUGGEST CHOCOLATE ON THE TOP AND VANILLA ON THE BOTTOM...

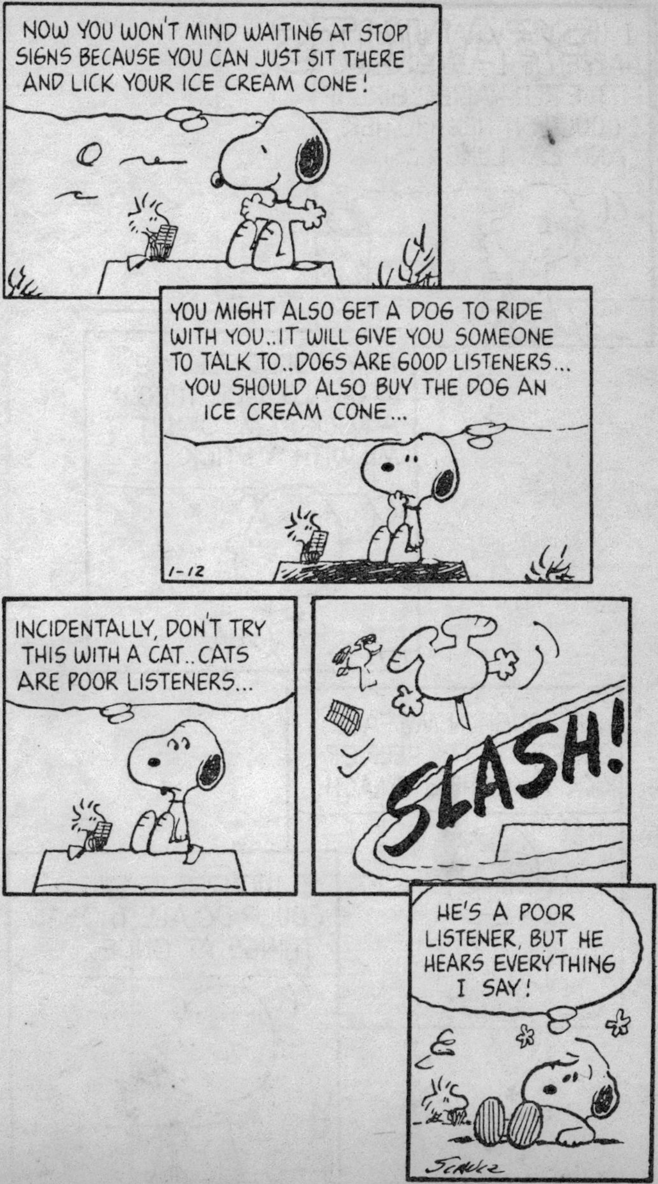
NOW YOU WON'T MIND WAITING AT STOP SIGNS BECAUSE YOU CAN JUST SIT THERE AND LICK YOUR ICE CREAM CONE!
YOU MIGHT ALSO GET A DOG TO RIDE WITH YOU..IT WILL GIVE YOU SOMEONE TO TALK TO..DOGS ARE GOOD LISTENERS... YOU SHOULD ALSO BUY THE DOG AN ICE CREAM CONE...
1-12
INCIDENTALLY, DON'T TRY THIS WITH A CAT..CATS ARE POOR LISTENERS...
SLASH!
HE'S A POOR LISTENER, BUT HE HEARS EVERYTHING I SAY!
SCHULZ

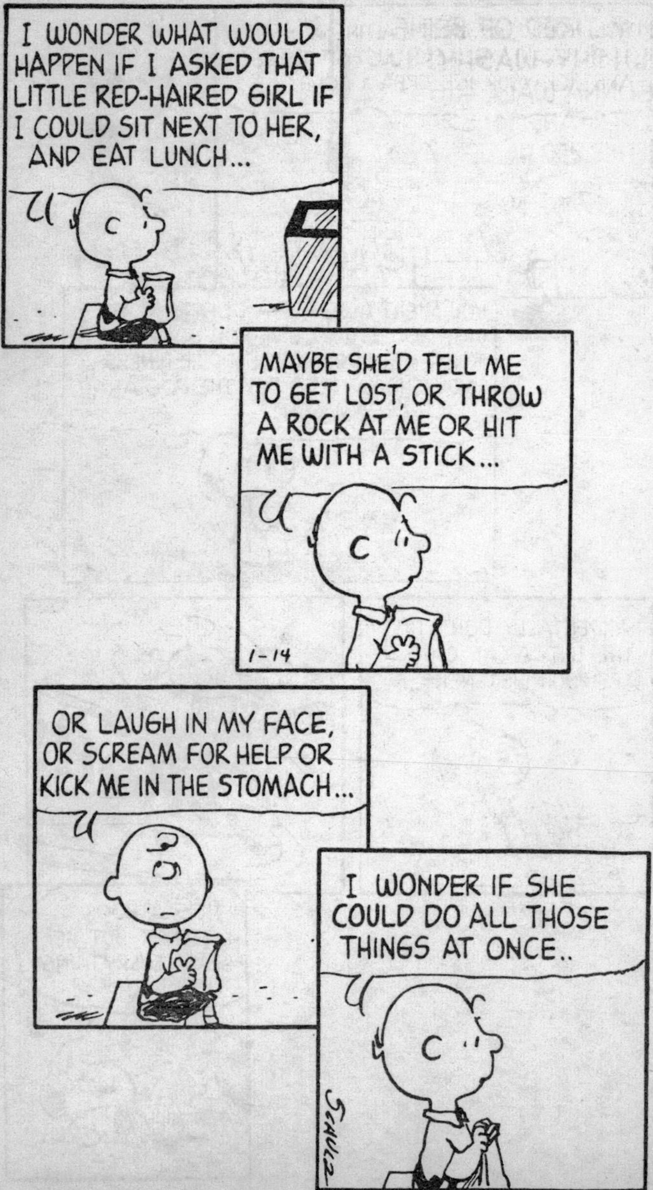
I WONDER WHAT WOULD HAPPEN IF I ASKED THAT LITTLE RED-HAIRED GIRL IF I COULD SIT NEXT TO HER, AND EAT LUNCH...
MAYBE SHE'D TELL ME TO GET LOST, OR THROW A ROCK AT ME OR HIT ME WITH A STICK...
1-14
OR LAUGH IN MY FACE, OR SCREAM FOR HELP OR KICK ME IN THE STOMACH...
I WONDER IF SHE COULD DO ALL THOSE THINGS AT ONCE..
SCHULZ

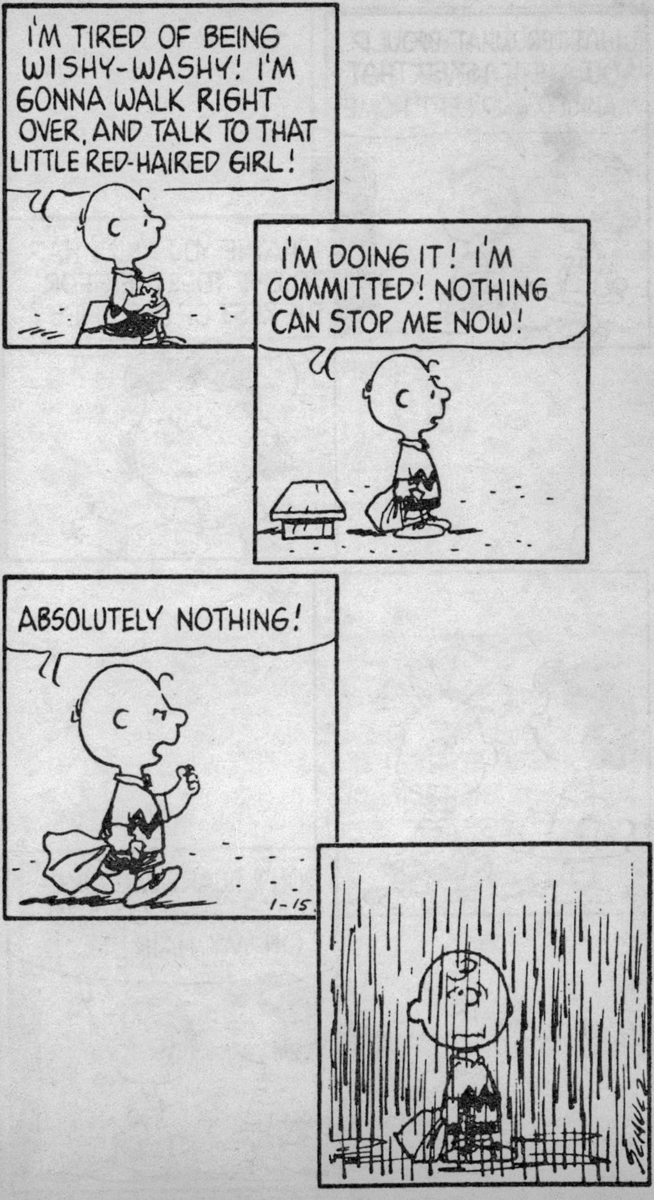
I'M TIRED OF BEING WISHY-WASHY! I'M GONNA WALK RIGHT OVER, AND TALK TO THAT LITTLE RED-HAIRED GIRL!
I'M DOING IT! I'M COMMITTED! NOTHING CAN STOP ME NOW!
ABSOLUTELY NOTHING!
1-15
SCHULZ

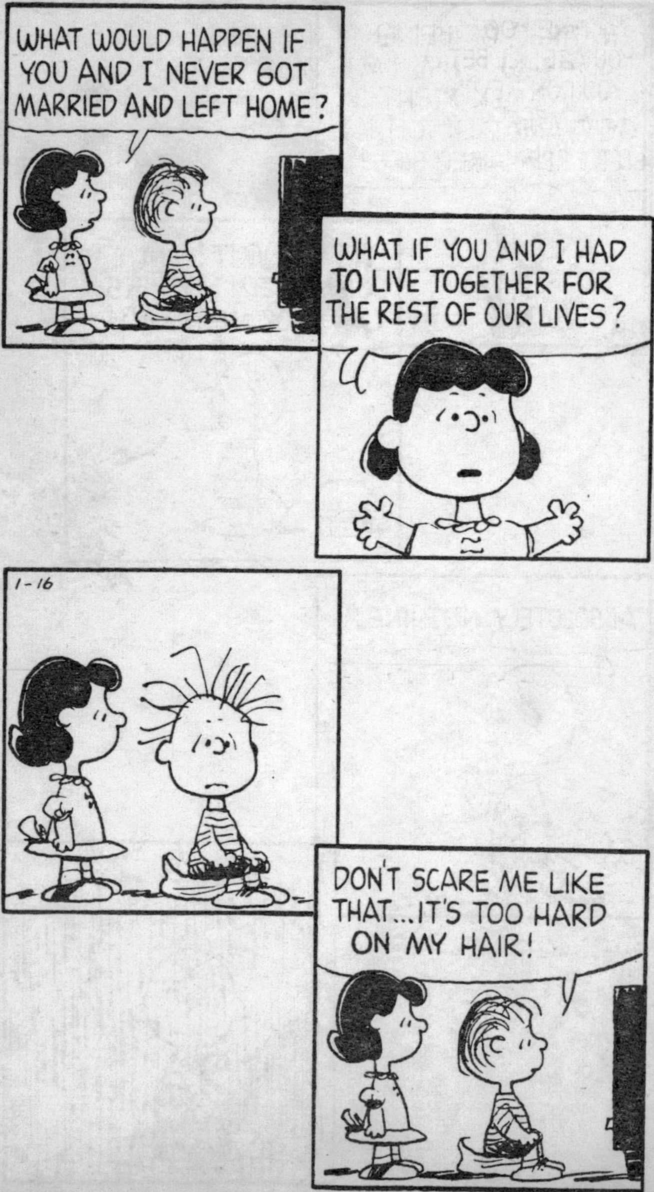
WHAT WOULD HAPPEN IF YOU AND I NEVER GOT MARRIED AND LEFT HOME?
WHAT IF YOU AND I HAD TO LIVE TOGETHER FOR THE REST OF OUR LIVES?
1-16
DON'T SCARE ME LIKE THAT...IT'S TOO HARD ON MY HAIR!

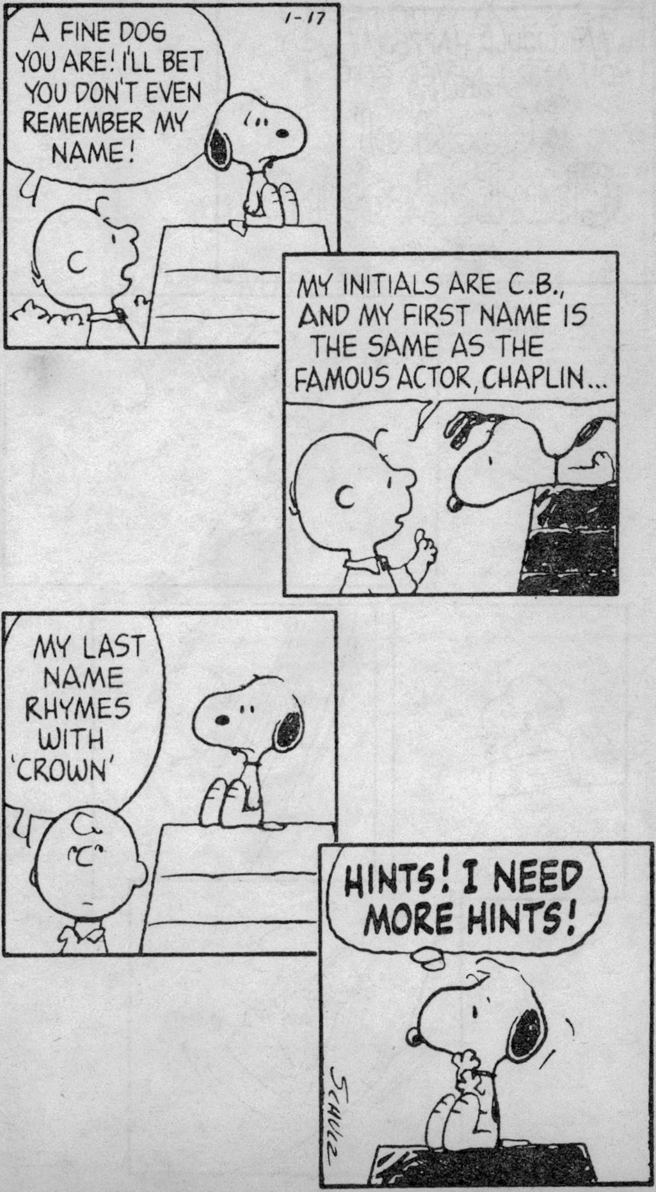
1-17
A FINE DOG YOU ARE! I'LL BET YOU DON'T EVEN REMEMBER MY NAME!
MY INITIALS ARE C.B., AND MY FIRST NAME IS THE SAME AS THE FAMOUS ACTOR, CHAPLIN...
MY LAST NAME RHYMES WITH 'CROWN'
HINTS! I NEED MORE HINTS!
SCHULZ

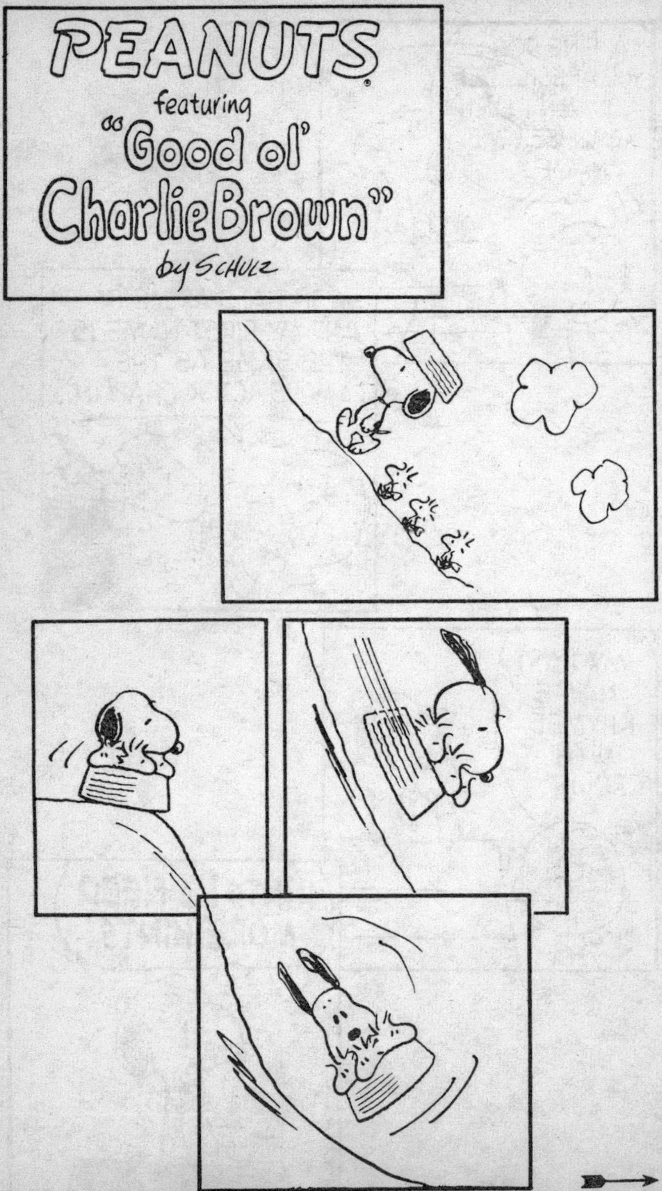
PEANUTS
featuring
"Good ol' Charlie Brown"
by SCHULZ

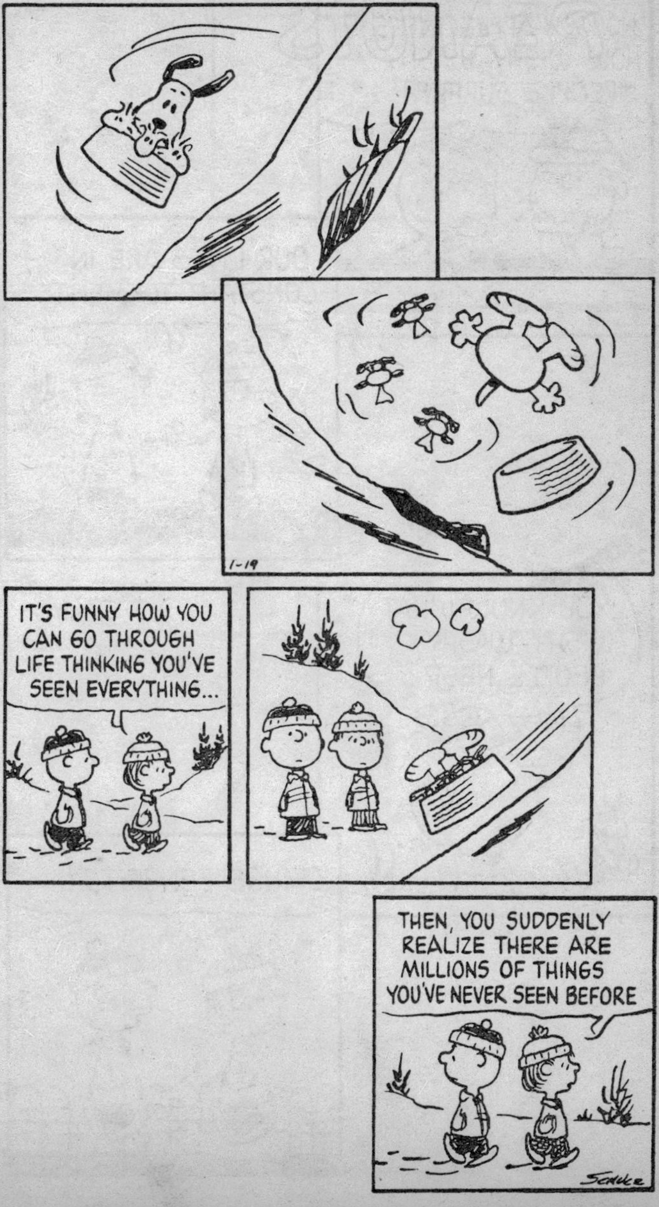
1-19
IT'S FUNNY HOW YOU CAN GO THROUGH LIFE THINKING YOU'VE SEEN EVERYTHING...
THEN, YOU SUDDENLY REALIZE THERE ARE MILLIONS OF THINGS YOU'VE NEVER SEEN BEFORE
SCHULZ

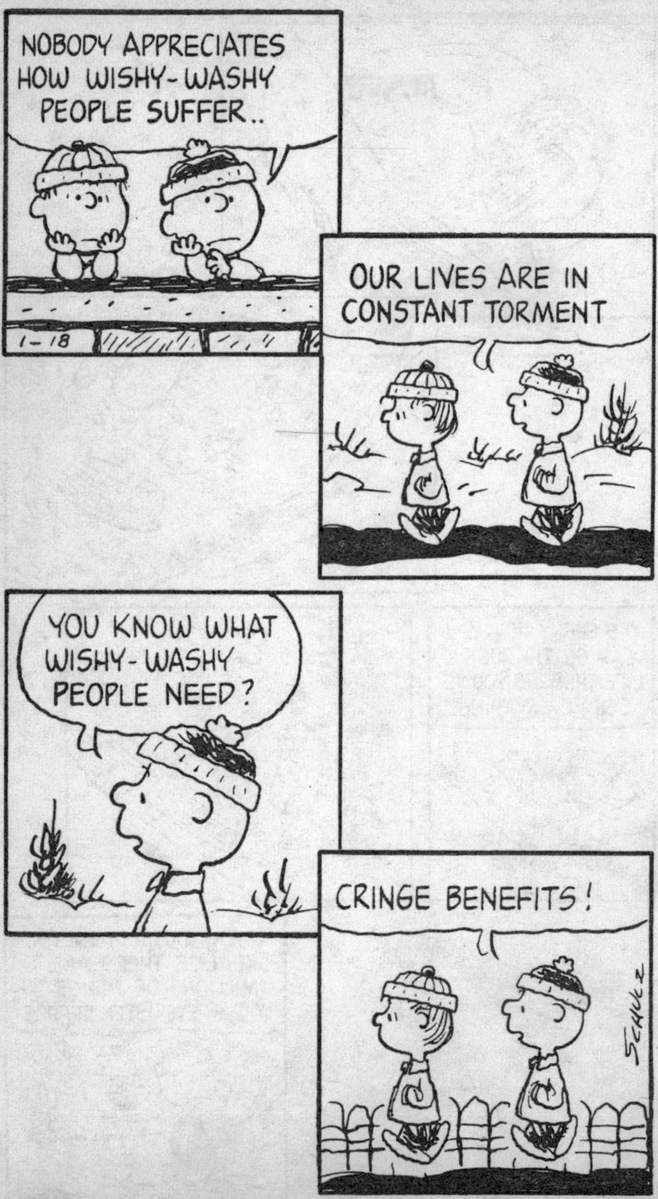
NOBODY APPRECIATES HOW WISHY-WASHY PEOPLE SUFFER..
1-18
OUR LIVES ARE IN CONSTANT TORMENT
YOU KNOW WHAT WISHY-WASHY PEOPLE NEED?
CRINGE BENEFITS!
SCHULZ

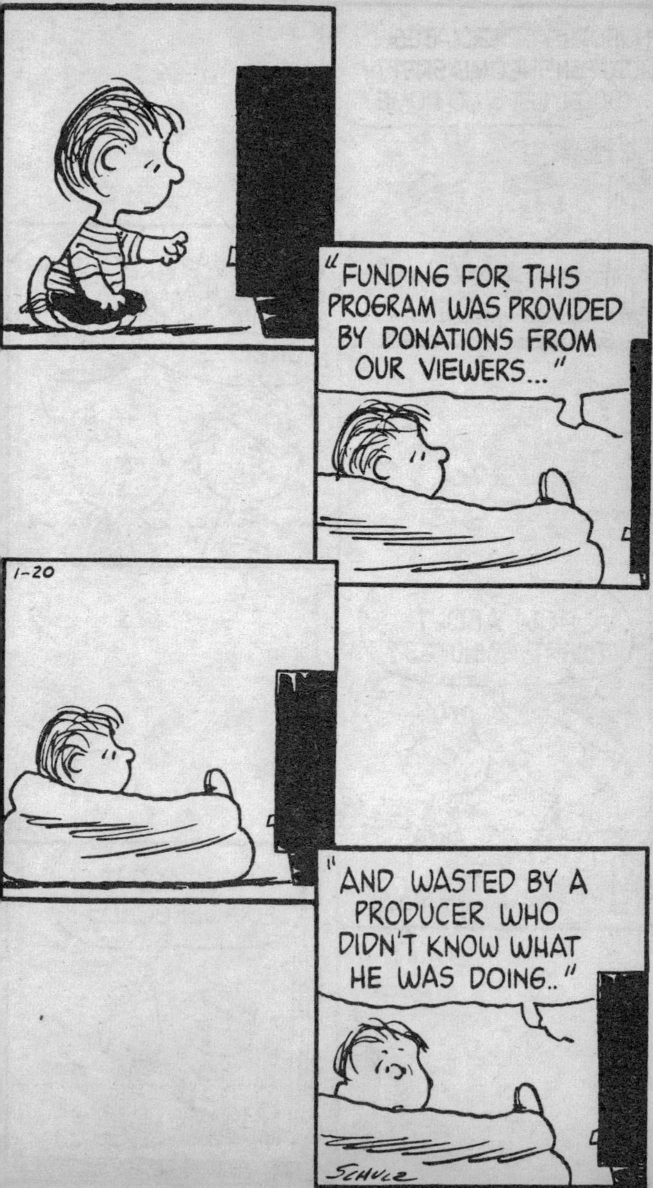
1-20
"FUNDING FOR THIS PROGRAM WAS PROVIDED BY DONATIONS FROM OUR VIEWERS..."
"AND WASTED BY A PRODUCER WHO DIDN'T KNOW WHAT HE WAS DOING.."
SCHULZ

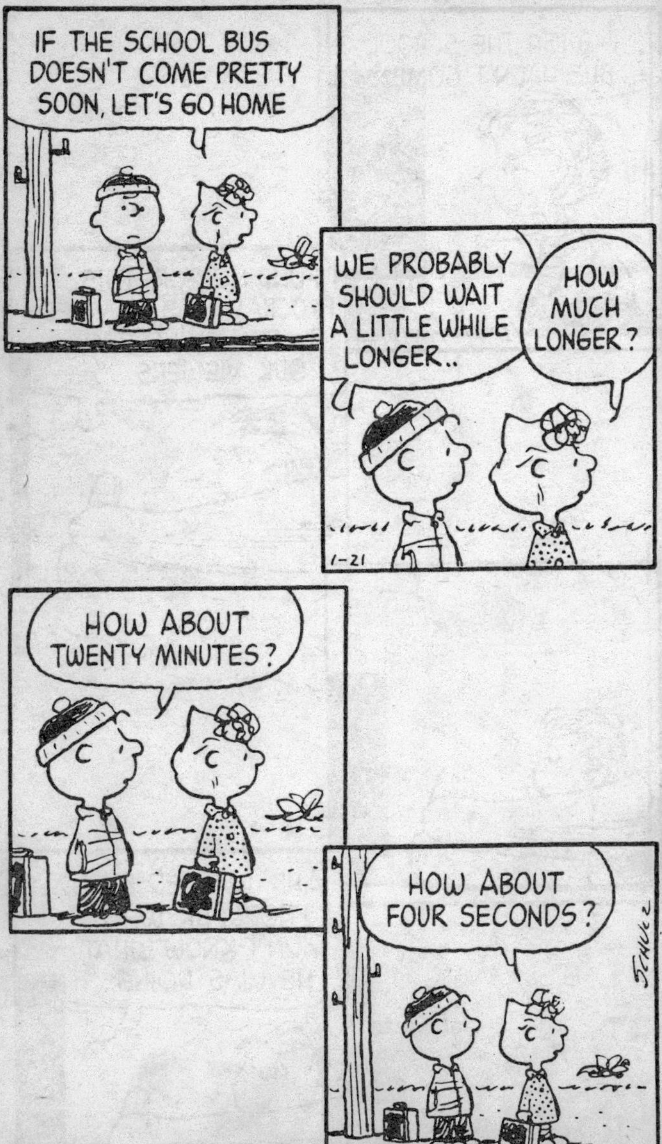
IF THE SCHOOL BUS DOESN'T COME PRETTY SOON, LET'S GO HOME
WE PROBABLY SHOULD WAIT A LITTLE WHILE LONGER..
HOW MUCH LONGER?
1-21
HOW ABOUT TWENTY MINUTES?
HOW ABOUT FOUR SECONDS?
SCHULZ

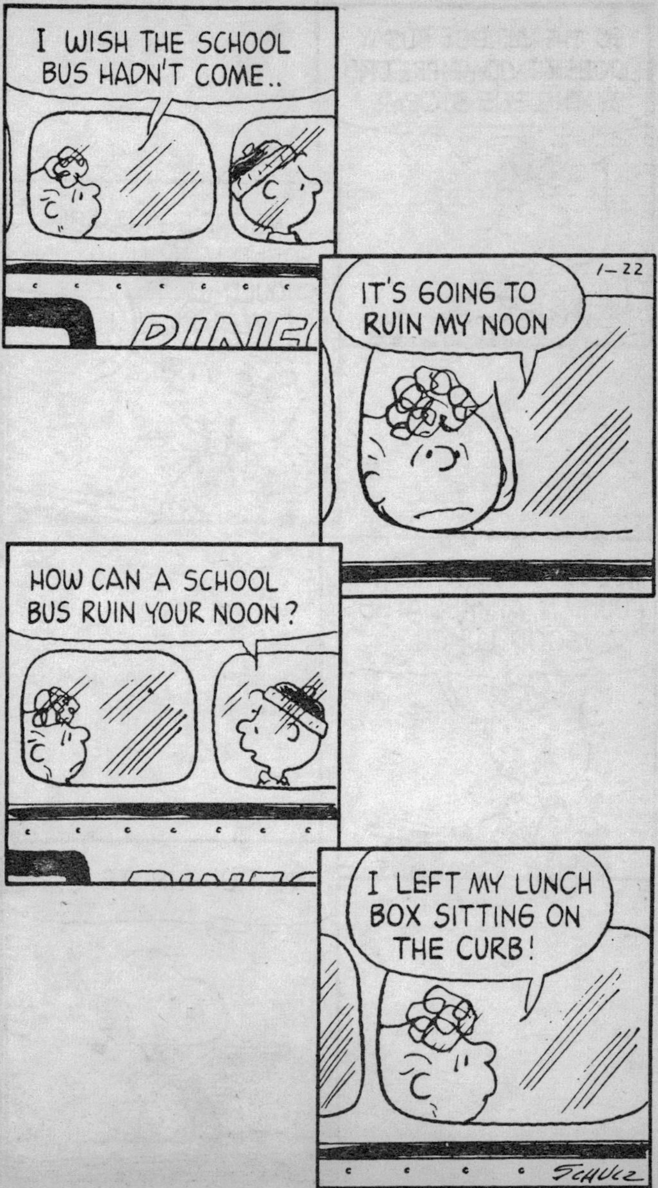
I WISH THE SCHOOL BUS HADN'T COME..
1-22
IT'S GOING TO RUIN MY NOON
HOW CAN A SCHOOL BUS RUIN YOUR NOON?
I LEFT MY LUNCH BOX SITTING ON THE CURB!
SCHULZ

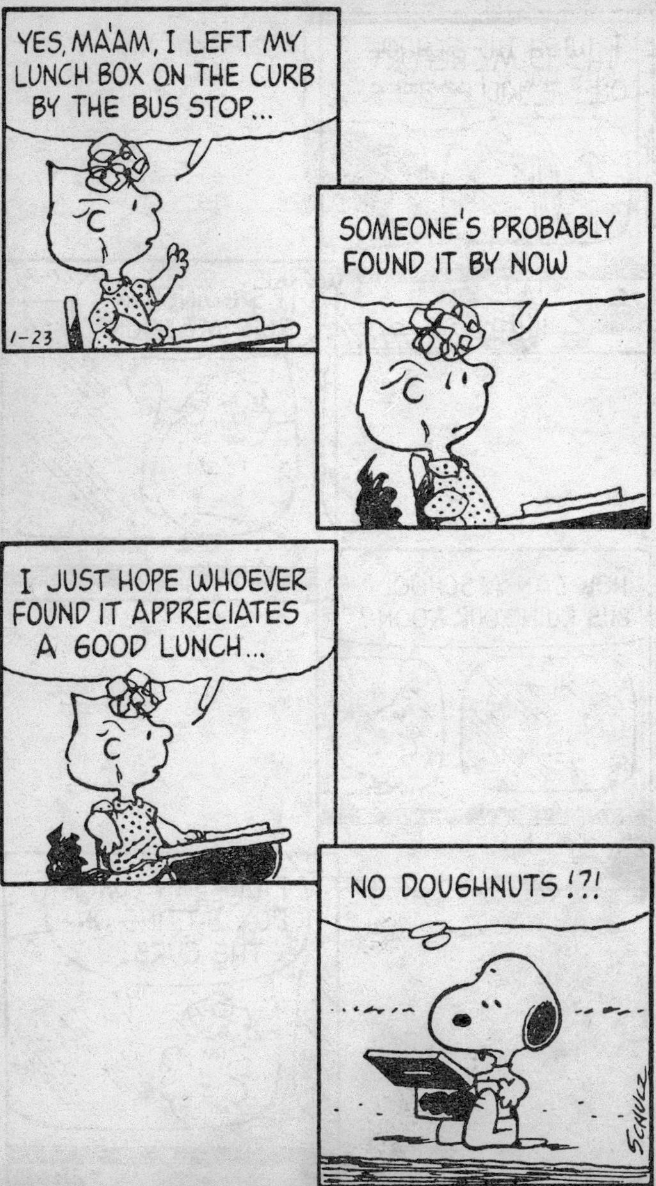
YES, MA'AM, I LEFT MY LUNCH BOX ON THE CURB BY THE BUS STOP...
1-23
SOMEONE'S PROBABLY FOUND IT BY NOW
I JUST HOPE WHOEVER FOUND IT APPRECIATES A GOOD LUNCH...
NO DOUGHNUTS !?!
SCHULZ

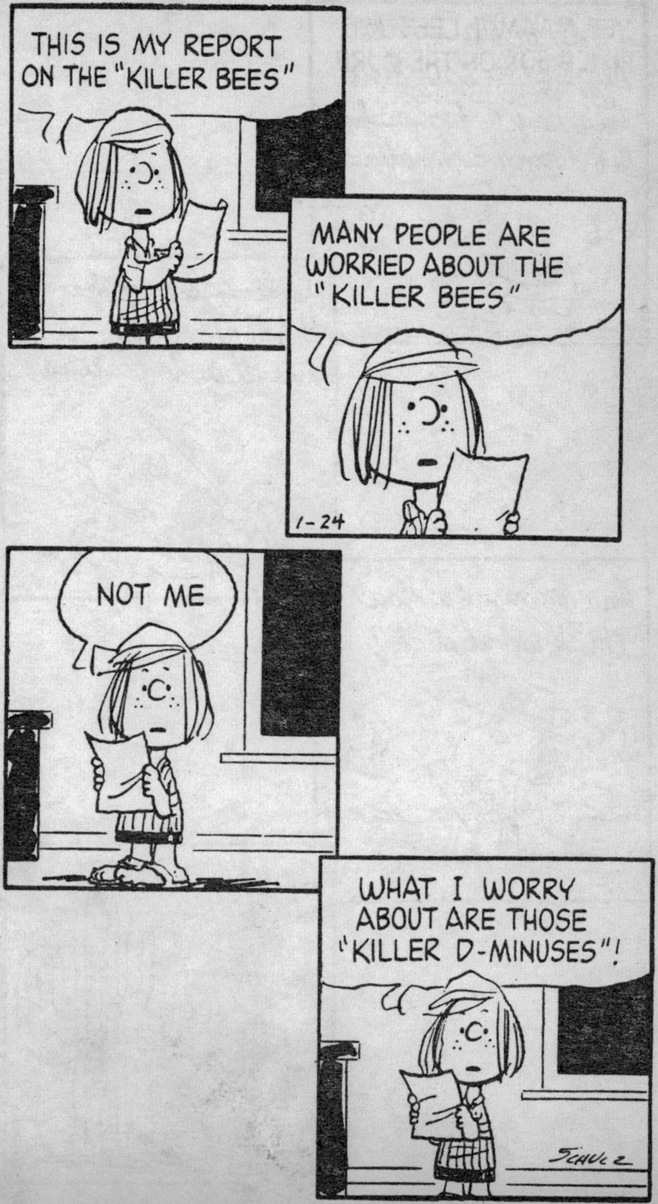
THIS IS MY REPORT ON THE "KILLER BEES"
MANY PEOPLE ARE WORRIED ABOUT THE "KILLER BEES"
1-24
NOT ME
WHAT I WORRY ABOUT ARE THOSE "KILLER D-MINUSES"!
SCHULZ

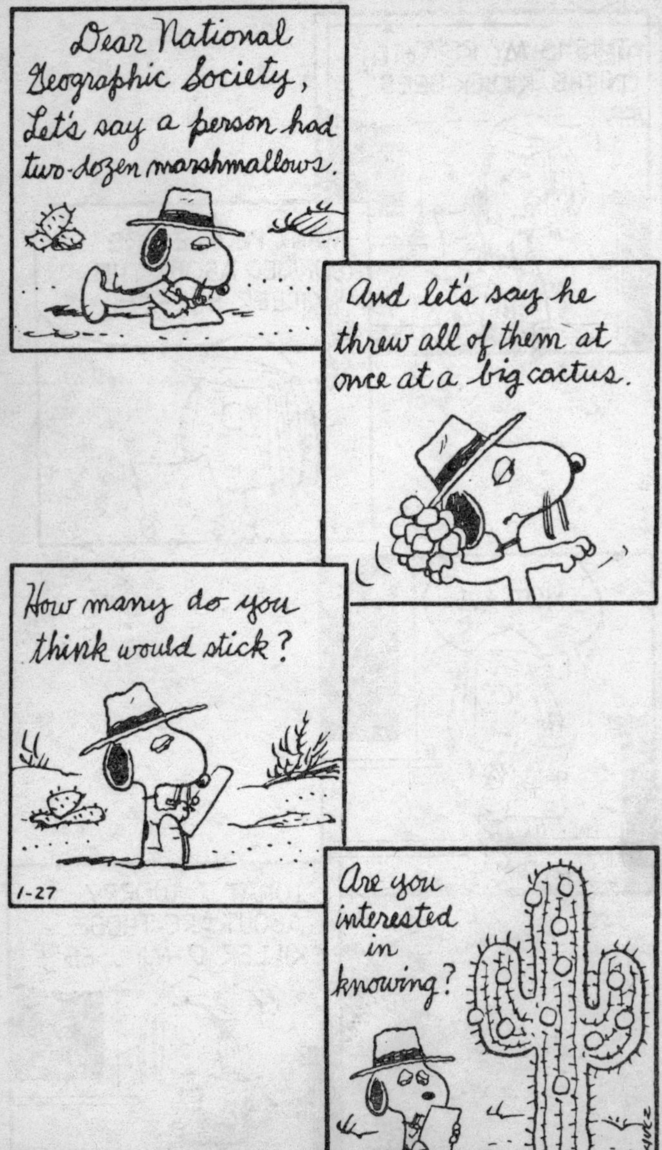
Dear National Geographic Society,
Let's say a person had two-dozen marshmallows.
And let's say he threw all of them at once at a big cactus.
How many do you think would stick?
1-27
Are you interested in knowing?
SCHULZ

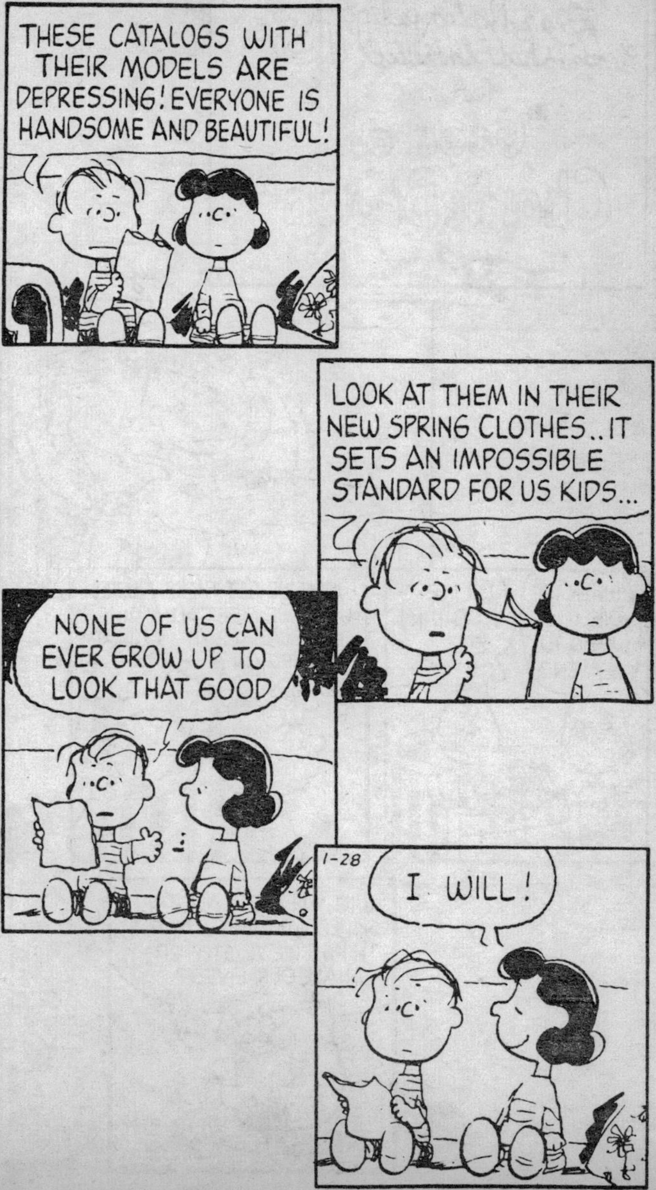
THESE CATALOGS WITH THEIR MODELS ARE DEPRESSING! EVERYONE IS HANDSOME AND BEAUTIFUL!
LOOK AT THEM IN THEIR NEW SPRING CLOTHES.. IT SETS AN IMPOSSIBLE STANDARD FOR US KIDS...
NONE OF US CAN EVER GROW UP TO LOOK THAT GOOD
1-28
I WILL!

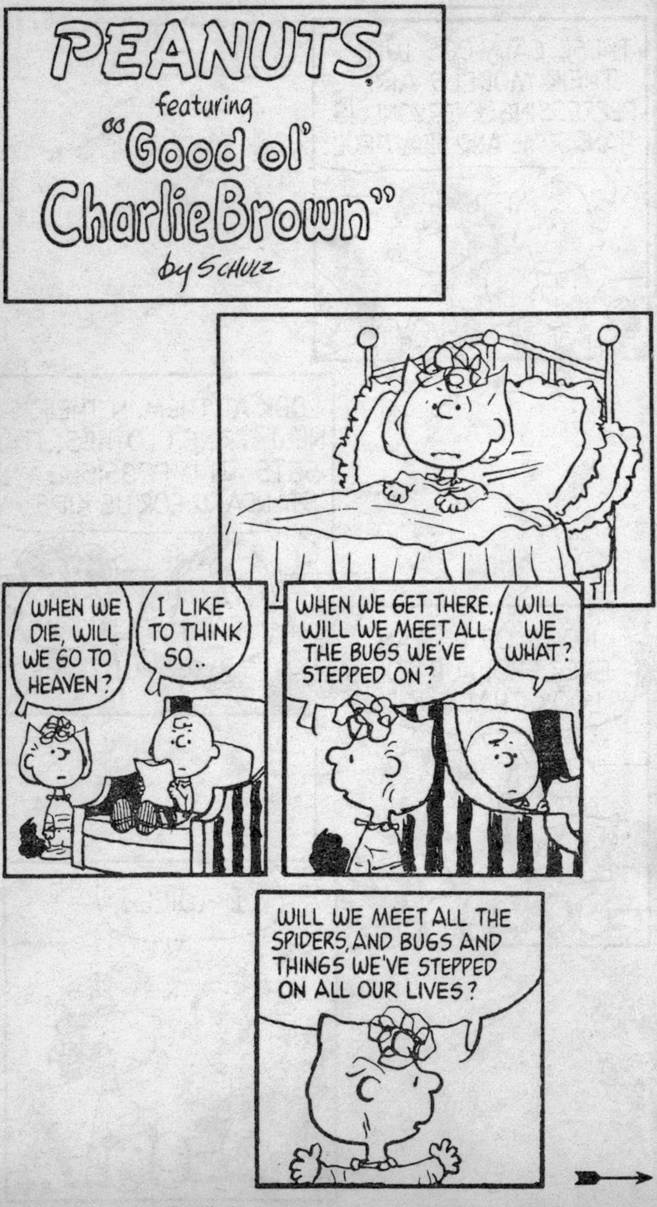
PEANUTS
featuring
"Good ol' Charlie Brown"
by SCHULZ
WHEN WE DIE, WILL WE GO TO HEAVEN?
I LIKE TO THINK SO..
WHEN WE GET THERE, WILL WE MEET ALL THE BUGS WE'VE STEPPED ON?
WILL WE WHAT?
WILL WE MEET ALL THE SPIDERS, AND BUGS AND THINGS WE'VE STEPPED ON ALL OUR LIVES?

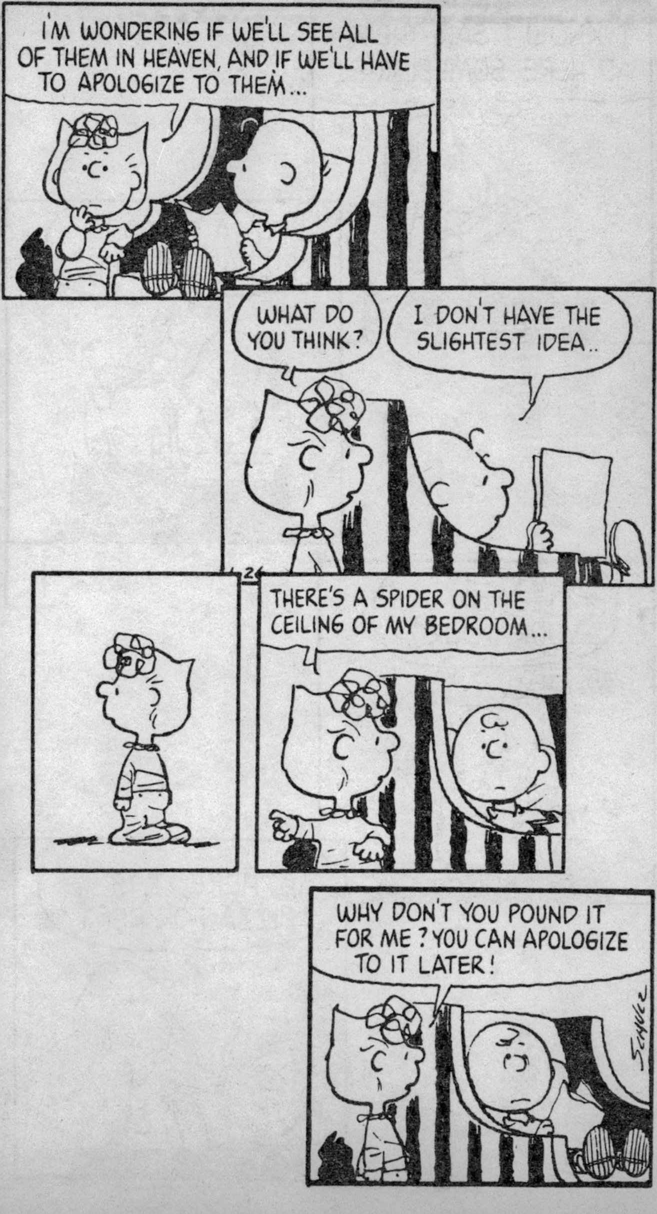
I'M WONDERING IF WE'LL SEE ALL OF THEM IN HEAVEN, AND IF WE'LL HAVE TO APOLOGIZE TO THEM...
WHAT DO YOU THINK?
I DON'T HAVE THE SLIGHTEST IDEA..
THERE'S A SPIDER ON THE CEILING OF MY BEDROOM...
WHY DON'T YOU POUND IT FOR ME? YOU CAN APOLOGIZE TO IT LATER!

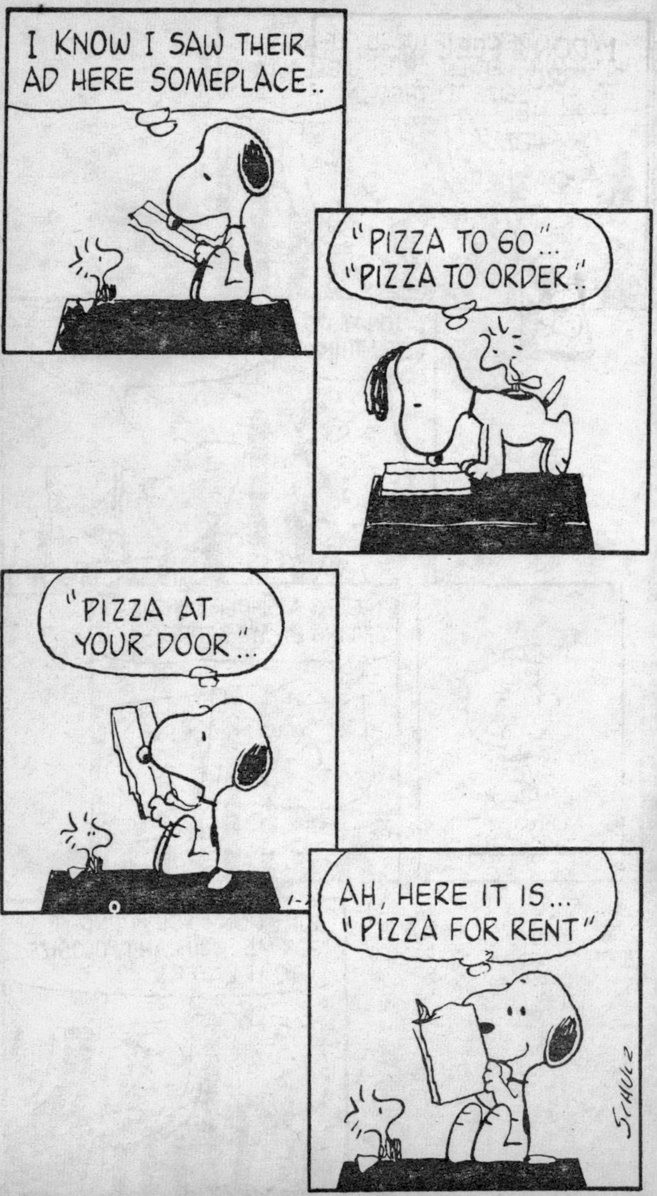
I KNOW I SAW THEIR AD HERE SOMEPLACE..
"PIZZA TO GO"... "PIZZA TO ORDER"..
"PIZZA AT YOUR DOOR"...
AH, HERE IT IS... "PIZZA FOR RENT"

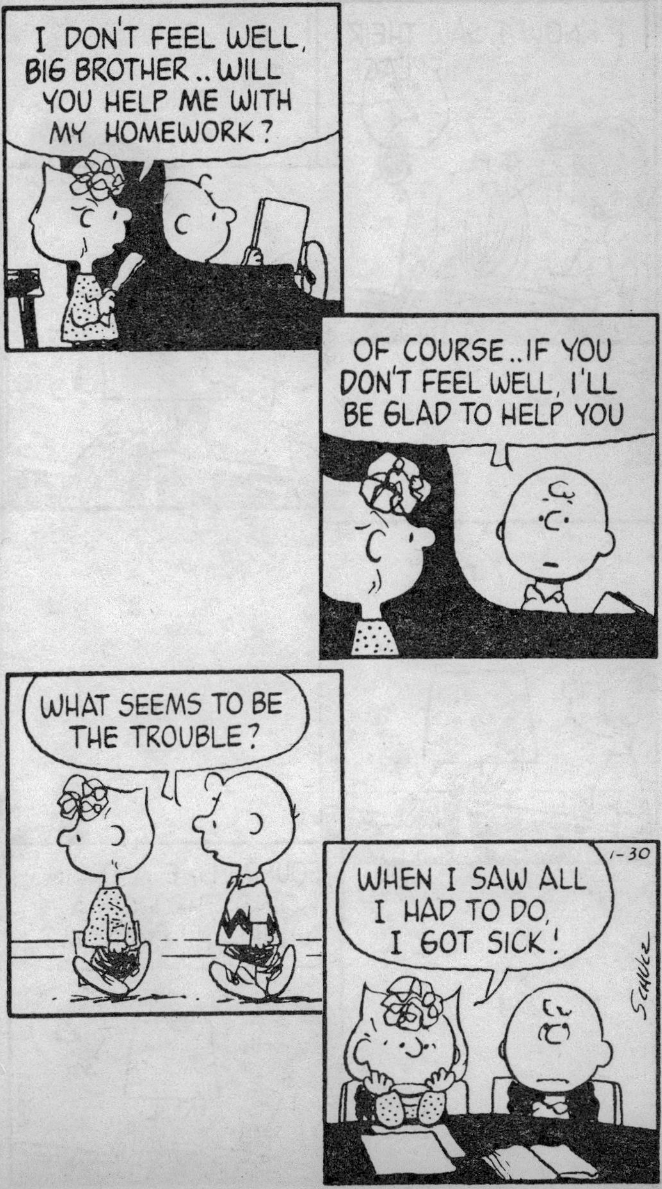
I DON'T FEEL WELL, BIG BROTHER.. WILL YOU HELP ME WITH MY HOMEWORK?
OF COURSE..IF YOU DON'T FEEL WELL, I'LL BE GLAD TO HELP YOU
WHAT SEEMS TO BE THE TROUBLE?
1-30
WHEN I SAW ALL I HAD TO DO, I GOT SICK!
SCHULZ

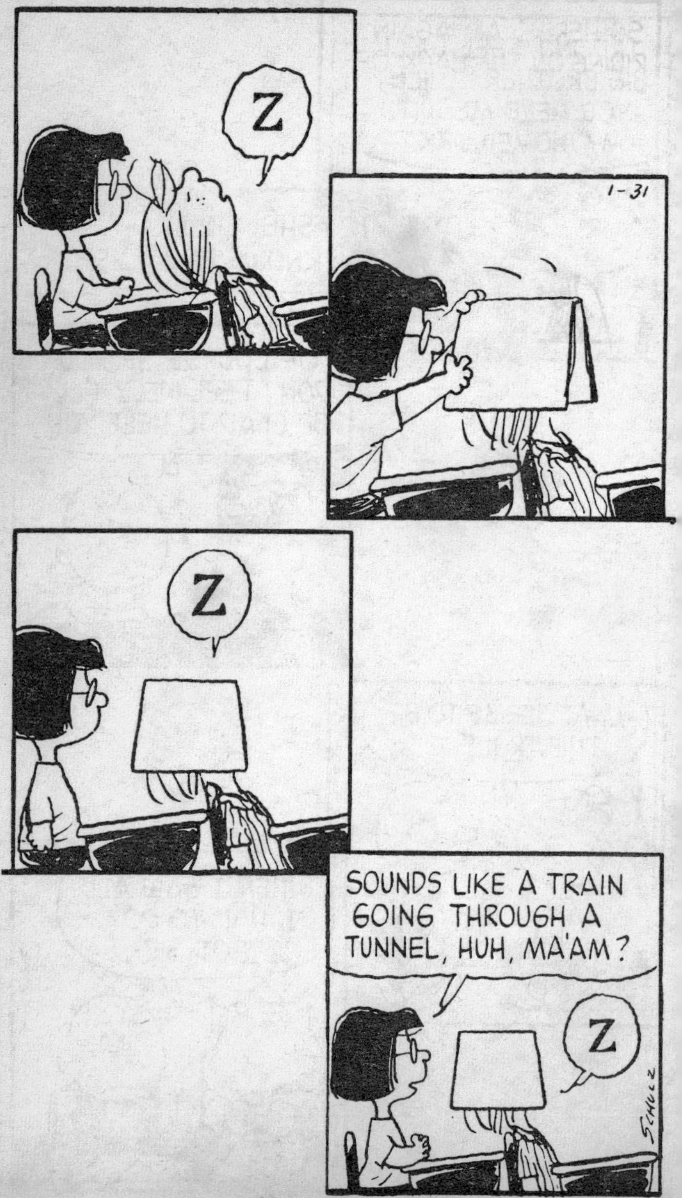
Z
1-31
Z
SOUNDS LIKE A TRAIN GOING THROUGH A TUNNEL, HUH, MA'AM?
Z
SCHULZ

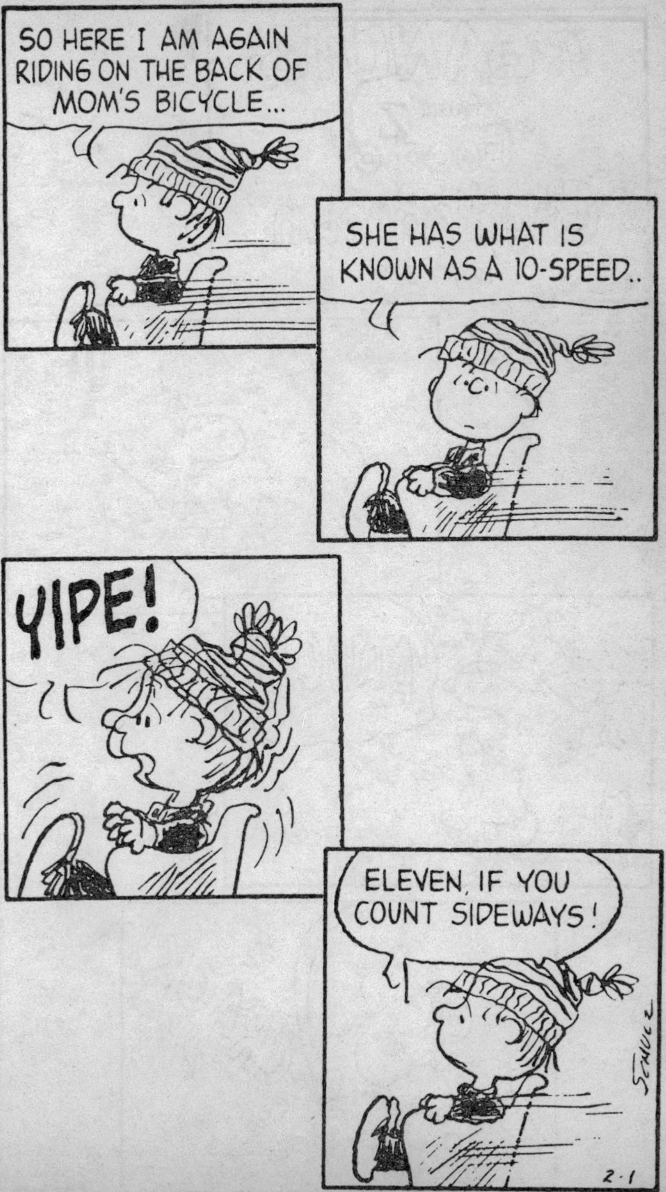
SO HERE I AM AGAIN RIDING ON THE BACK OF MOM'S BICYCLE...
SHE HAS WHAT IS KNOWN AS A 10-SPEED..
YIPE!
ELEVEN, IF YOU COUNT SIDEWAYS!
SCHULZ
2-1

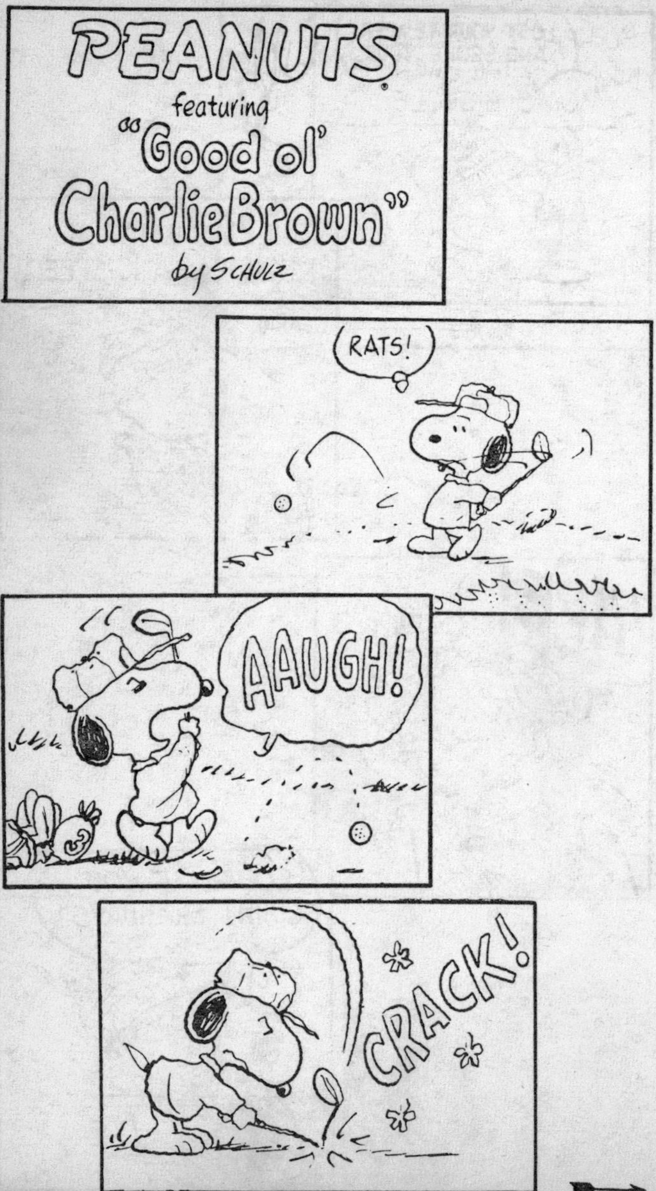
PEANUTS
featuring
"Good ol' Charlie Brown"
by SCHULZ
RATS!
AAUGH!
CRACK!

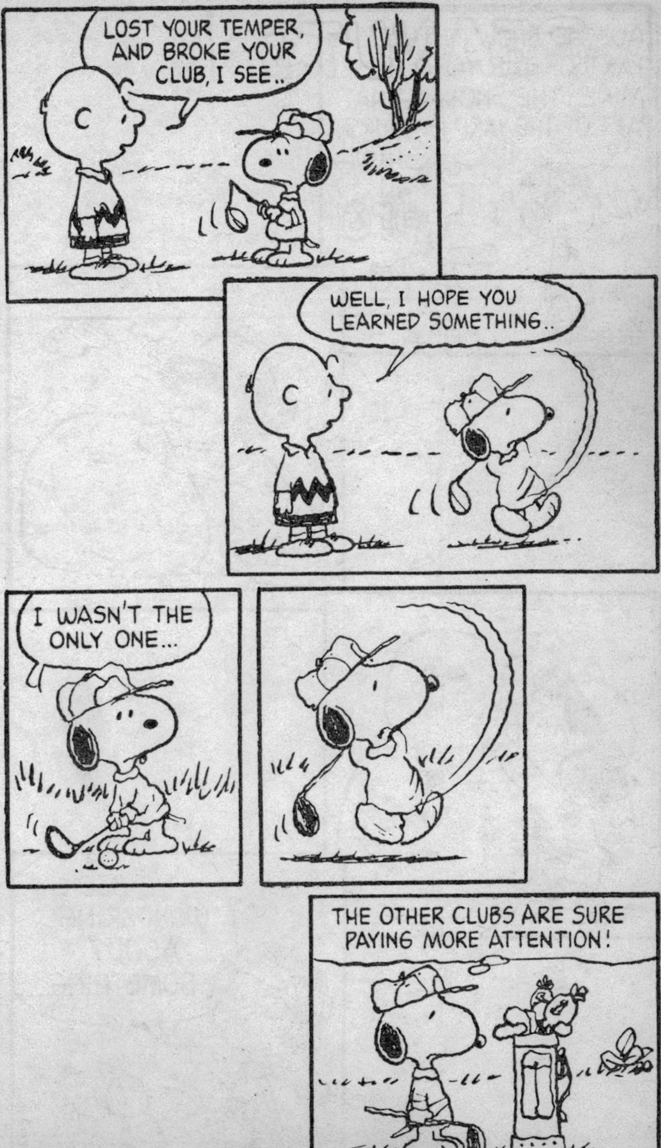
LOST YOUR TEMPER, AND BROKE YOUR CLUB, I SEE..
WELL, I HOPE YOU LEARNED SOMETHING..
I WASN'T THE ONLY ONE...
THE OTHER CLUBS ARE SURE PAYING MORE ATTENTION!
SCHULZ
2-2

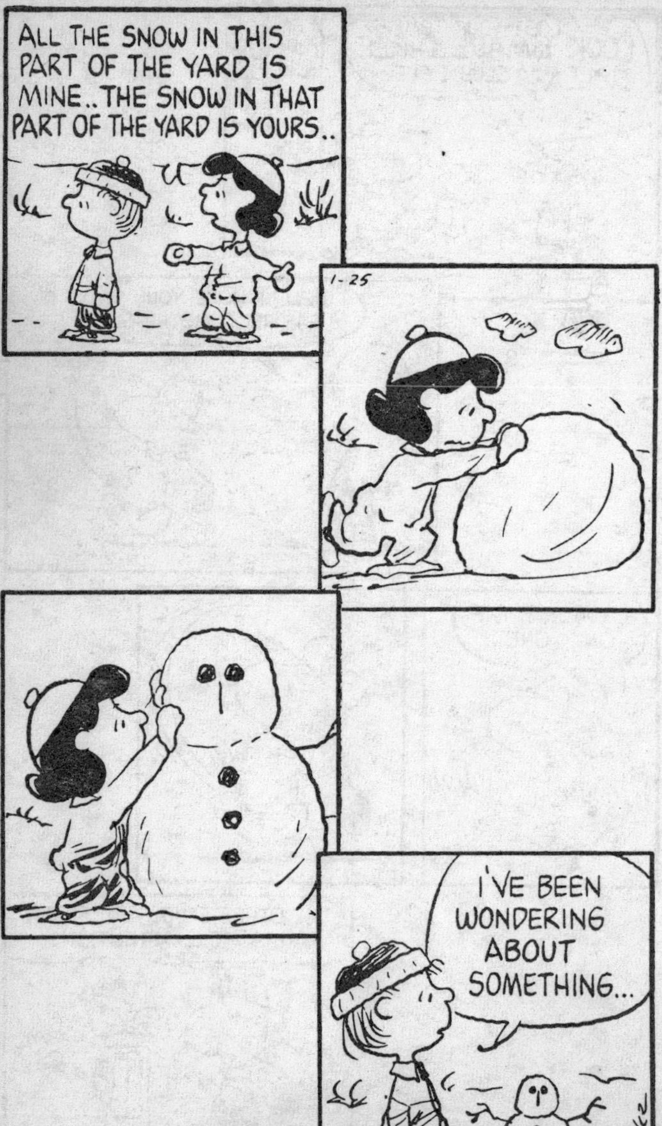
ALL THE SNOW IN THIS PART OF THE YARD IS MINE..THE SNOW IN THAT PART OF THE YARD IS YOURS..
1-25
I'VE BEEN WONDERING ABOUT SOMETHING...
SCHULZ

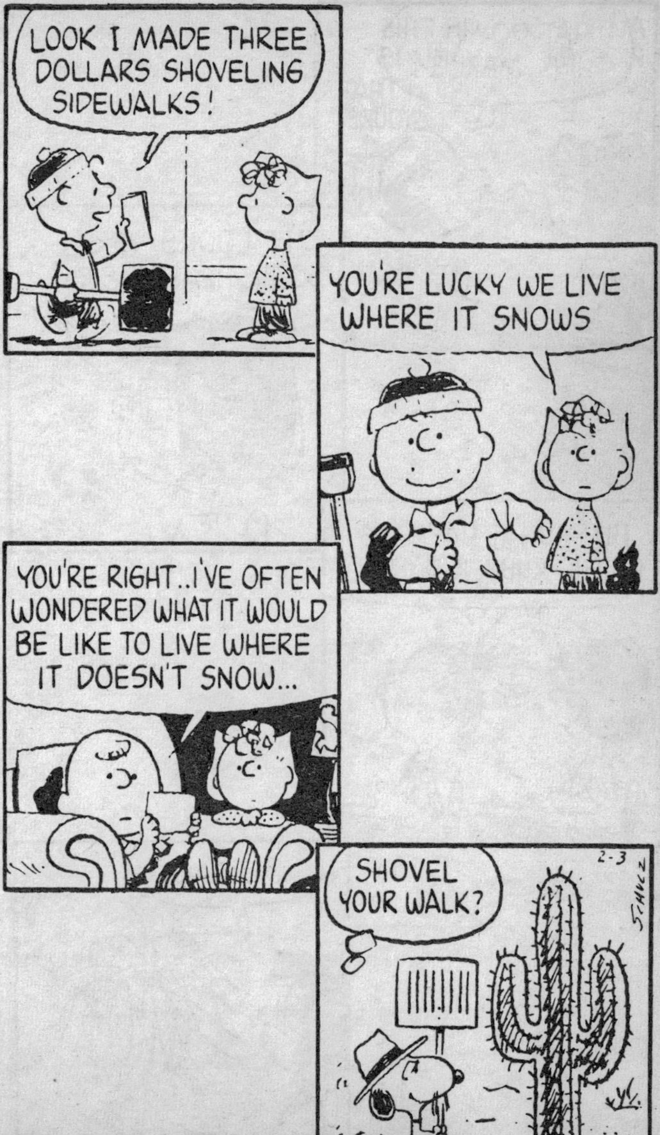
LOOK I MADE THREE DOLLARS SHOVELING SIDEWALKS!
YOU'RE LUCKY WE LIVE WHERE IT SNOWS
YOU'RE RIGHT..I'VE OFTEN WONDERED WHAT IT WOULD BE LIKE TO LIVE WHERE IT DOESN'T SNOW...
SHOVEL YOUR WALK?
2-3
SCHULZ

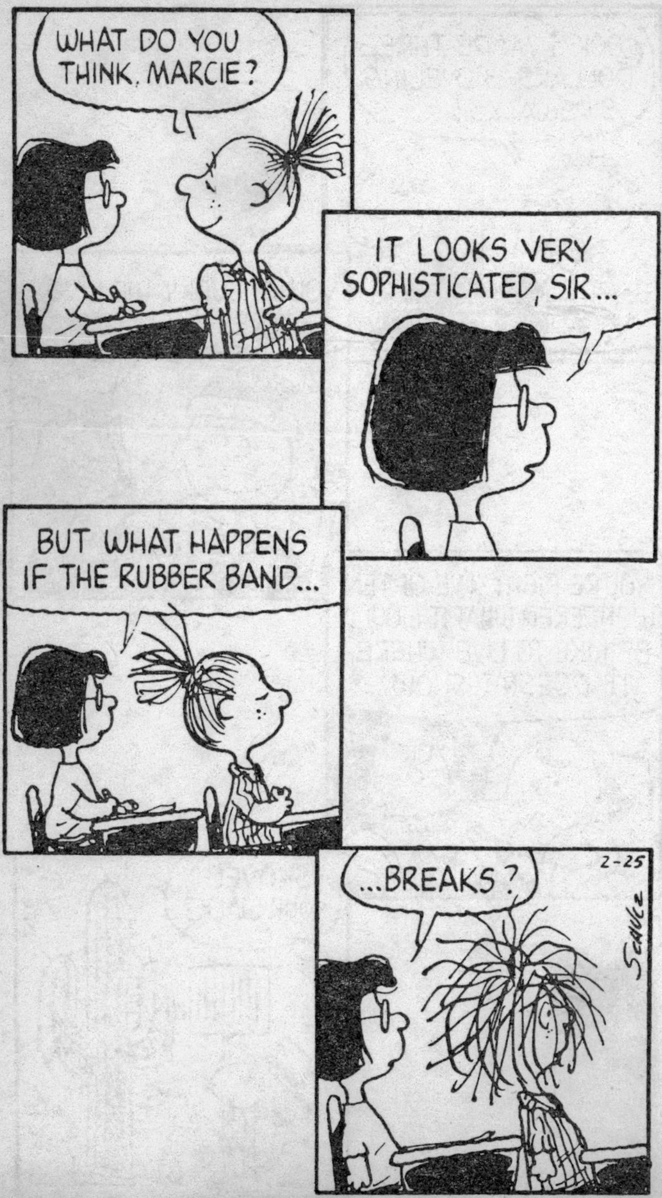
WHAT DO YOU THINK, MARCIE?
IT LOOKS VERY SOPHISTICATED, SIR...
BUT WHAT HAPPENS IF THE RUBBER BAND...
...BREAKS?
2-25
SCHULZ

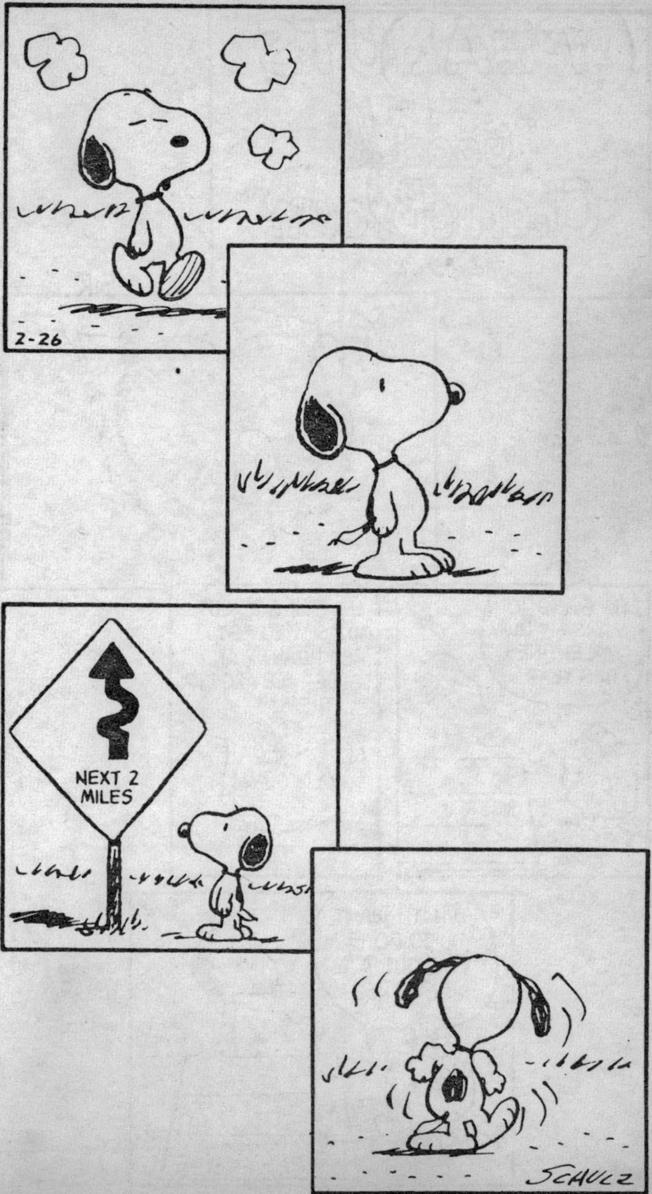
2-26
NEXT 2
MILES
SCHULZ

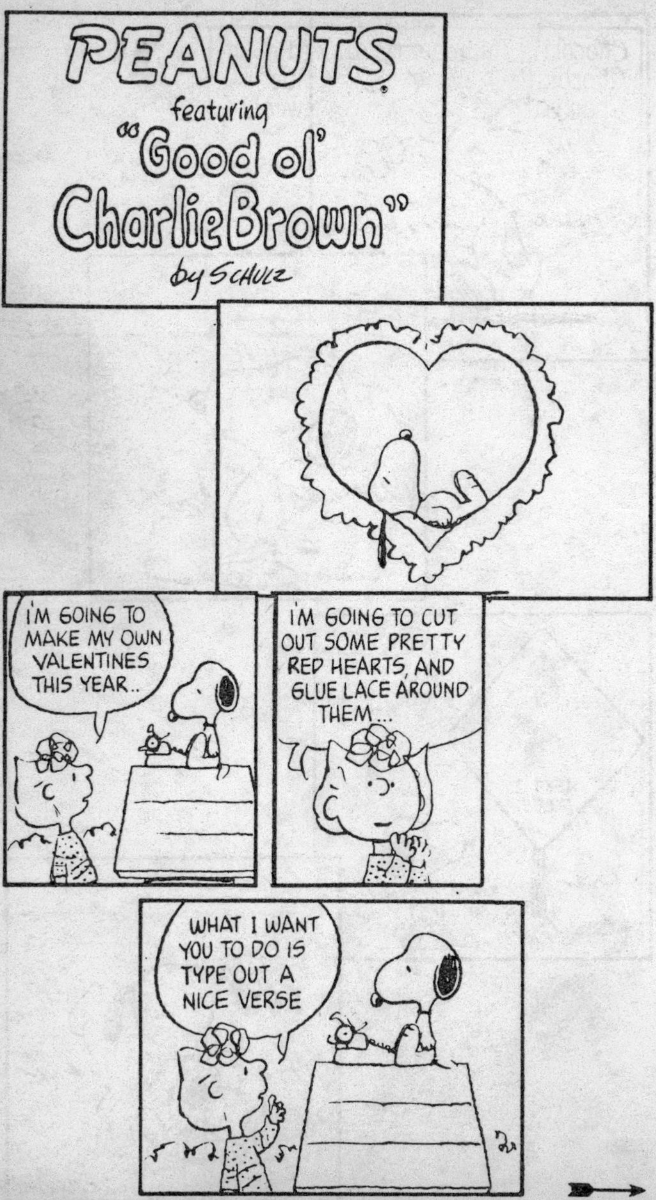
PEANUTS
featuring
"Good ol' Charlie Brown"
by SCHULZ
I'M GOING TO MAKE MY OWN VALENTINES THIS YEAR..
I'M GOING TO CUT OUT SOME PRETTY RED HEARTS, AND GLUE LACE AROUND THEM...
WHAT I WANT YOU TO DO IS TYPE OUT A NICE VERSE

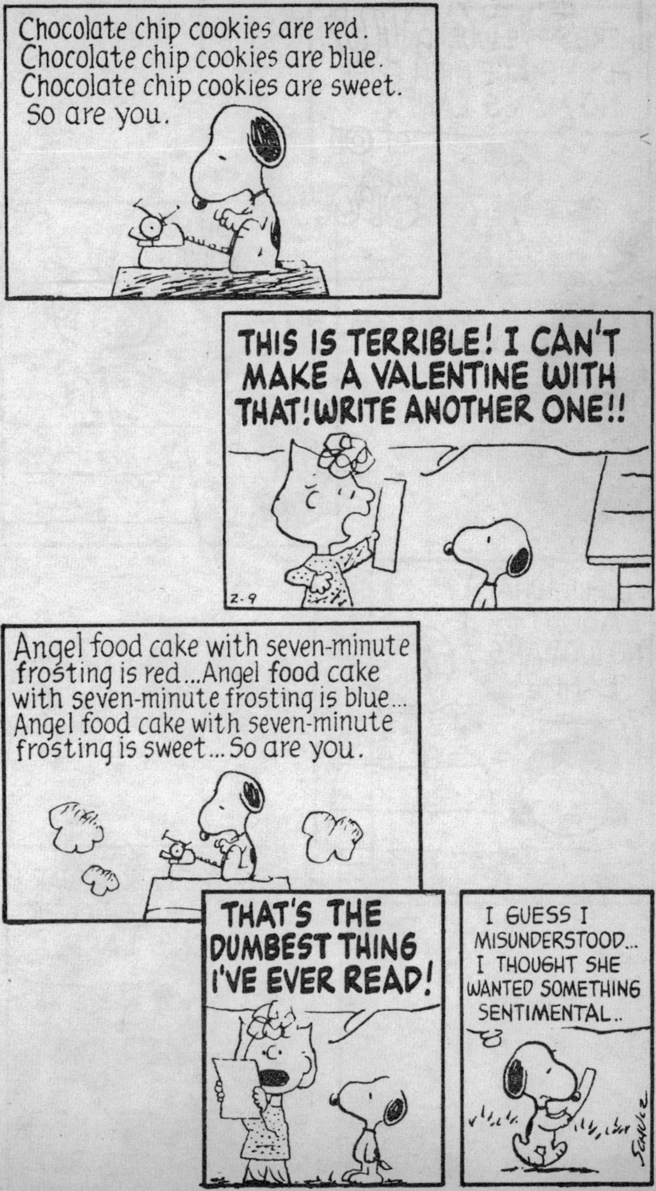
Chocolate chip cookies are red.
Chocolate chip cookies are blue.
Chocolate chip cookies are sweet.
So are you.
THIS IS TERRIBLE! I CAN'T MAKE A VALENTINE WITH THAT! WRITE ANOTHER ONE!!
2-9
Angel food cake with seven-minute frosting is red...Angel food cake with seven-minute frosting is blue... Angel food cake with seven-minute frosting is sweet... So are you.
THAT'S THE DUMBEST THING I'VE EVER READ!
I GUESS I MISUNDERSTOOD... I THOUGHT SHE WANTED SOMETHING SENTIMENTAL..
SCHULZ

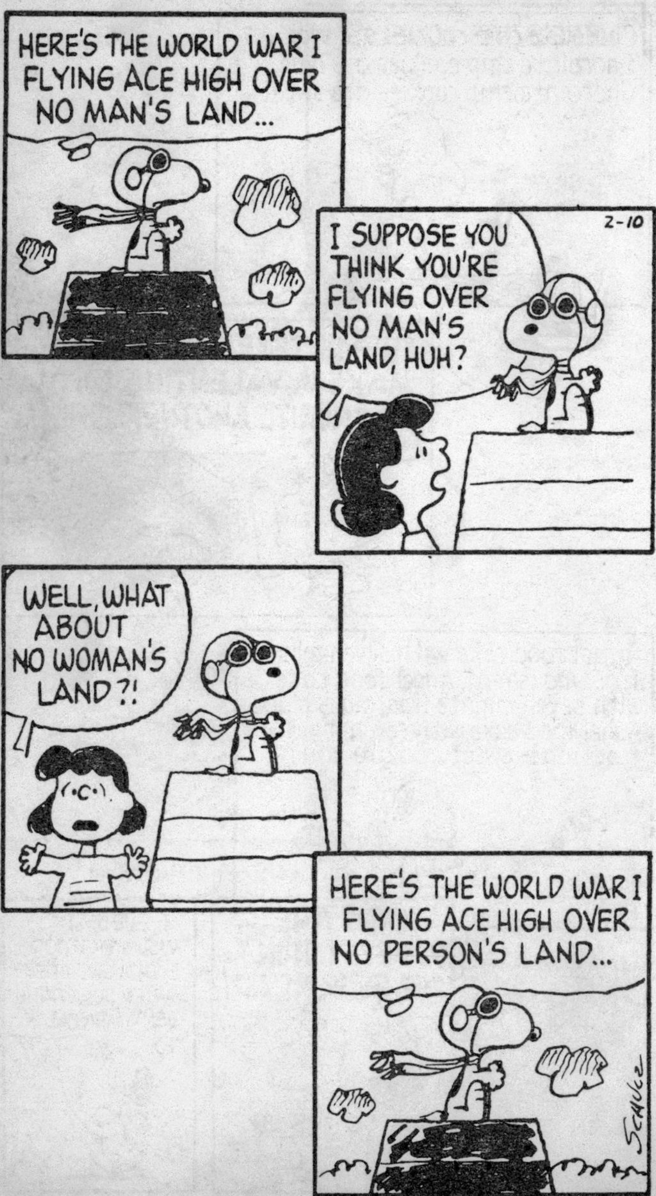
HERE'S THE WORLD WAR I FLYING ACE HIGH OVER NO MAN'S LAND...
2-10
I SUPPOSE YOU THINK YOU'RE FLYING OVER NO MAN'S LAND, HUH?
WELL, WHAT ABOUT NO WOMAN'S LAND?!
HERE'S THE WORLD WAR I FLYING ACE HIGH OVER NO PERSON'S LAND...
SCHULZ

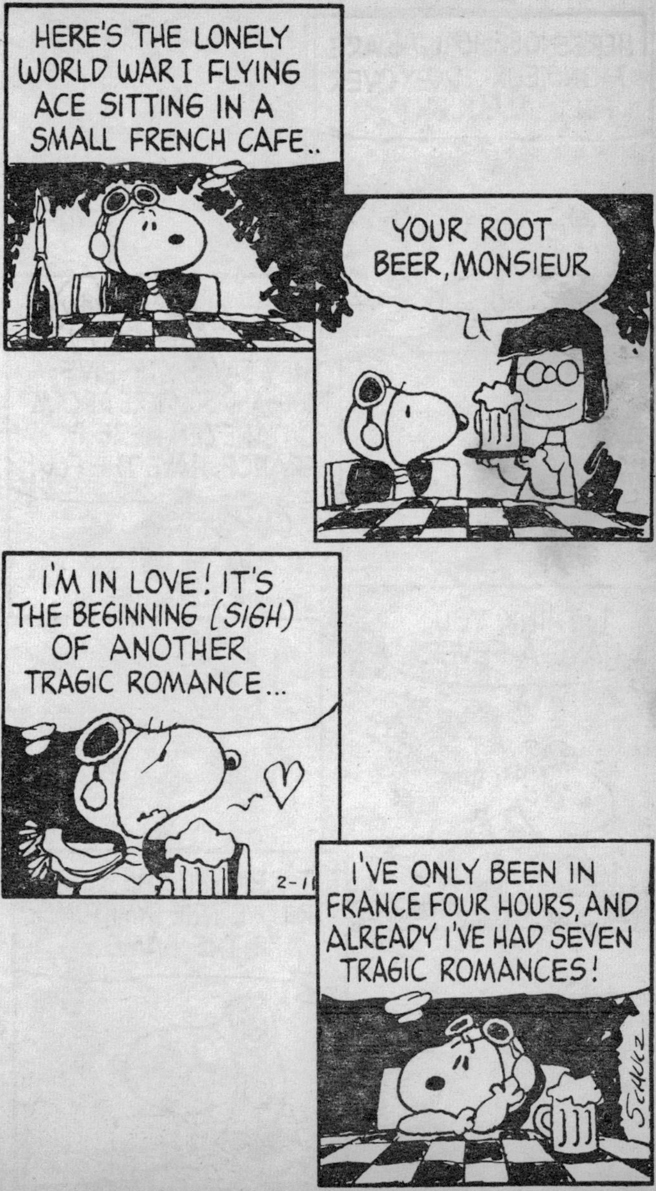
HERE'S THE LONELY WORLD WAR I FLYING ACE SITTING IN A SMALL FRENCH CAFE..
YOUR ROOT BEER, MONSIEUR
I'M IN LOVE! IT'S THE BEGINNING (SIGH) OF ANOTHER TRAGIC ROMANCE...
I'VE ONLY BEEN IN FRANCE FOUR HOURS, AND ALREADY I'VE HAD SEVEN TRAGIC ROMANCES!
SCHULZ

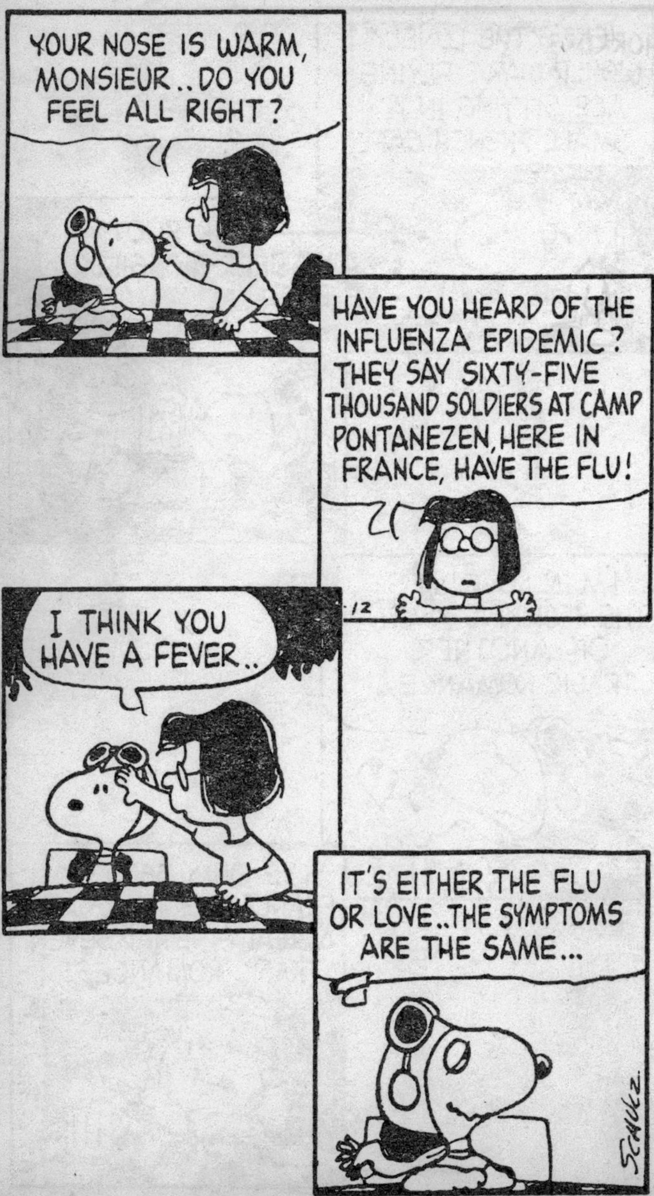
YOUR NOSE IS WARM, MONSIEUR..DO YOU FEEL ALL RIGHT?
HAVE YOU HEARD OF THE INFLUENZA EPIDEMIC? THEY SAY SIXTY-FIVE THOUSAND SOLDIERS AT CAMP PONTANEZEN, HERE IN FRANCE, HAVE THE FLU!
I THINK YOU HAVE A FEVER..
IT'S EITHER THE FLU OR LOVE..THE SYMPTOMS ARE THE SAME...
SCHULZ

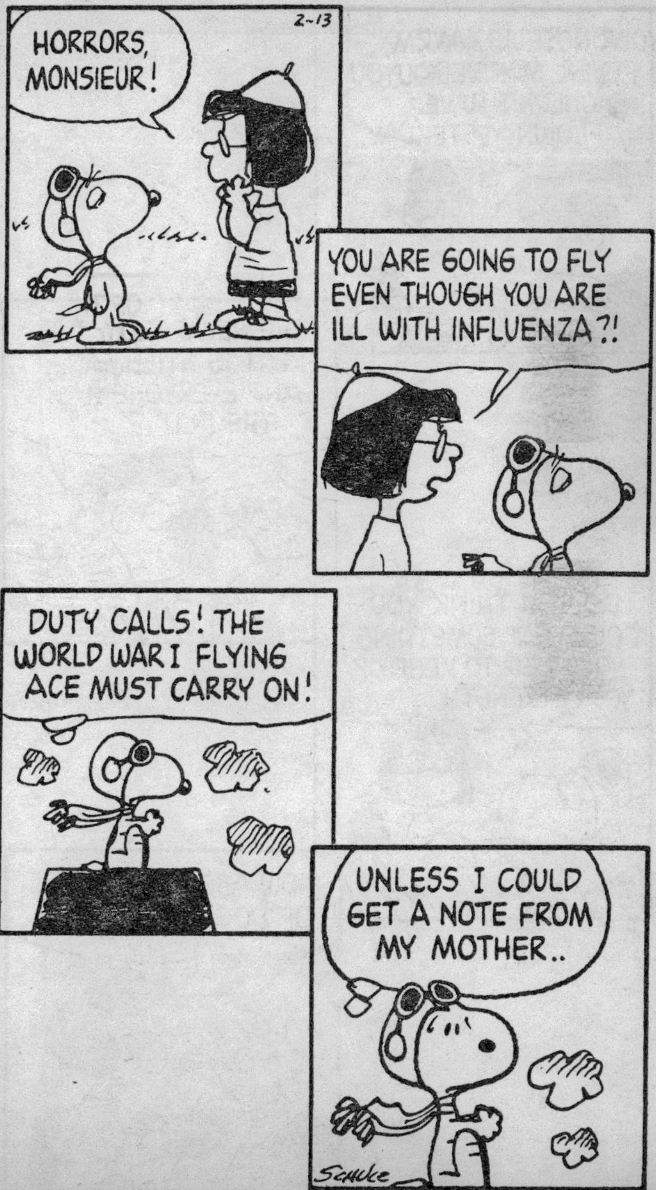
2-13
HORRORS, MONSIEUR!
YOU ARE GOING TO FLY EVEN THOUGH YOU ARE ILL WITH INFLUENZA?!
DUTY CALLS! THE WORLD WAR I FLYING ACE MUST CARRY ON!
UNLESS I COULD GET A NOTE FROM MY MOTHER..
SCHULZ

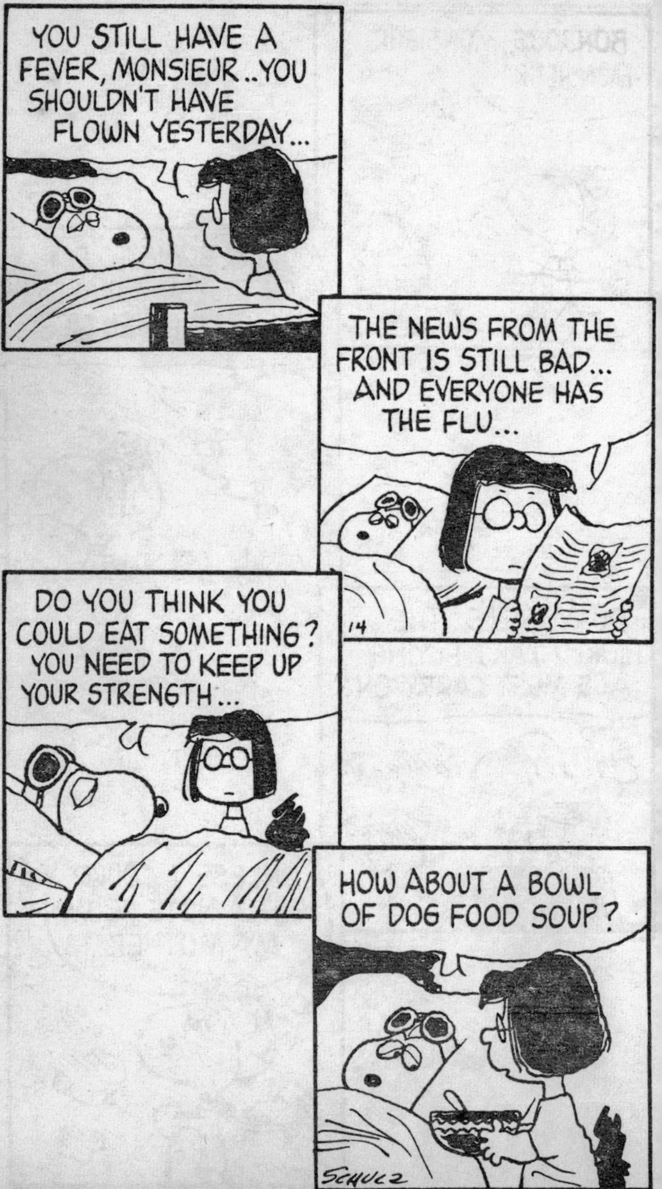
YOU STILL HAVE A FEVER, MONSIEUR..YOU SHOULDN'T HAVE FLOWN YESTERDAY...
THE NEWS FROM THE FRONT IS STILL BAD... AND EVERYONE HAS THE FLU...
DO YOU THINK YOU COULD EAT SOMETHING? YOU NEED TO KEEP UP YOUR STRENGTH...
HOW ABOUT A BOWL OF DOG FOOD SOUP?
SCHULZ

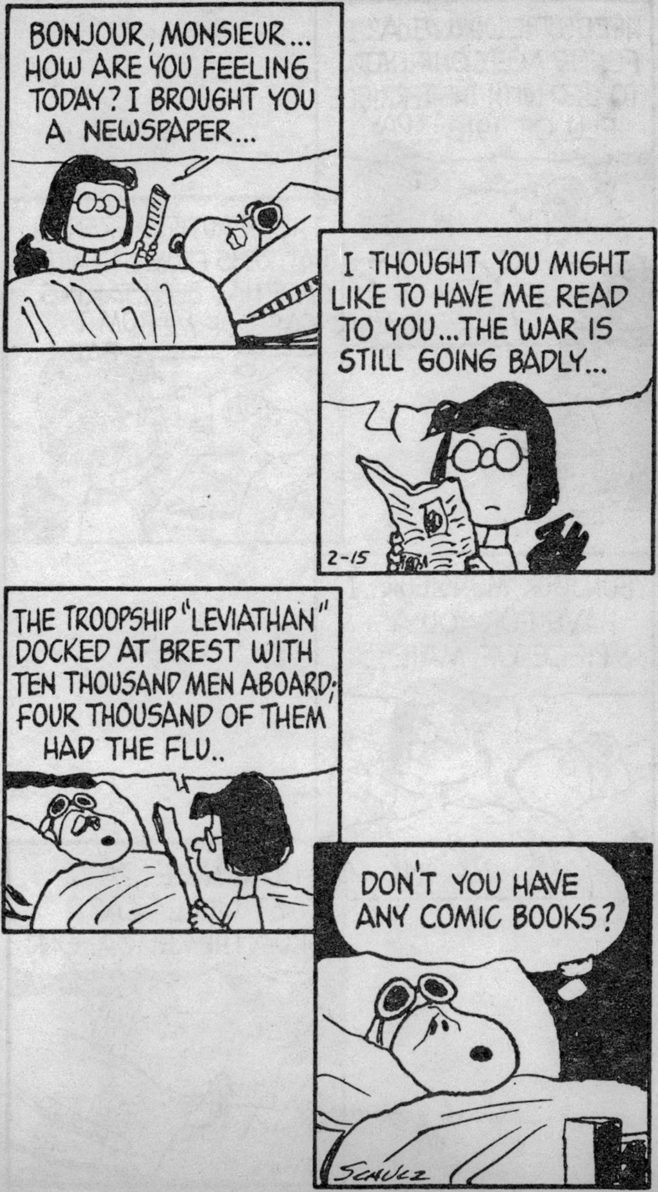
BONJOUR, MONSIEUR... HOW ARE YOU FEELING TODAY? I BROUGHT YOU A NEWSPAPER...
I THOUGHT YOU MIGHT LIKE TO HAVE ME READ TO YOU...THE WAR IS STILL GOING BADLY...
2-15
THE TROOPSHIP "LEVIATHAN" DOCKED AT BREST WITH TEN THOUSAND MEN ABOARD; FOUR THOUSAND OF THEM HAD THE FLU..
DON'T YOU HAVE ANY COMIC BOOKS?
SCHULZ

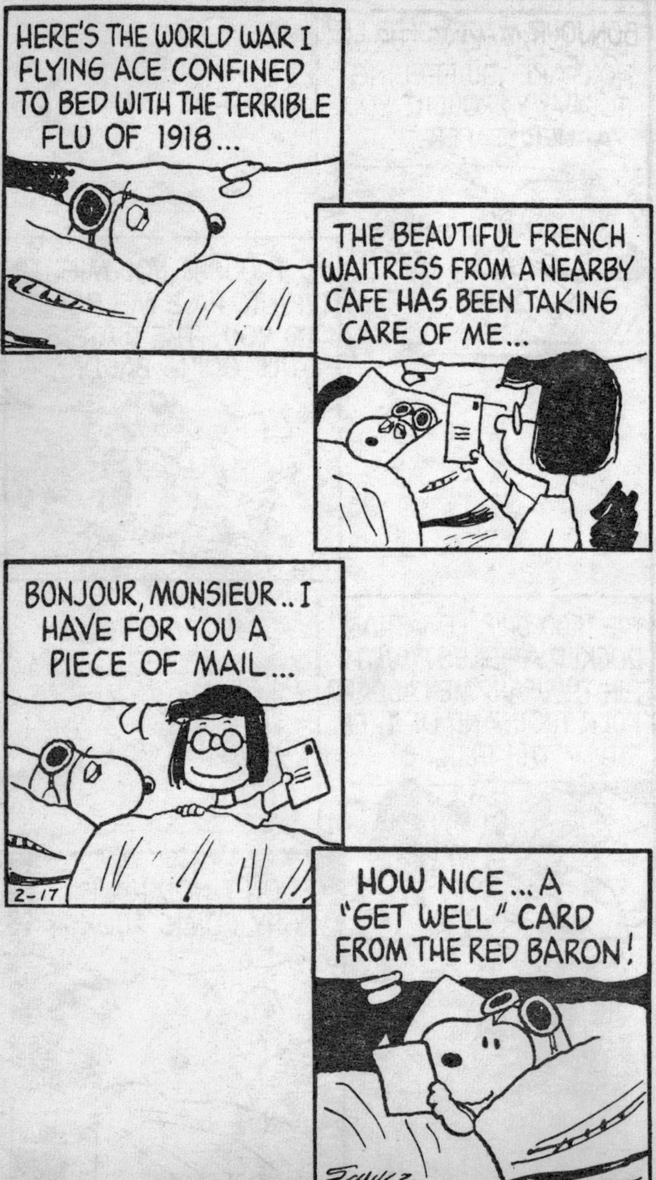
HERE'S THE WORLD WAR I FLYING ACE CONFINED TO BED WITH THE TERRIBLE FLU OF 1918...
THE BEAUTIFUL FRENCH WAITRESS FROM A NEARBY CAFE HAS BEEN TAKING CARE OF ME...
BONJOUR, MONSIEUR.. I HAVE FOR YOU A PIECE OF MAIL...
2-17
HOW NICE... A "GET WELL" CARD FROM THE RED BARON!
SCHULZ

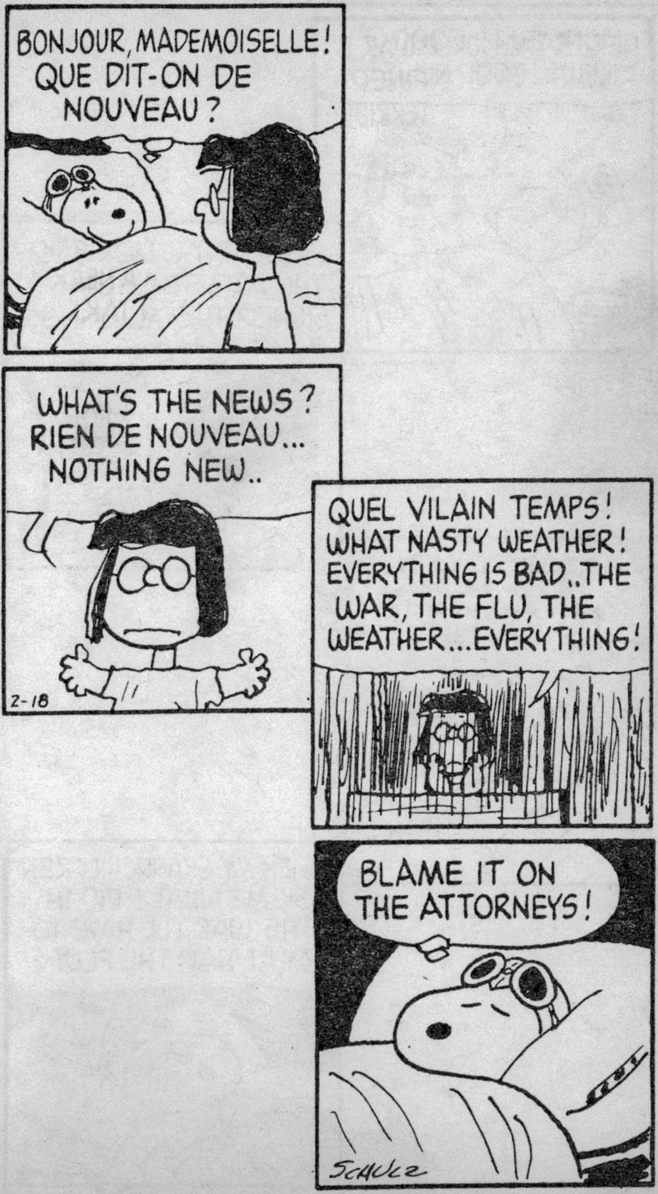
BONJOUR, MADEMOISELLE! QUE DIT-ON DE NOUVEAU?
WHAT'S THE NEWS? RIEN DE NOUVEAU... NOTHING NEW..
2-18
QUEL VILAIN TEMPS! WHAT NASTY WEATHER! EVERYTHING IS BAD..THE WAR, THE FLU, THE WEATHER...EVERYTHING!
BLAME IT ON THE ATTORNEYS!
SCHULZ

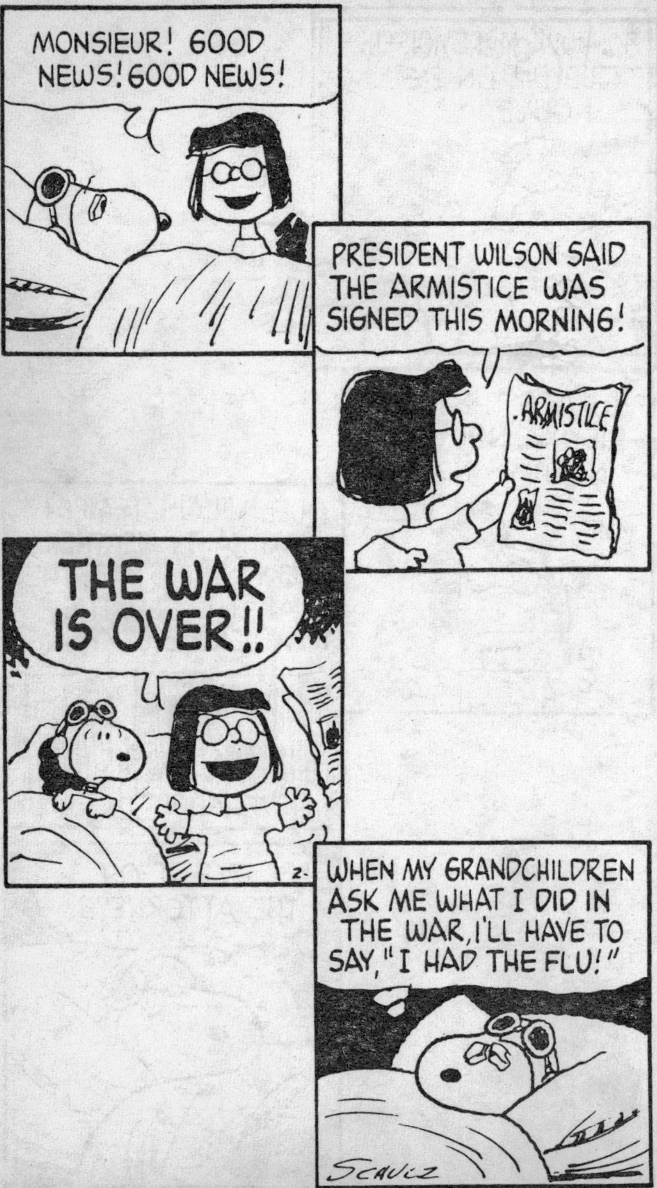

MONSIEUR! GOOD NEWS! GOOD NEWS!
PRESIDENT WILSON SAID THE ARMISTICE WAS SIGNED THIS MORNING!
ARMISTICE
THE WAR IS OVER!!
WHEN MY GRANDCHILDREN ASK ME WHAT I DID IN THE WAR, I'LL HAVE TO SAY, "I HAD THE FLU!"
SCHULZ

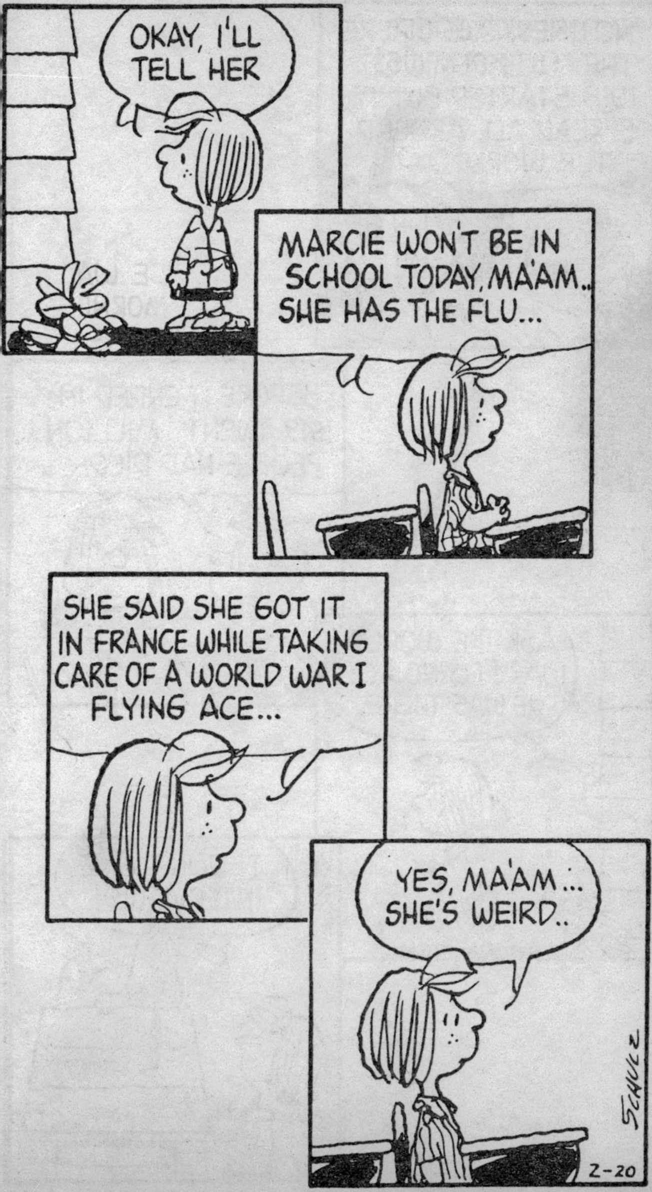
OKAY, I'LL TELL HER
MARCIE WON'T BE IN SCHOOL TODAY, MA'AM.. SHE HAS THE FLU...
SHE SAID SHE GOT IT IN FRANCE WHILE TAKING CARE OF A WORLD WAR I FLYING ACE...
YES, MA'AM... SHE'S WEIRD..
SCHULZ
2-20

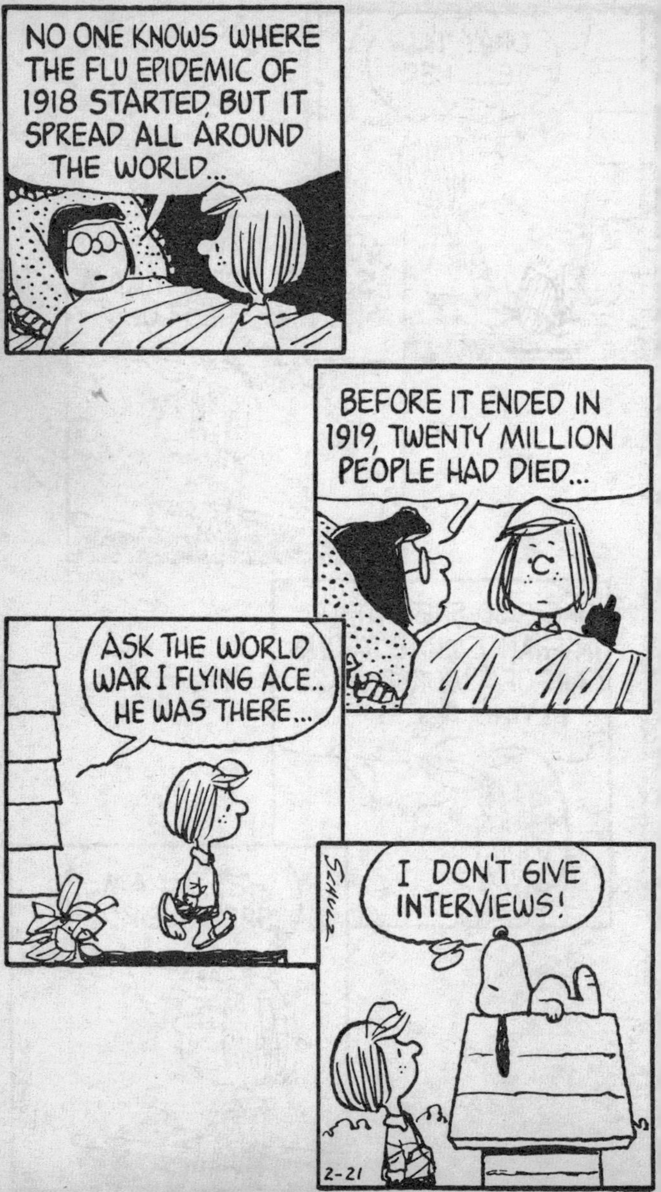
NO ONE KNOWS WHERE THE FLU EPIDEMIC OF 1918 STARTED, BUT IT SPREAD ALL AROUND THE WORLD...
BEFORE IT ENDED IN 1919, TWENTY MILLION PEOPLE HAD DIED...
ASK THE WORLD WAR I FLYING ACE.. HE WAS THERE...
I DON'T GIVE INTERVIEWS!
SCHULZ
2-21

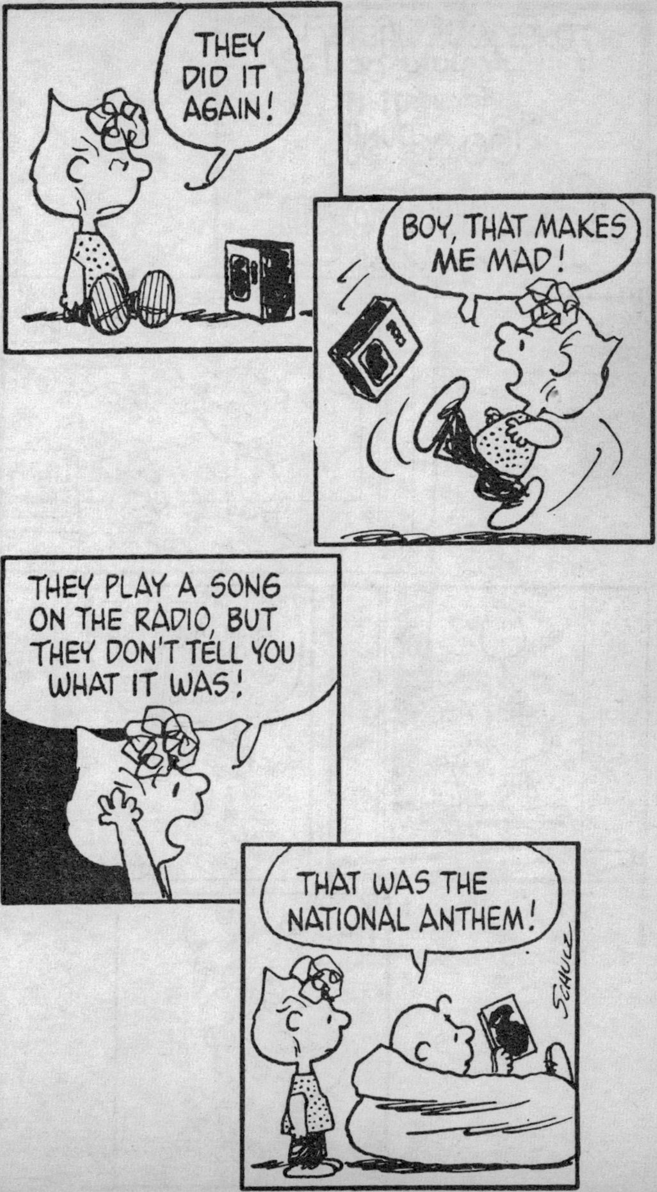
THEY DID IT AGAIN!
BOY, THAT MAKES ME MAD!
THEY PLAY A SONG ON THE RADIO, BUT THEY DON'T TELL YOU WHAT IT WAS!
THAT WAS THE NATIONAL ANTHEM!
SCHULZ

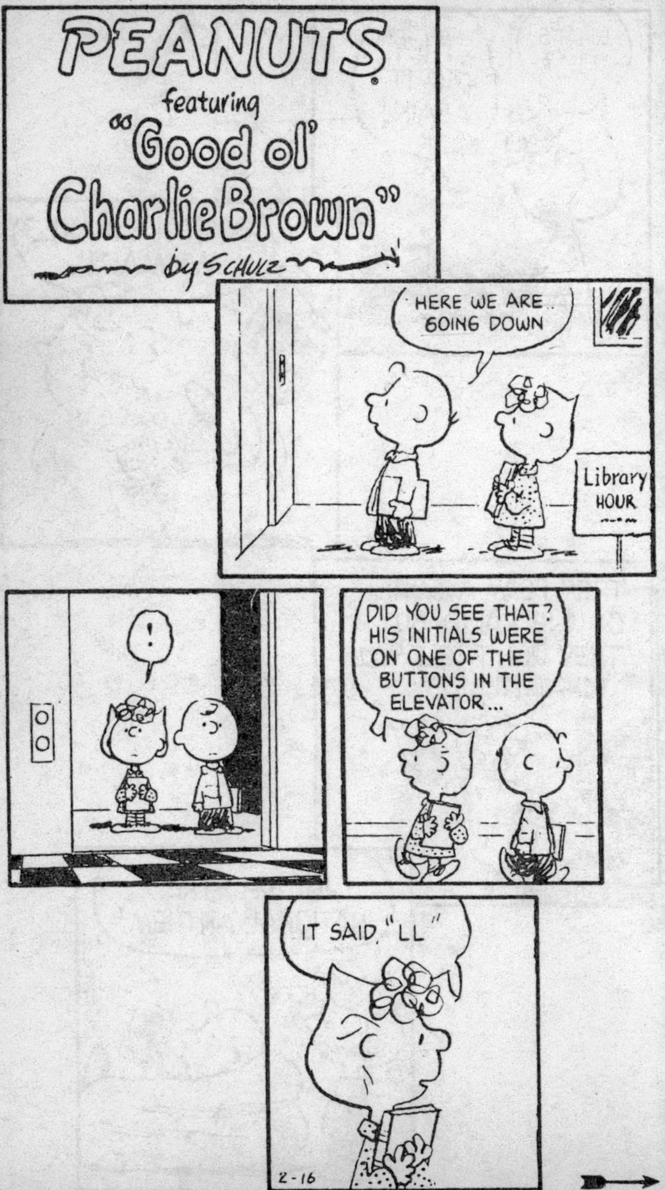
PEANUTS
featuring
"Good ol' Charlie Brown"
by SCHULZ
HERE WE ARE.. GOING DOWN
Library HOUR
!
DID YOU SEE THAT? HIS INITIALS WERE ON ONE OF THE BUTTONS IN THE ELEVATOR...
IT SAID, "LL"
2-16

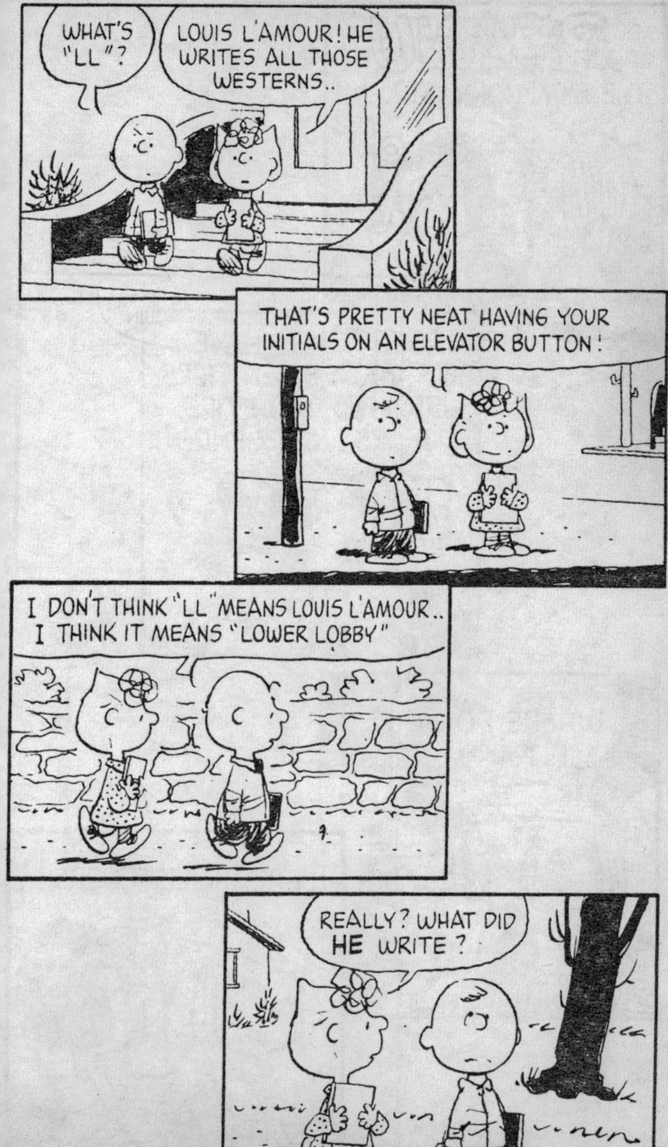
WHAT'S "LL"?
LOUIS L'AMOUR! HE WRITES ALL THOSE WESTERNS..
THAT'S PRETTY NEAT HAVING YOUR INITIALS ON AN ELEVATOR BUTTON!
I DON'T THINK "LL" MEANS LOUIS L'AMOUR.. I THINK IT MEANS "LOWER LOBBY"
REALLY? WHAT DID HE WRITE?
SCHULZ

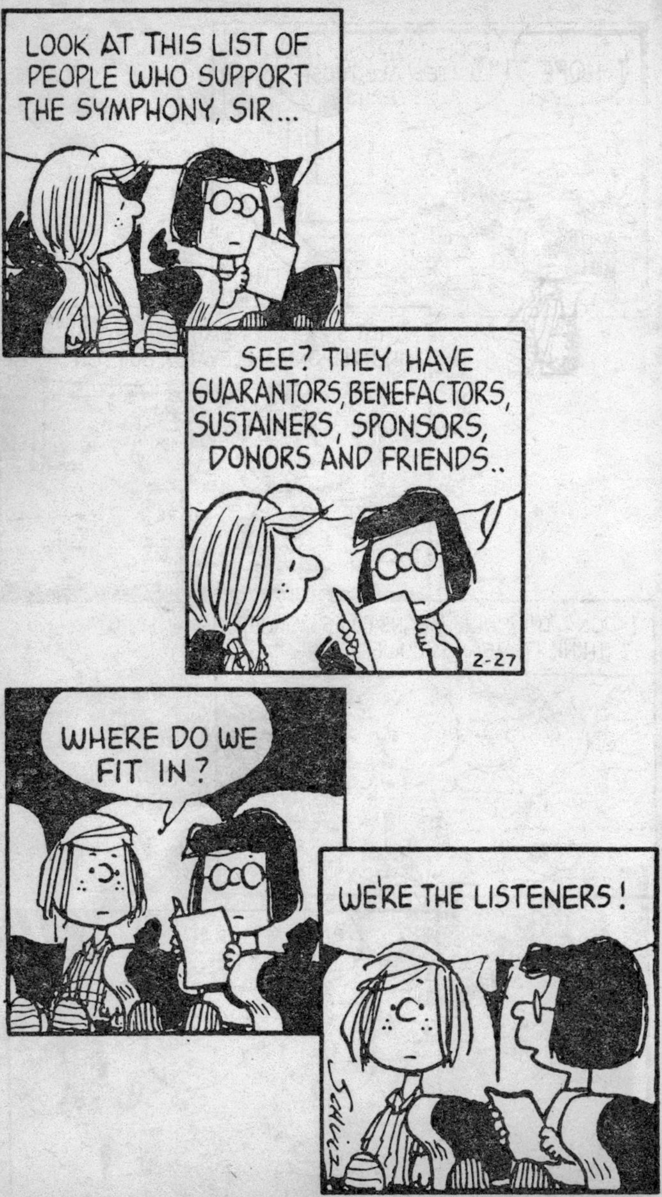
LOOK AT THIS LIST OF PEOPLE WHO SUPPORT THE SYMPHONY, SIR...
SEE? THEY HAVE GUARANTORS, BENEFACTORS, SUSTAINERS, SPONSORS, DONORS AND FRIENDS..
2-27
WHERE DO WE FIT IN?
WE'RE THE LISTENERS!
SCHULZ

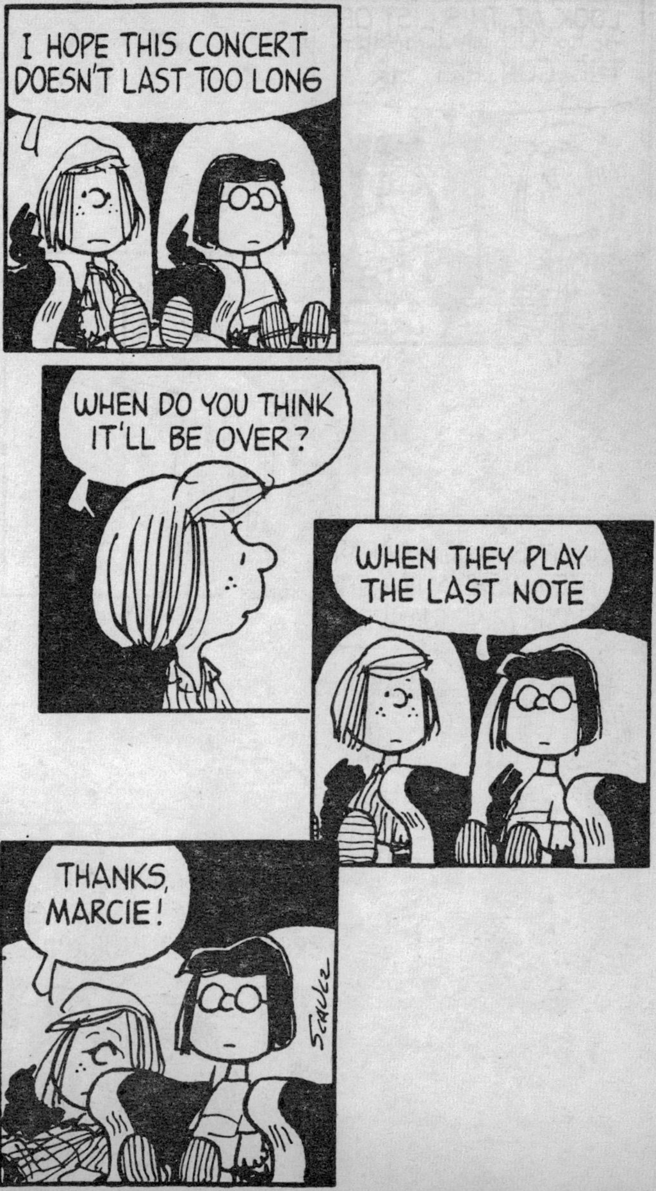
I HOPE THIS CONCERT DOESN'T LAST TOO LONG
WHEN DO YOU THINK IT'LL BE OVER?
WHEN THEY PLAY THE LAST NOTE
THANKS, MARCIE!
SCHULZ

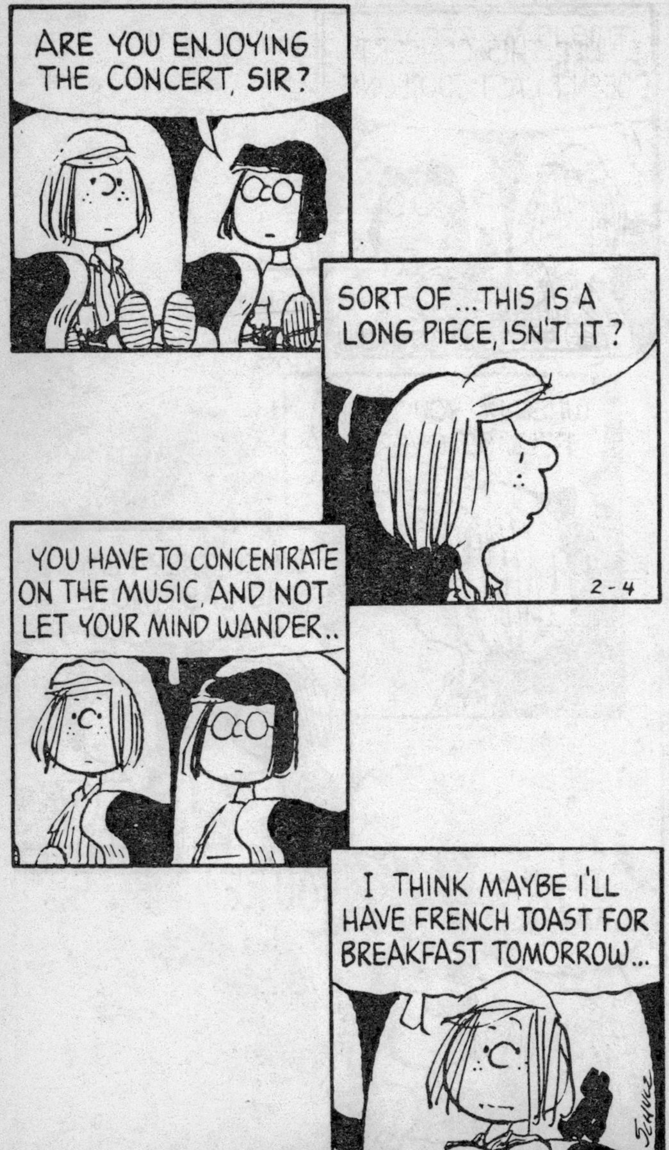
ARE YOU ENJOYING THE CONCERT, SIR?
SORT OF...THIS IS A LONG PIECE, ISN'T IT?
2-4
YOU HAVE TO CONCENTRATE ON THE MUSIC, AND NOT LET YOUR MIND WANDER..
I THINK MAYBE I'LL HAVE FRENCH TOAST FOR BREAKFAST TOMORROW...
SCHULZ

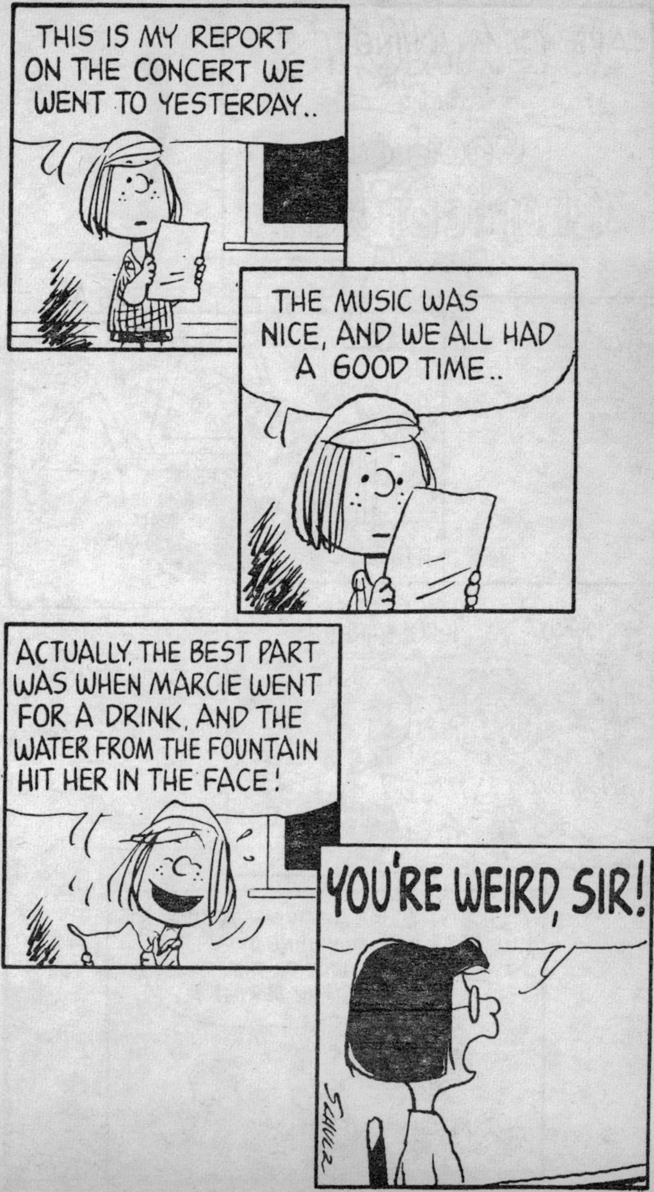
THIS IS MY REPORT ON THE CONCERT WE WENT TO YESTERDAY..
THE MUSIC WAS NICE, AND WE ALL HAD A GOOD TIME..
ACTUALLY, THE BEST PART WAS WHEN MARCIE WENT FOR A DRINK, AND THE WATER FROM THE FOUNTAIN HIT HER IN THE FACE!
YOU'RE WEIRD, SIR!
SCHULZ

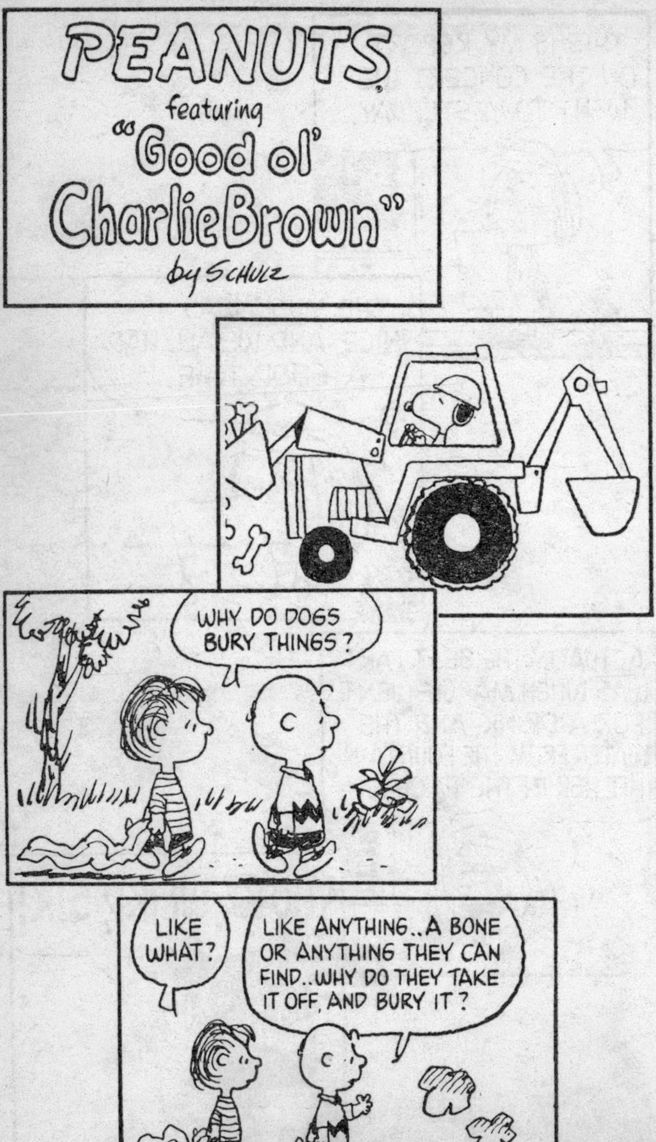
PEANUTS
featuring
"Good ol' Charlie Brown"
by SCHULZ
WHY DO DOGS BURY THINGS?
LIKE WHAT?
LIKE ANYTHING..A BONE OR ANYTHING THEY CAN FIND..WHY DO THEY TAKE IT OFF, AND BURY IT?

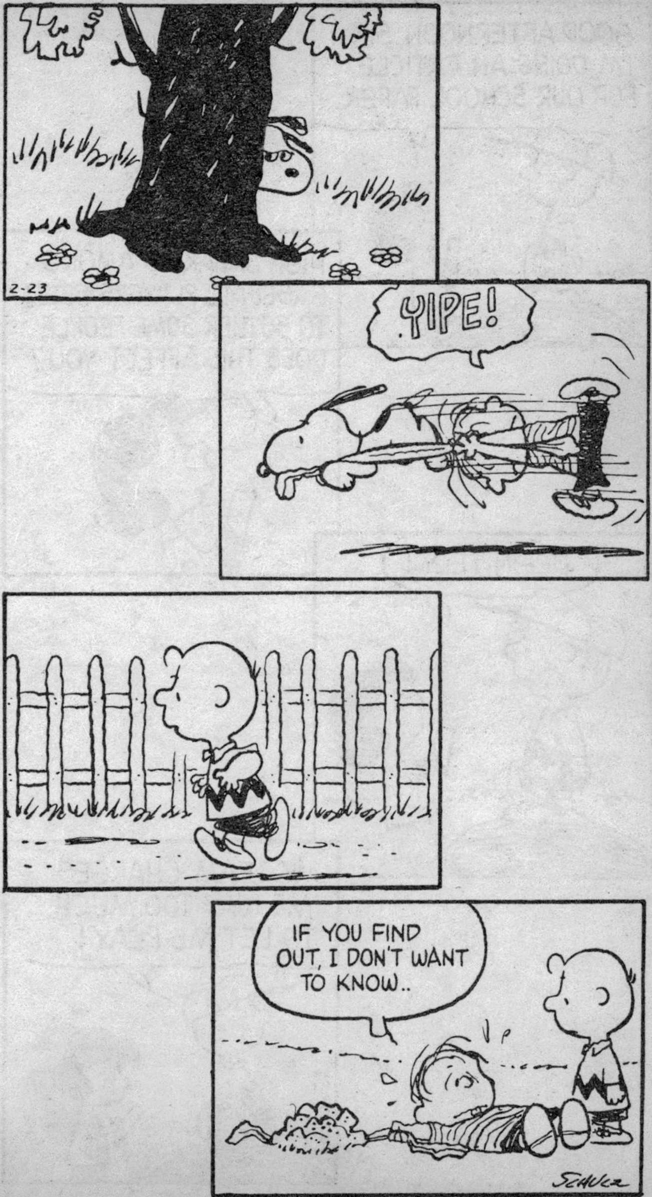
2-23
YIPE!
IF YOU FIND OUT, I DON'T WANT TO KNOW..
SCHULZ

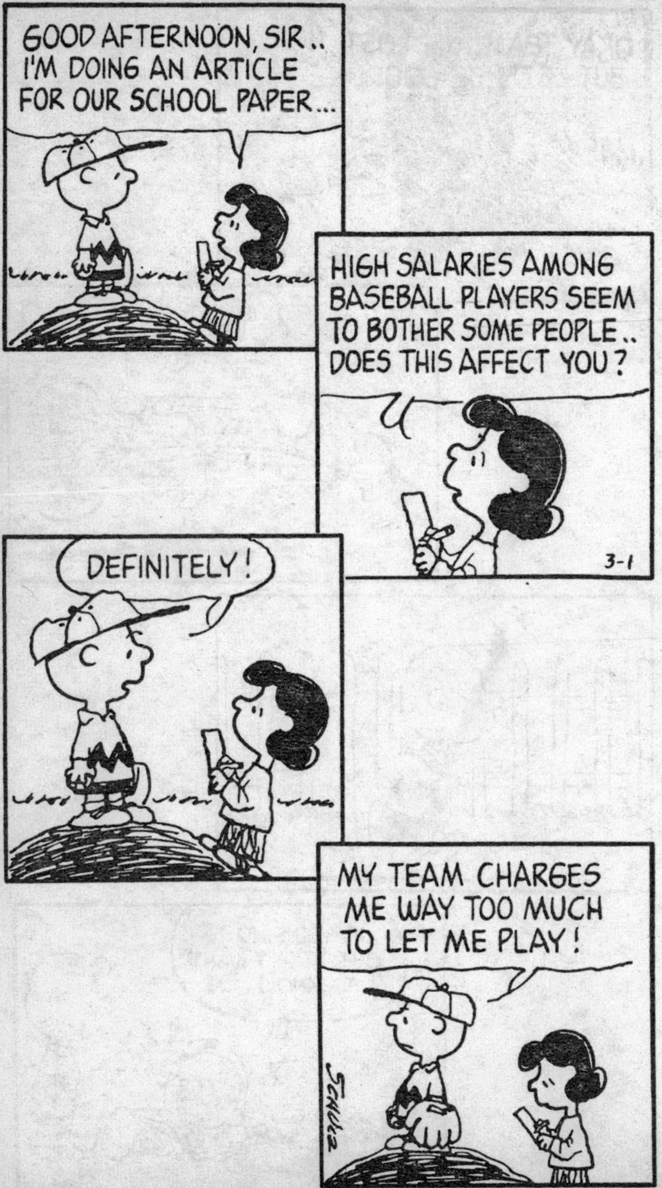
GOOD AFTERNOON, SIR.. I'M DOING AN ARTICLE FOR OUR SCHOOL PAPER...
HIGH SALARIES AMONG BASEBALL PLAYERS SEEM TO BOTHER SOME PEOPLE.. DOES THIS AFFECT YOU?
3-1
DEFINITELY!
MY TEAM CHARGES ME WAY TOO MUCH TO LET ME PLAY!
SCHULZ

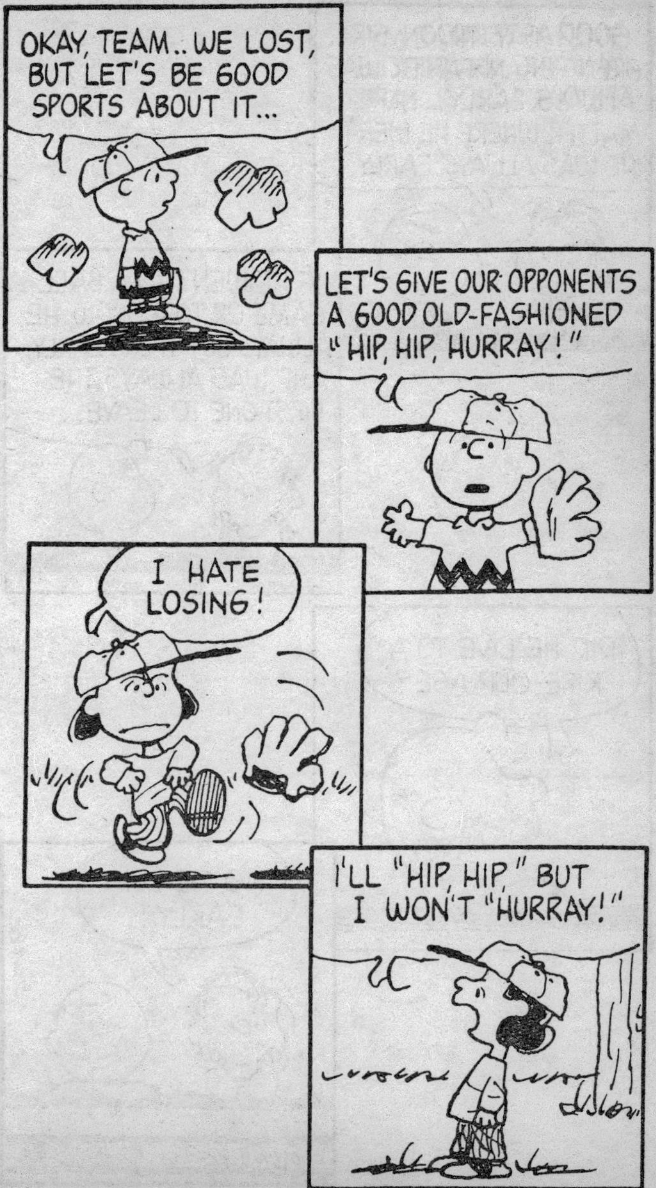
OKAY, TEAM.. WE LOST, BUT LET'S BE GOOD SPORTS ABOUT IT...
LET'S GIVE OUR OPPONENTS A GOOD OLD-FASHIONED "HIP, HIP, HURRAY!"
I HATE LOSING!
I'LL "HIP, HIP," BUT I WON'T "HURRAY!"

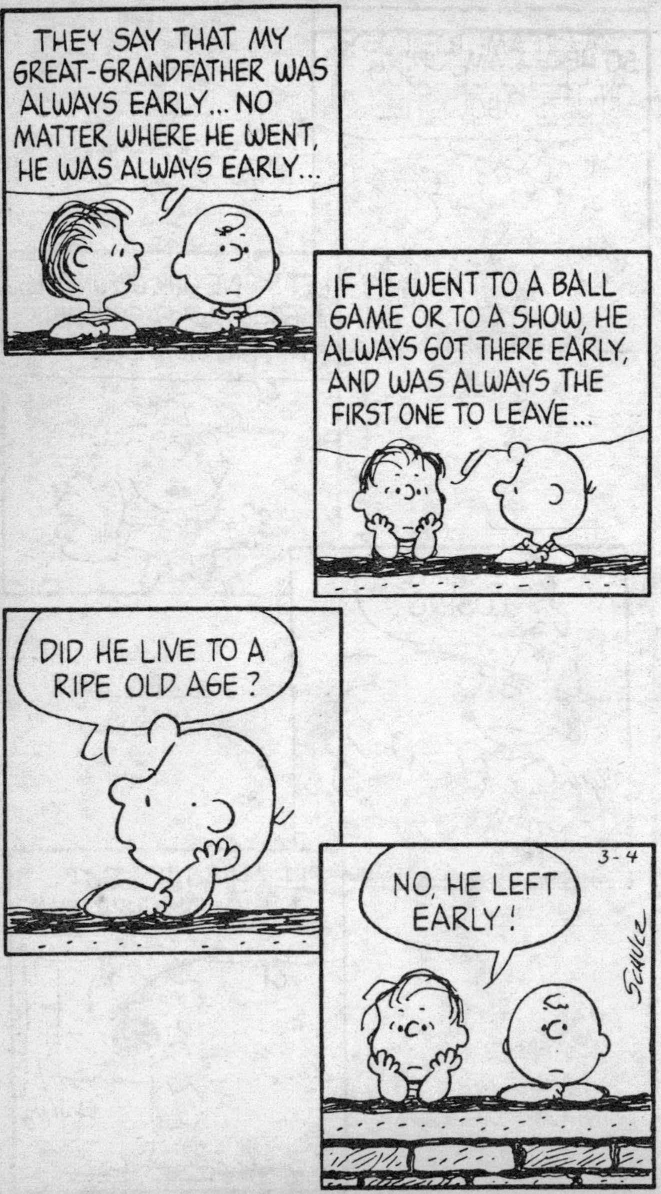
THEY SAY THAT MY GREAT-GRANDFATHER WAS ALWAYS EARLY... NO MATTER WHERE HE WENT, HE WAS ALWAYS EARLY...
IF HE WENT TO A BALL GAME OR TO A SHOW, HE ALWAYS GOT THERE EARLY, AND WAS ALWAYS THE FIRST ONE TO LEAVE...
DID HE LIVE TO A RIPE OLD AGE?
NO, HE LEFT EARLY!
3-4
SCHULZ

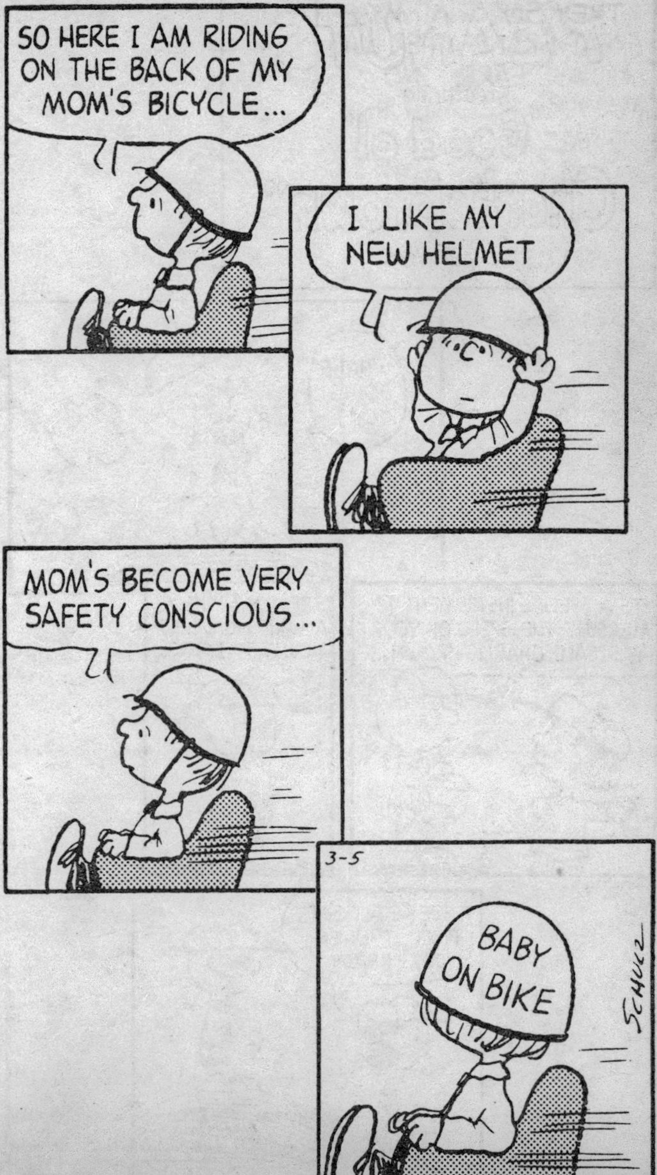

SO HERE I AM RIDING ON THE BACK OF MY MOM'S BICYCLE...
I LIKE MY NEW HELMET
MOM'S BECOME VERY SAFETY CONSCIOUS...
3-5
BABY ON BIKE
SCHULZ

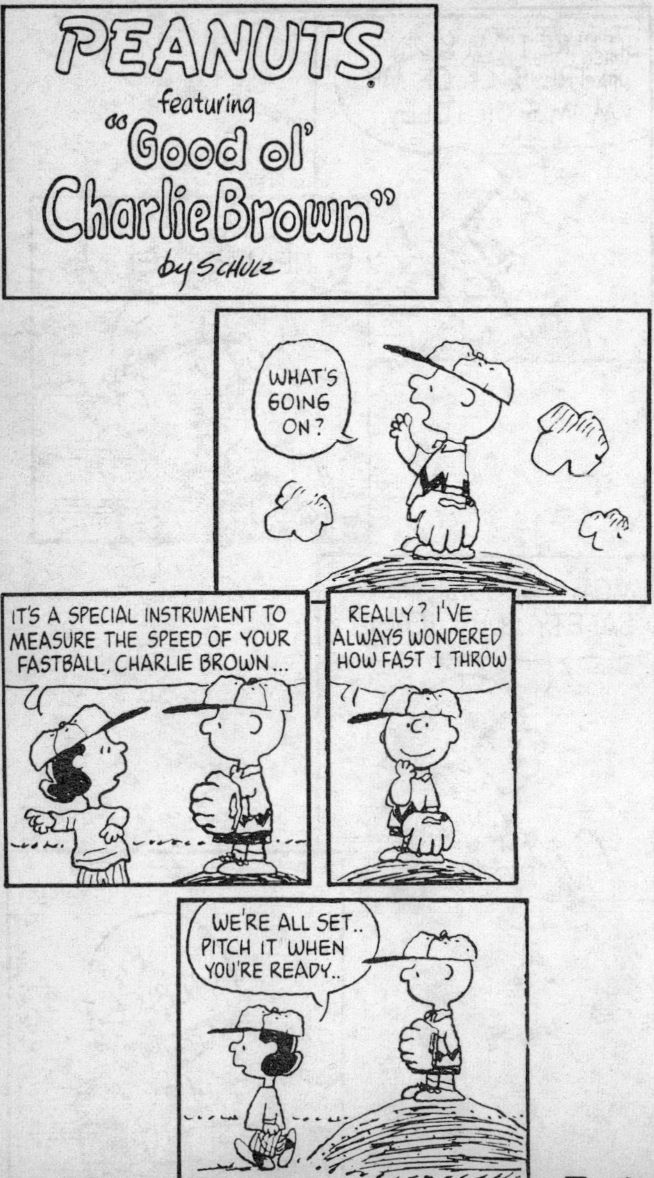
PEANUTS®
featuring
"Good ol' Charlie Brown"
by SCHULZ
WHAT'S GOING ON?
IT'S A SPECIAL INSTRUMENT TO MEASURE THE SPEED OF YOUR FASTBALL, CHARLIE BROWN...
REALLY? I'VE ALWAYS WONDERED HOW FAST I THROW
WE'RE ALL SET.. PITCH IT WHEN YOU'RE READY..

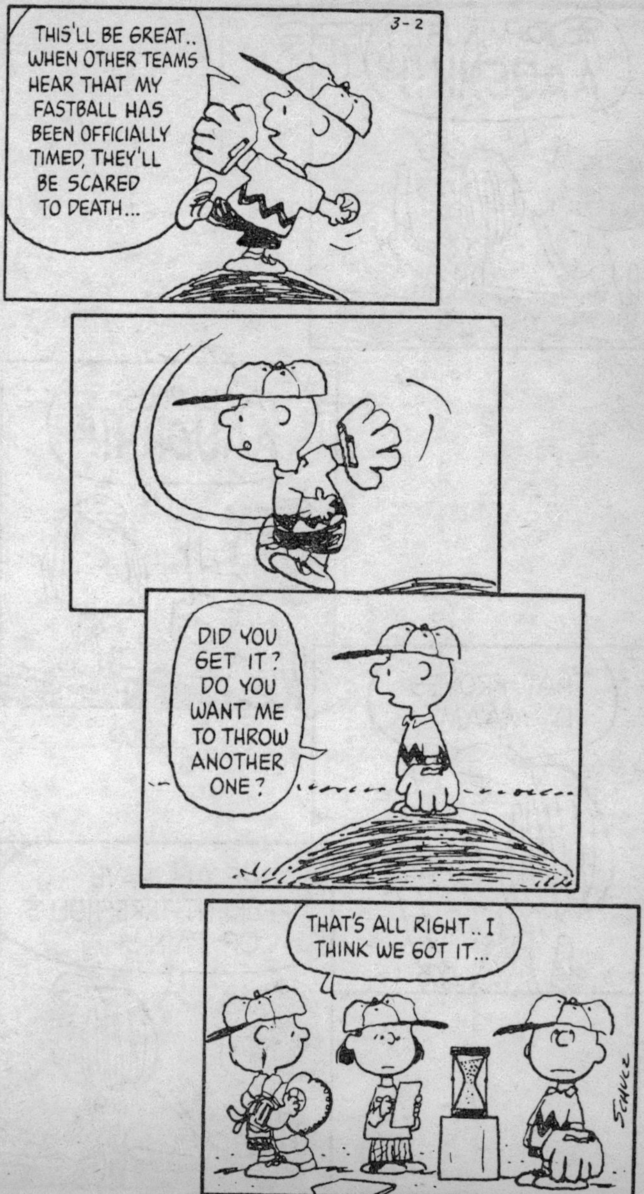
3-2
THIS'LL BE GREAT.. WHEN OTHER TEAMS HEAR THAT MY FASTBALL HAS BEEN OFFICIALLY TIMED, THEY'LL BE SCARED TO DEATH...
DID YOU GET IT? DO YOU WANT ME TO THROW ANOTHER ONE?
THAT'S ALL RIGHT.. I THINK WE GOT IT...
SCHULZ

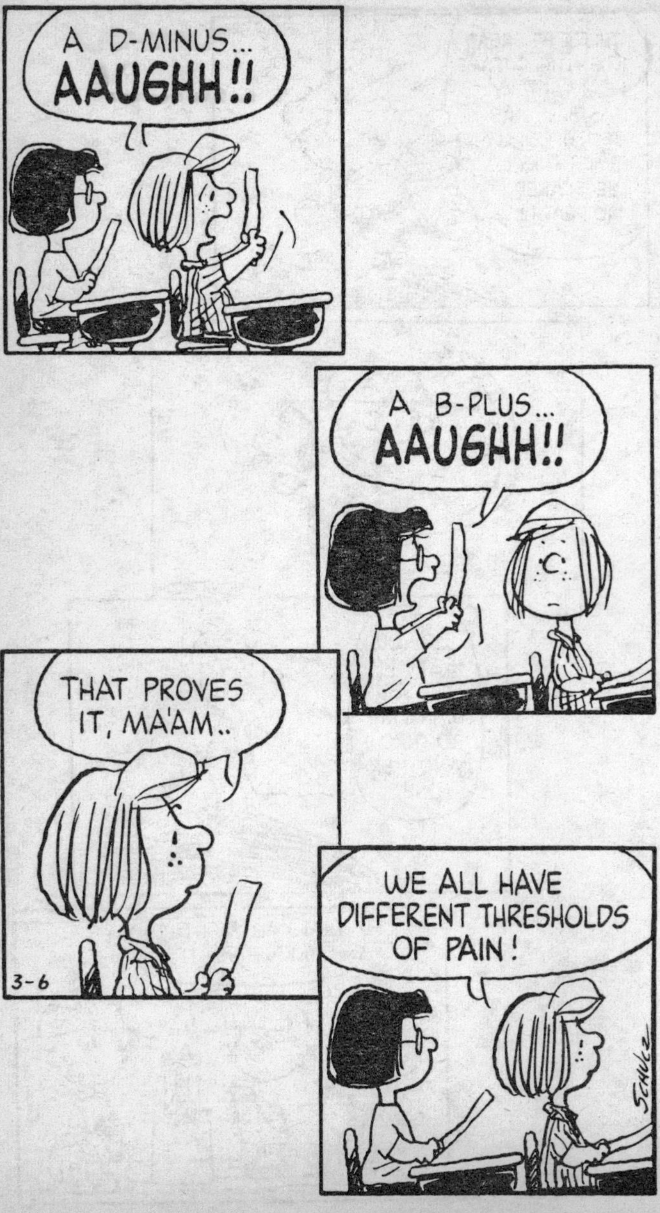
A D-MINUS... AAUGHH!!
A B-PLUS... AAUGHH!!
THAT PROVES IT, MA'AM..
WE ALL HAVE DIFFERENT THRESHOLDS OF PAIN!
3-6
SCHULZ

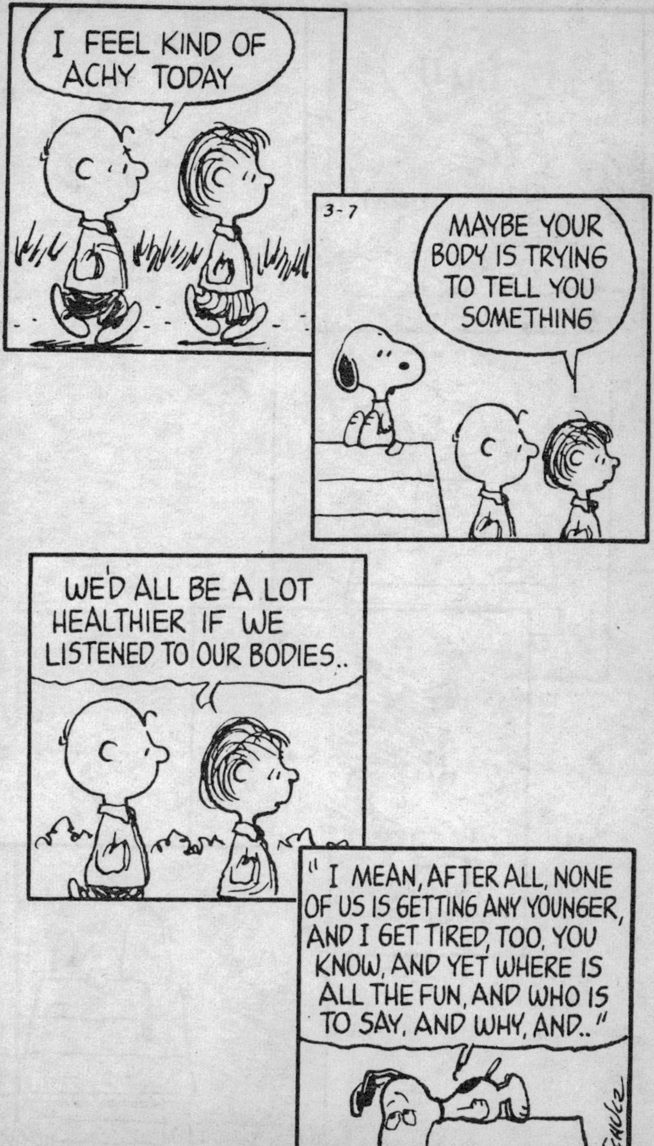
I FEEL KIND OF ACHY TODAY
3-7
MAYBE YOUR BODY IS TRYING TO TELL YOU SOMETHING
WE'D ALL BE A LOT HEALTHIER IF WE LISTENED TO OUR BODIES..
" I MEAN, AFTER ALL, NONE OF US IS GETTING ANY YOUNGER, AND I GET TIRED, TOO, YOU KNOW, AND YET WHERE IS ALL THE FUN, AND WHO IS TO SAY, AND WHY, AND.."
SCHULZ

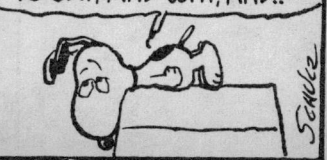

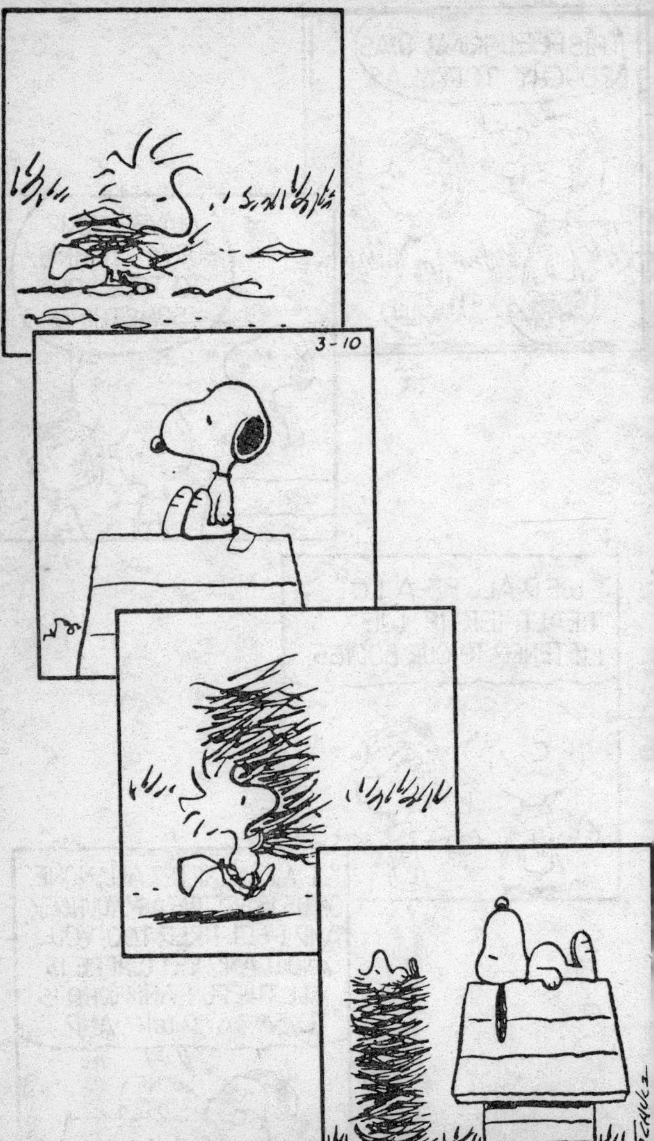
3-10
SCHULZ

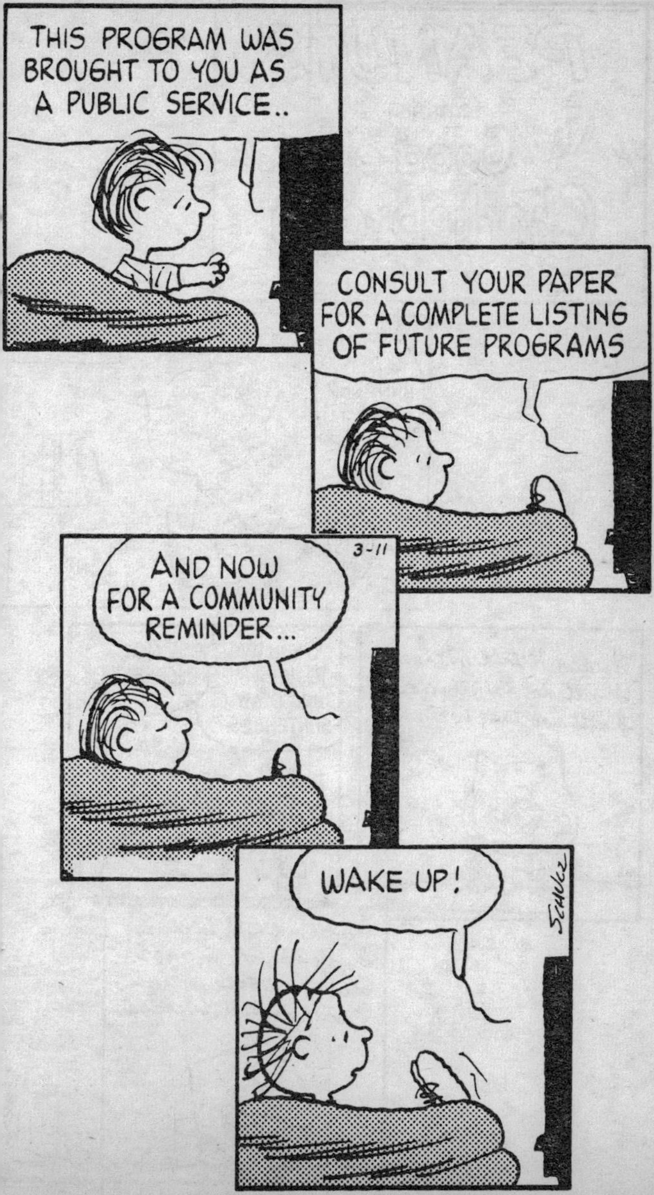
THIS PROGRAM WAS BROUGHT TO YOU AS A PUBLIC SERVICE..
CONSULT YOUR PAPER FOR A COMPLETE LISTING OF FUTURE PROGRAMS
3-11
AND NOW FOR A COMMUNITY REMINDER...
WAKE UP!
SCHULZ

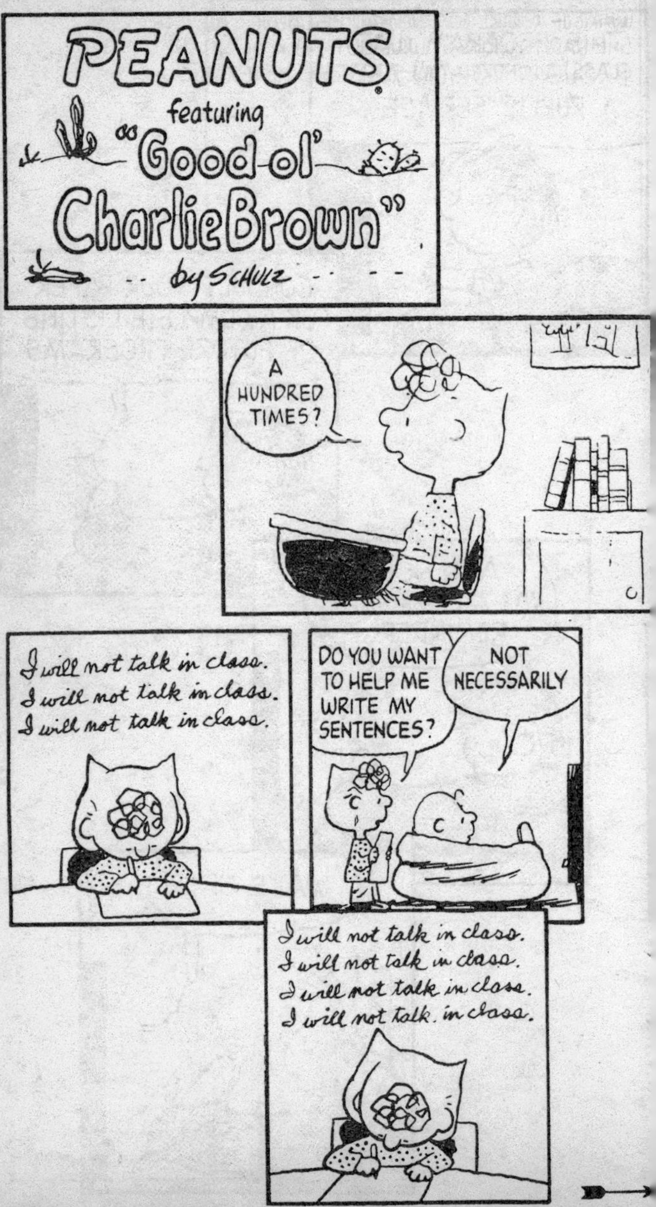
PEANUTS
featuring
"Good ol' Charlie Brown"
by SCHULZ
A HUNDRED TIMES?
I will not talk in class.
I will not talk in class.
I will not talk in class.
DO YOU WANT TO HELP ME WRITE MY SENTENCES?
NOT NECESSARILY
I will not talk in class.
I will not talk in class.
I will not talk in class.
I will not talk. in class.

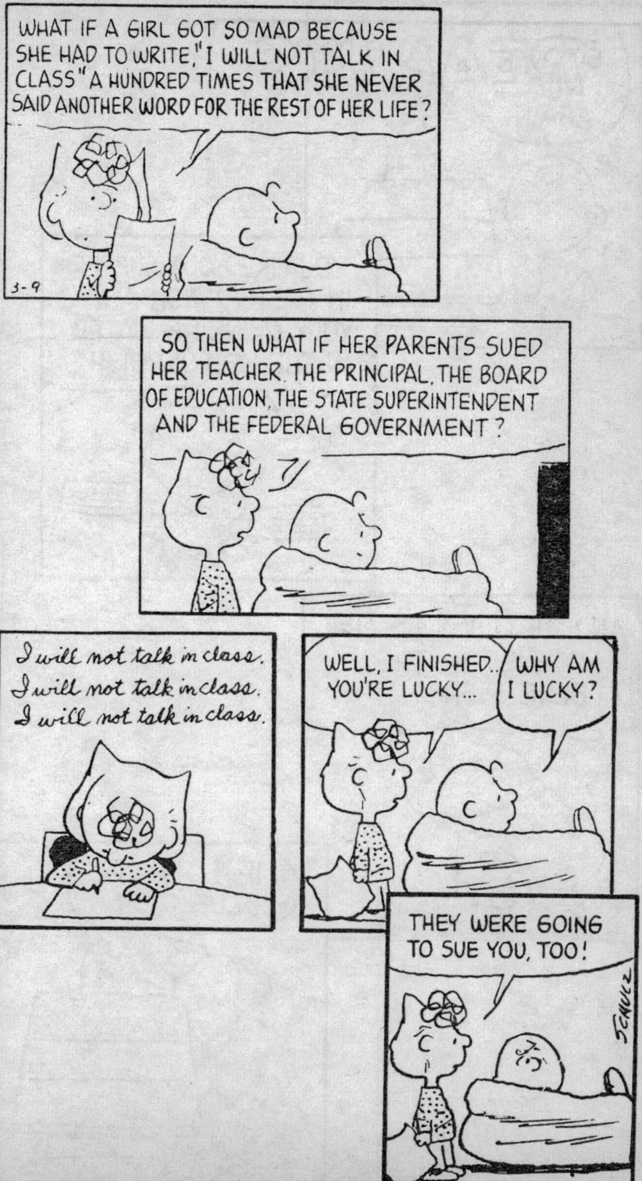
WHAT IF A GIRL GOT SO MAD BECAUSE SHE HAD TO WRITE, "I WILL NOT TALK IN CLASS" A HUNDRED TIMES THAT SHE NEVER SAID ANOTHER WORD FOR THE REST OF HER LIFE?
3-9
SO THEN WHAT IF HER PARENTS SUED HER TEACHER, THE PRINCIPAL, THE BOARD OF EDUCATION, THE STATE SUPERINTENDENT AND THE FEDERAL GOVERNMENT?
I will not talk in class.
I will not talk in class.
I will not talk in class.
WELL, I FINISHED.. YOU'RE LUCKY...
WHY AM I LUCKY?
THEY WERE GOING TO SUE YOU, TOO!
SCHULZ

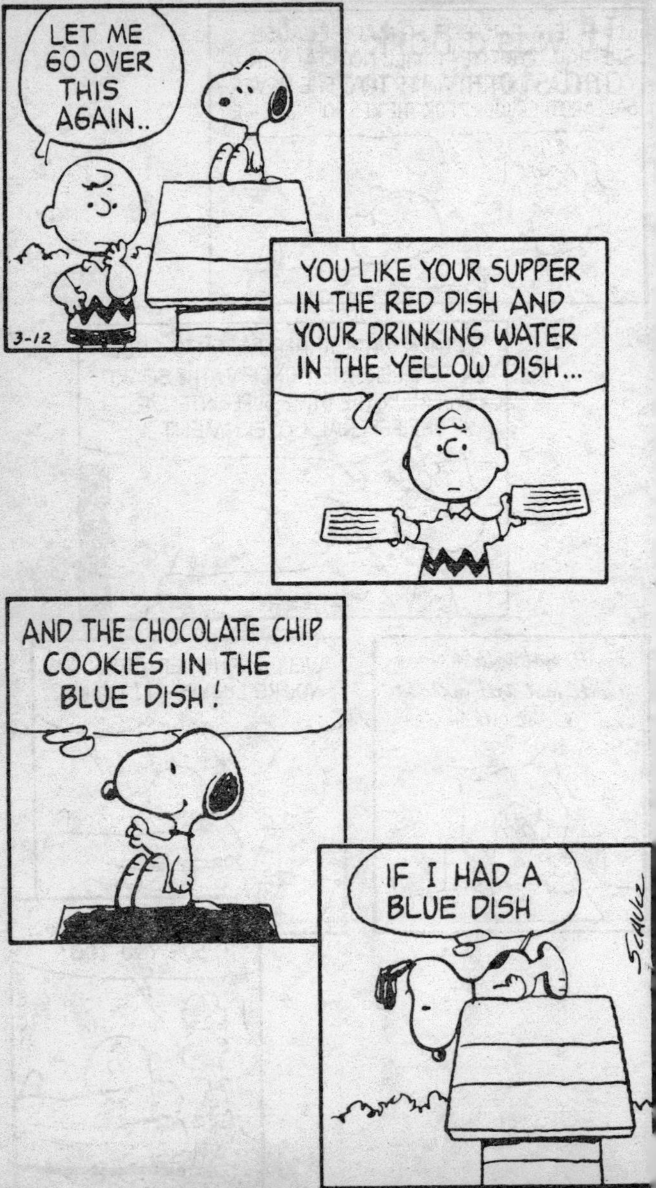
LET ME GO OVER THIS AGAIN..
3-12
YOU LIKE YOUR SUPPER IN THE RED DISH AND YOUR DRINKING WATER IN THE YELLOW DISH...
AND THE CHOCOLATE CHIP COOKIES IN THE BLUE DISH!
IF I HAD A BLUE DISH
SCHULZ

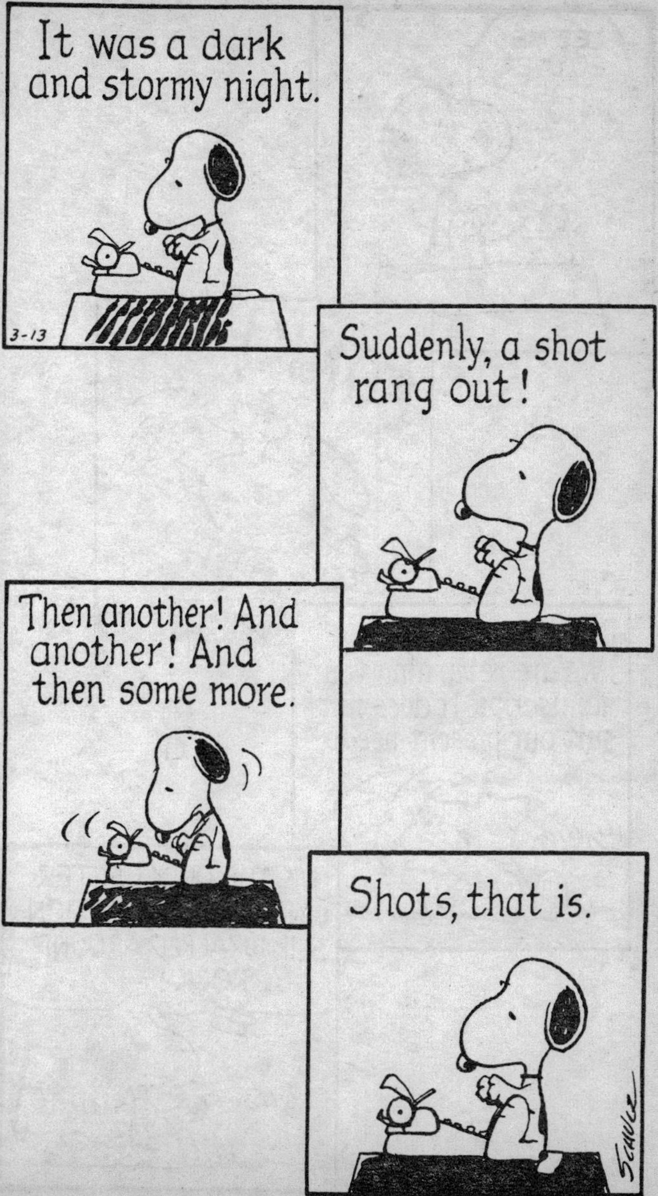

It was a dark and stormy night.
3-13
Suddenly, a shot rang out!
Then another! And another! And then some more.
Shots, that is.
SCHULZ

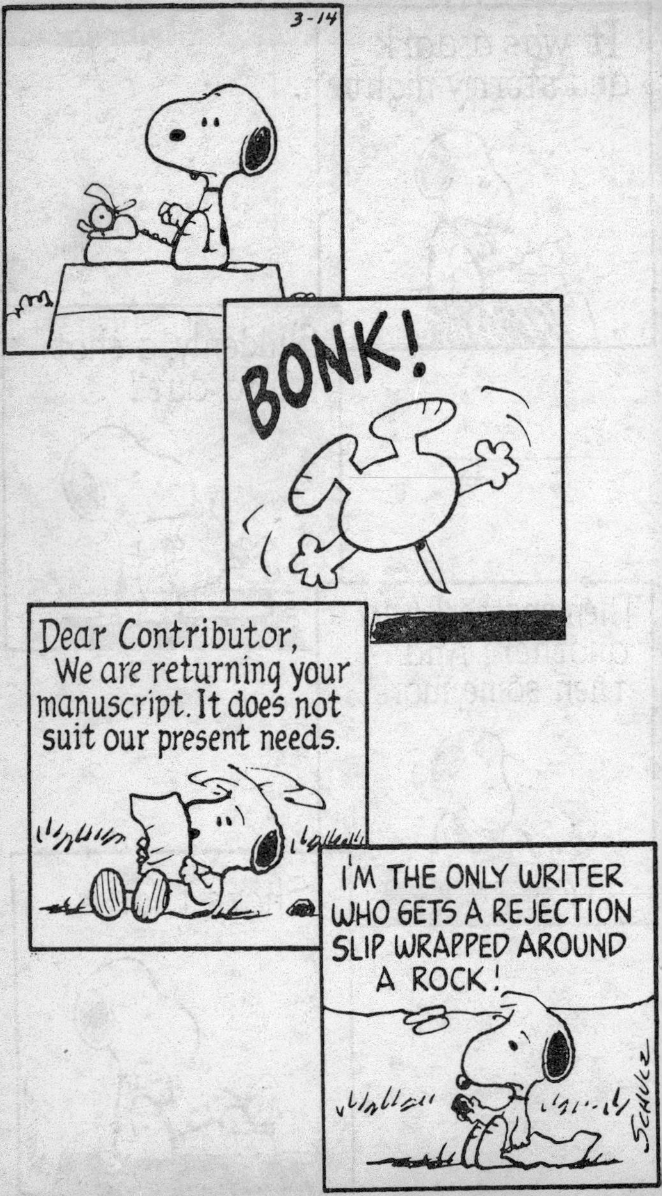
3-14
BONK!
Dear Contributor,
We are returning your manuscript. It does not suit our present needs.
I'M THE ONLY WRITER WHO GETS A REJECTION SLIP WRAPPED AROUND A ROCK!
SCHULZ

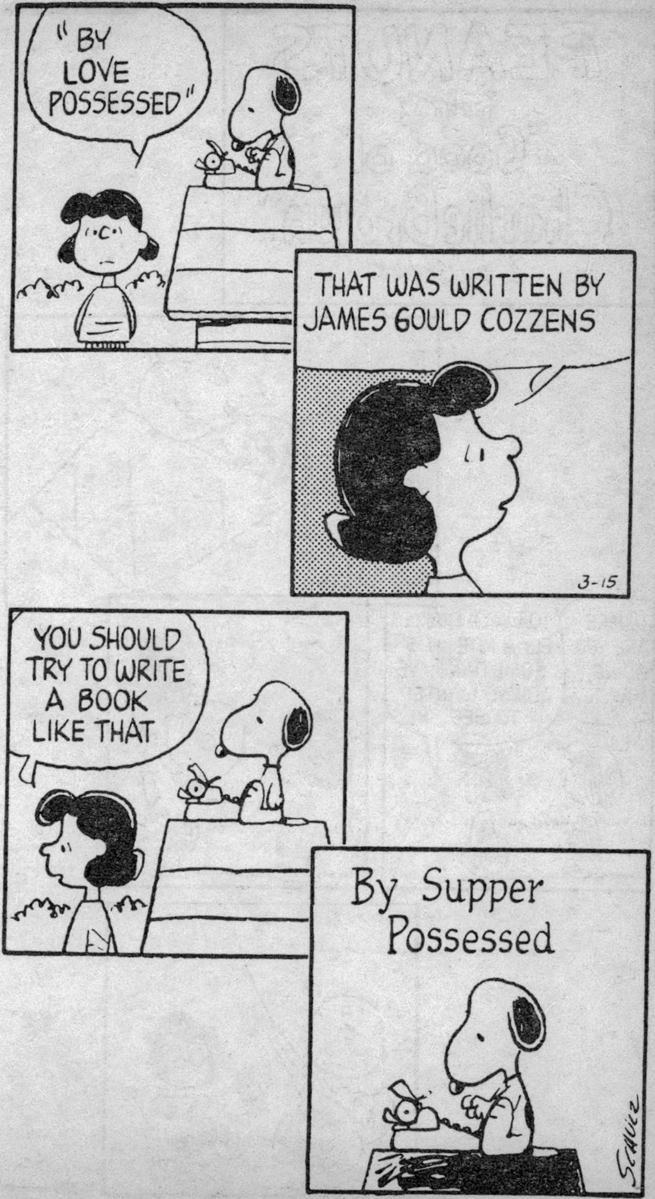
"BY LOVE POSSESSED"
THAT WAS WRITTEN BY JAMES GOULD COZZENS
3-15
YOU SHOULD TRY TO WRITE A BOOK LIKE THAT
By Supper Possessed
SCHULZ

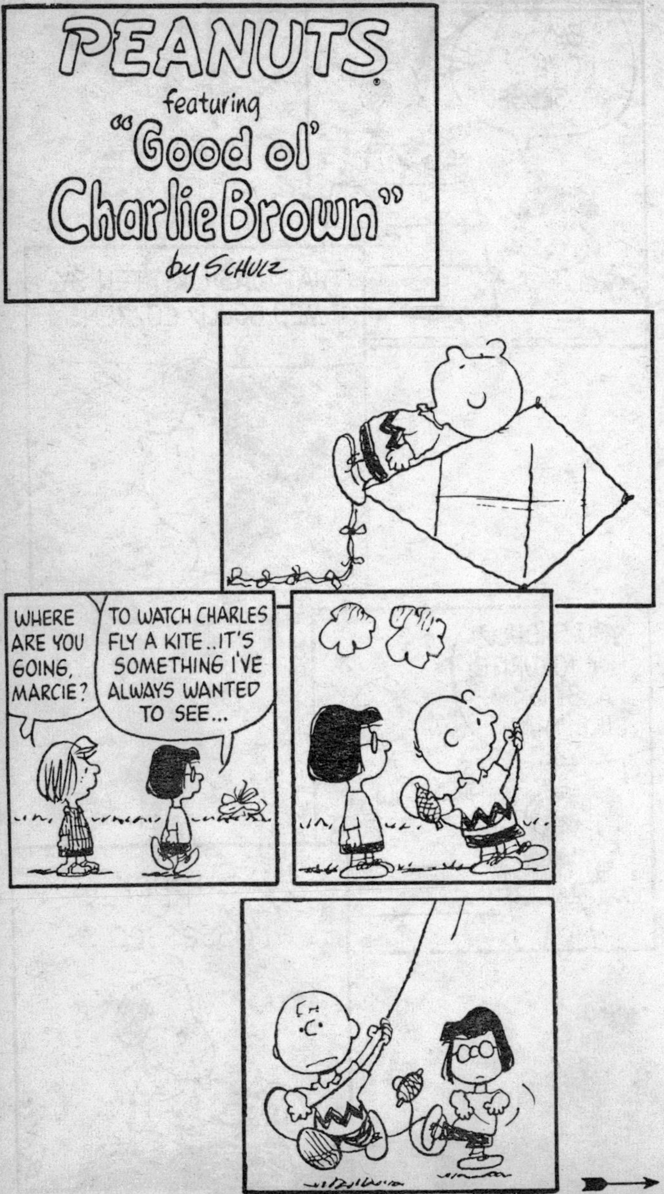

PEANUTS
featuring
"Good ol' Charlie Brown"
by SCHULZ
WHERE ARE YOU GOING, MARCIE?
TO WATCH CHARLES FLY A KITE..IT'S SOMETHING I'VE ALWAYS WANTED TO SEE...

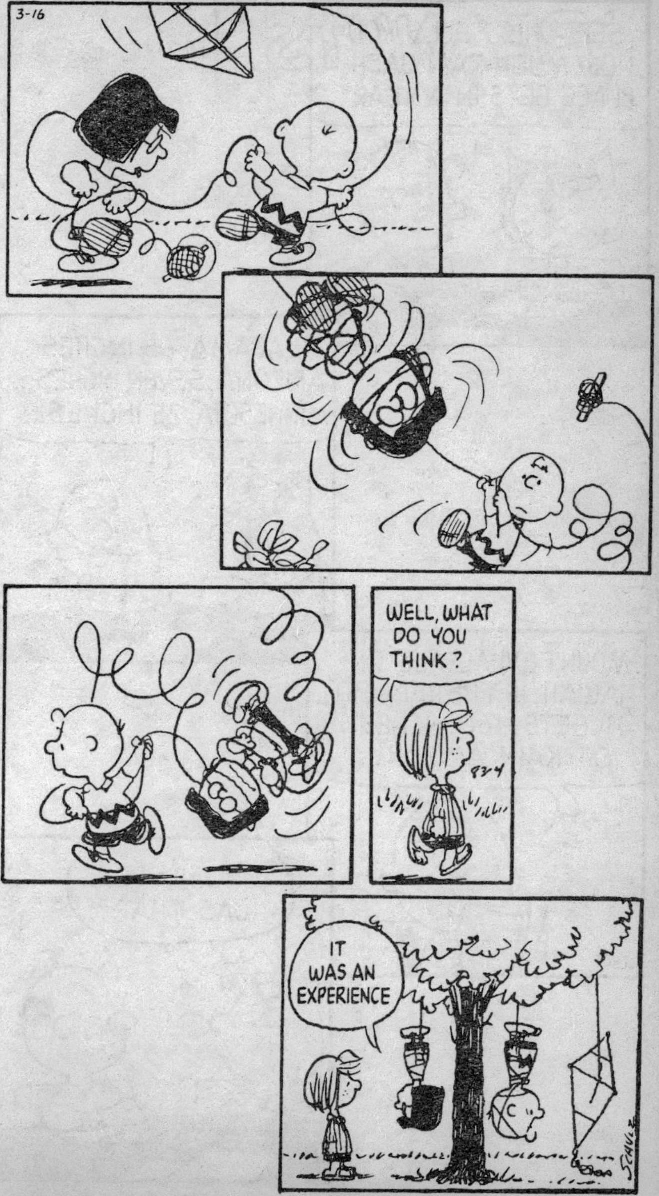
3-16
WELL, WHAT DO YOU THINK?
IT WAS AN EXPERIENCE
SCHULZ

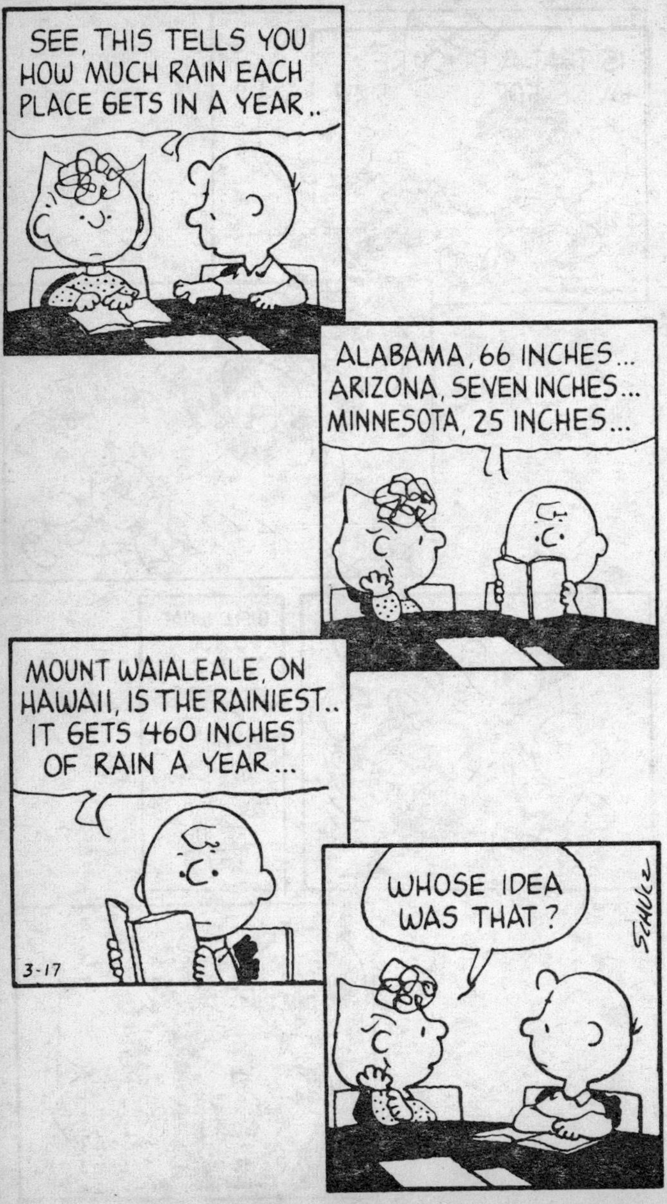
SEE, THIS TELLS YOU HOW MUCH RAIN EACH PLACE GETS IN A YEAR..
ALABAMA, 66 INCHES... ARIZONA, SEVEN INCHES... MINNESOTA, 25 INCHES...
MOUNT WAIALEALE, ON HAWAII, IS THE RAINIEST.. IT GETS 460 INCHES OF RAIN A YEAR...
3-17
WHOSE IDEA WAS THAT?
SCHULZ

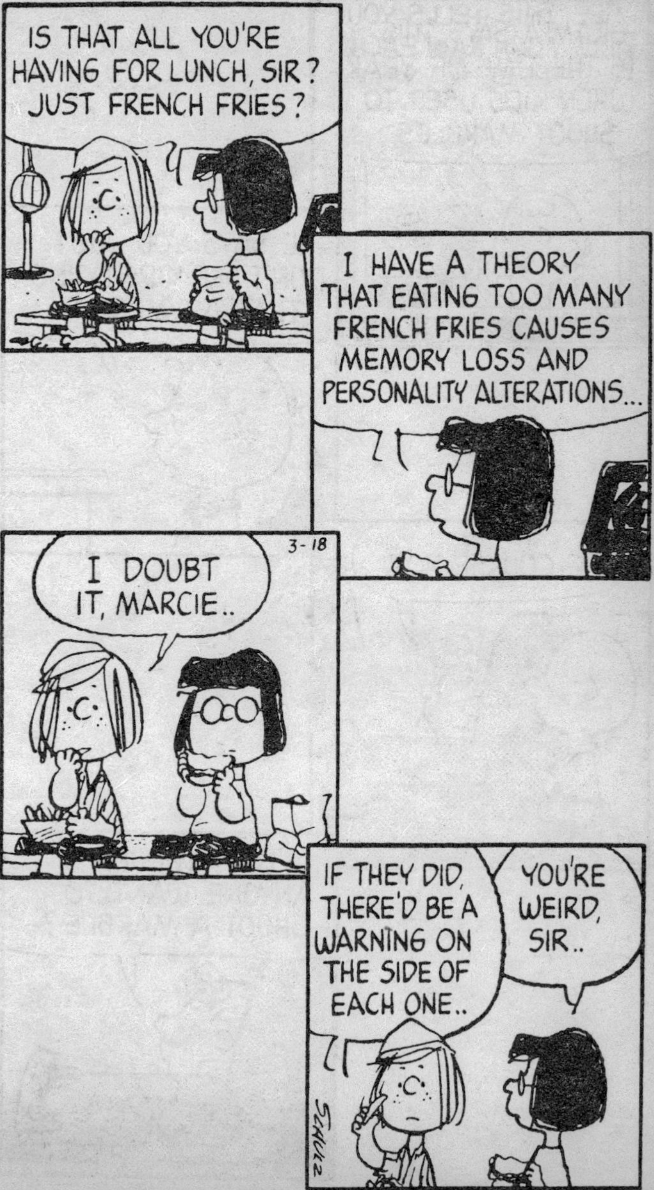
IS THAT ALL YOU'RE HAVING FOR LUNCH, SIR? JUST FRENCH FRIES?
I HAVE A THEORY THAT EATING TOO MANY FRENCH FRIES CAUSES MEMORY LOSS AND PERSONALITY ALTERATIONS...
3-18
I DOUBT IT, MARCIE..
IF THEY DID, THERE'D BE A WARNING ON THE SIDE OF EACH ONE..
YOU'RE WEIRD, SIR..
SCHULZ

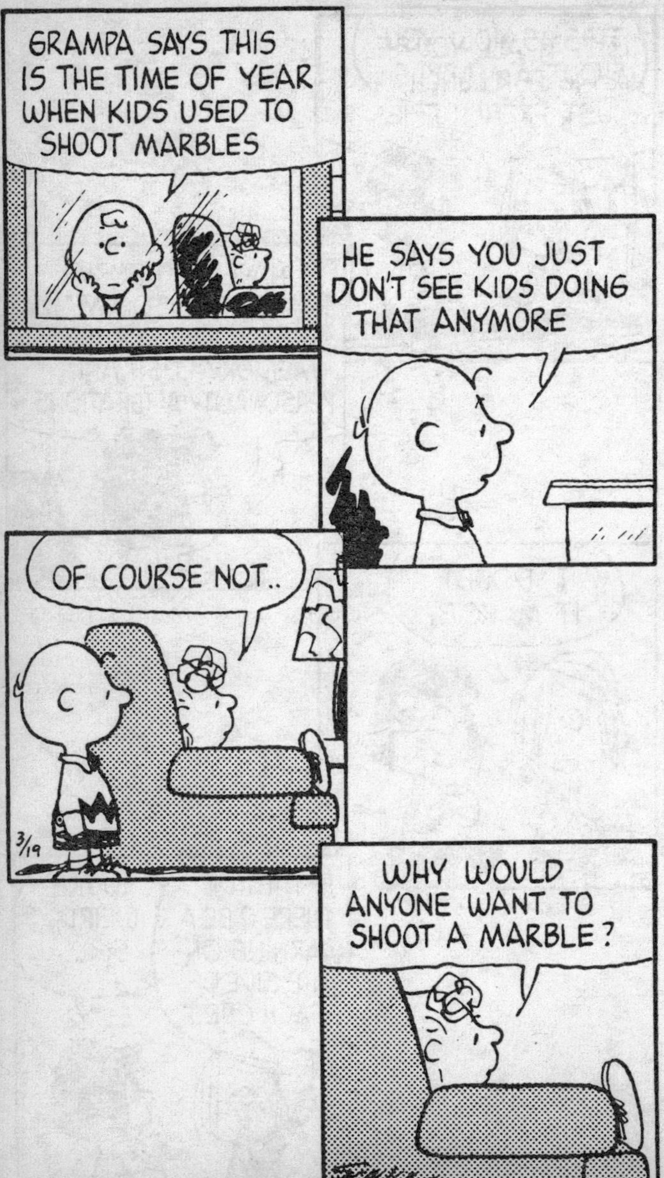
GRAMPA SAYS THIS IS THE TIME OF YEAR WHEN KIDS USED TO SHOOT MARBLES
HE SAYS YOU JUST DON'T SEE KIDS DOING THAT ANYMORE
OF COURSE NOT..
WHY WOULD ANYONE WANT TO SHOOT A MARBLE?
3/19

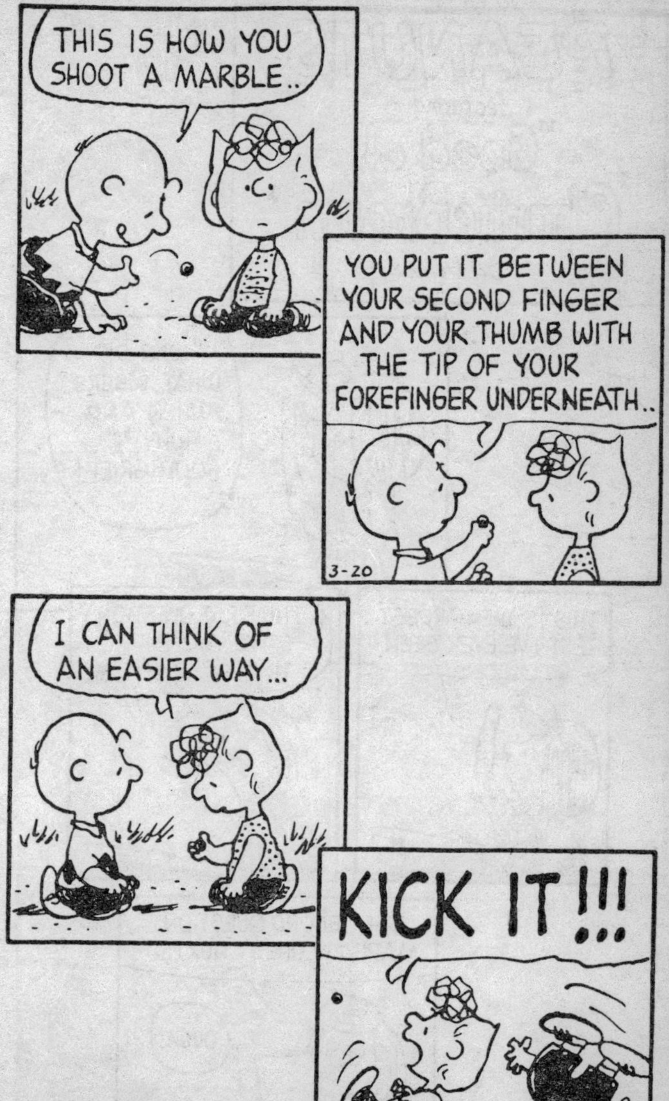
THIS IS HOW YOU SHOOT A MARBLE..
YOU PUT IT BETWEEN YOUR SECOND FINGER AND YOUR THUMB WITH THE TIP OF YOUR FOREFINGER UNDERNEATH..
3-20
I CAN THINK OF AN EASIER WAY...
KICK IT!!!
SCHULZ

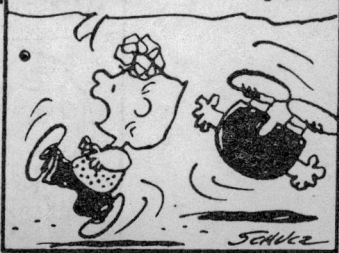

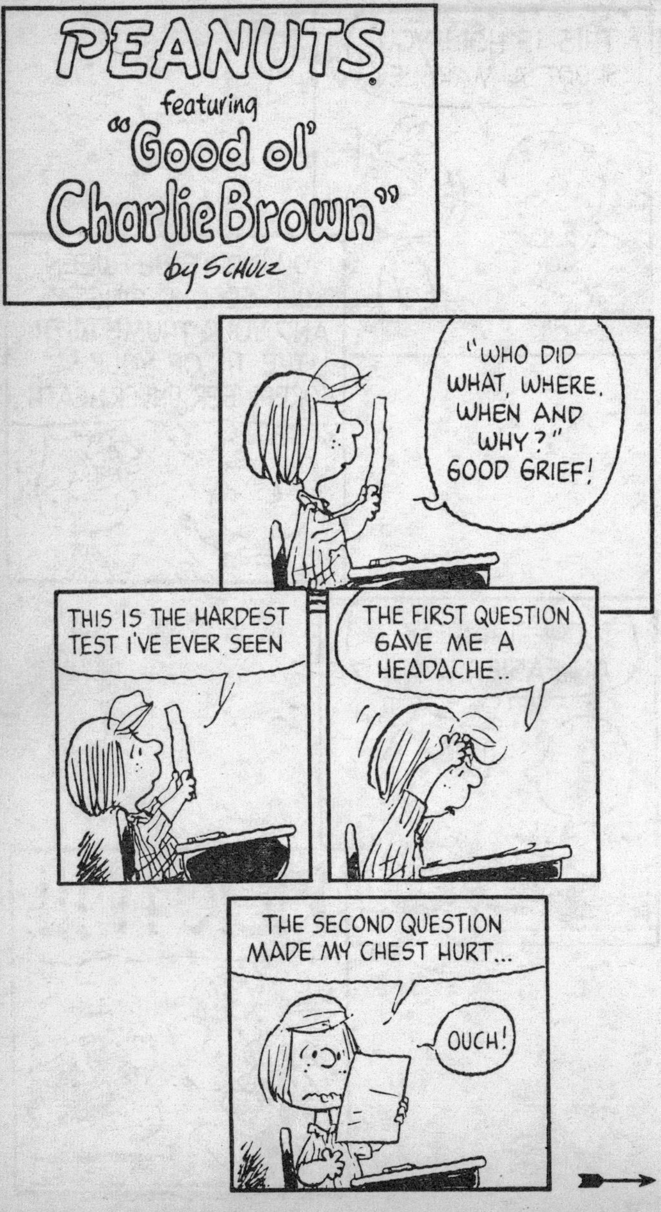
PEANUTS®
featuring
"Good ol' Charlie Brown"
by SCHULZ
"WHO DID WHAT, WHERE, WHEN AND WHY?" GOOD GRIEF!
THIS IS THE HARDEST TEST I'VE EVER SEEN
THE FIRST QUESTION GAVE ME A HEADACHE..
THE SECOND QUESTION MADE MY CHEST HURT...
OUCH!

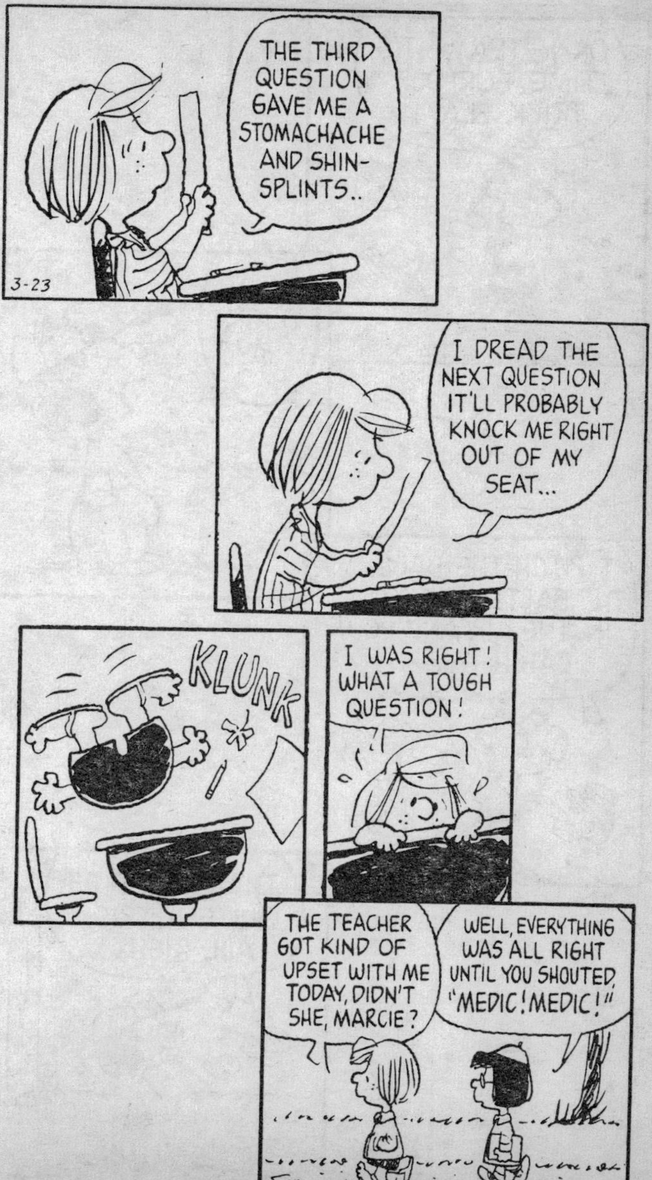

3-23
THE THIRD QUESTION GAVE ME A STOMACHACHE AND SHIN-SPLINTS..
I DREAD THE NEXT QUESTION IT'LL PROBABLY KNOCK ME RIGHT OUT OF MY SEAT...
KLUNK
I WAS RIGHT! WHAT A TOUGH QUESTION!
THE TEACHER GOT KIND OF UPSET WITH ME TODAY, DIDN'T SHE, MARCIE?
WELL, EVERYTHING WAS ALL RIGHT UNTIL YOU SHOUTED, "MEDIC! MEDIC!"

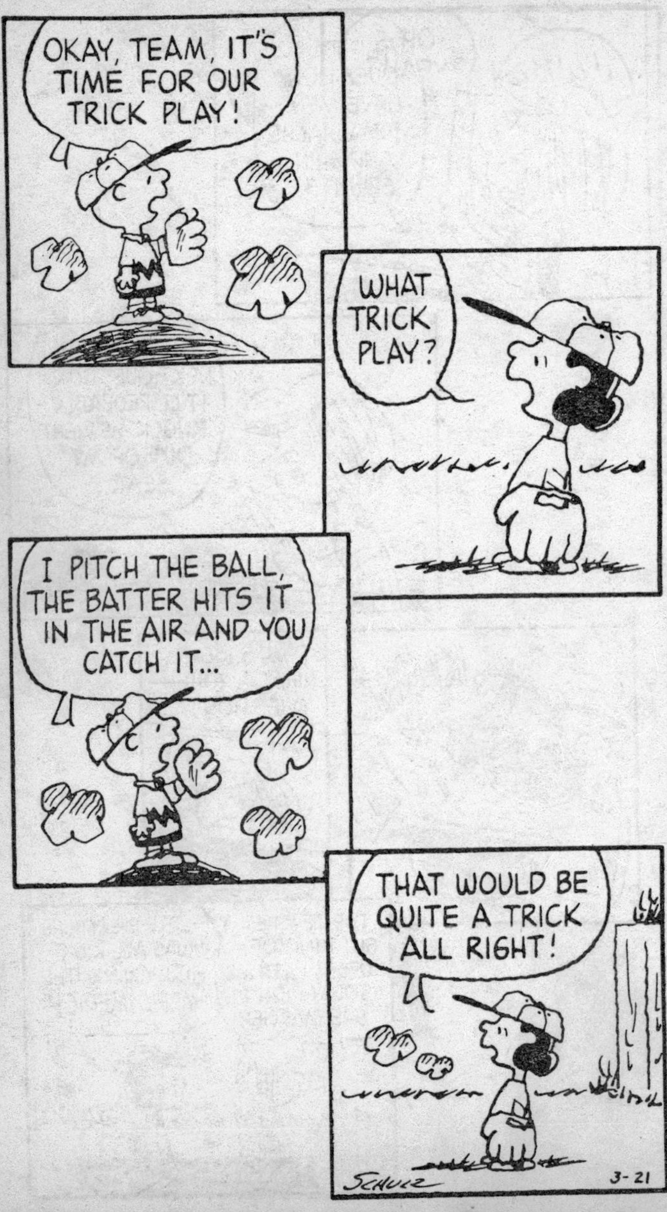
OKAY, TEAM, IT'S TIME FOR OUR TRICK PLAY!
WHAT TRICK PLAY?
I PITCH THE BALL, THE BATTER HITS IT IN THE AIR AND YOU CATCH IT...
THAT WOULD BE QUITE A TRICK ALL RIGHT!
SCHULZ
3-21

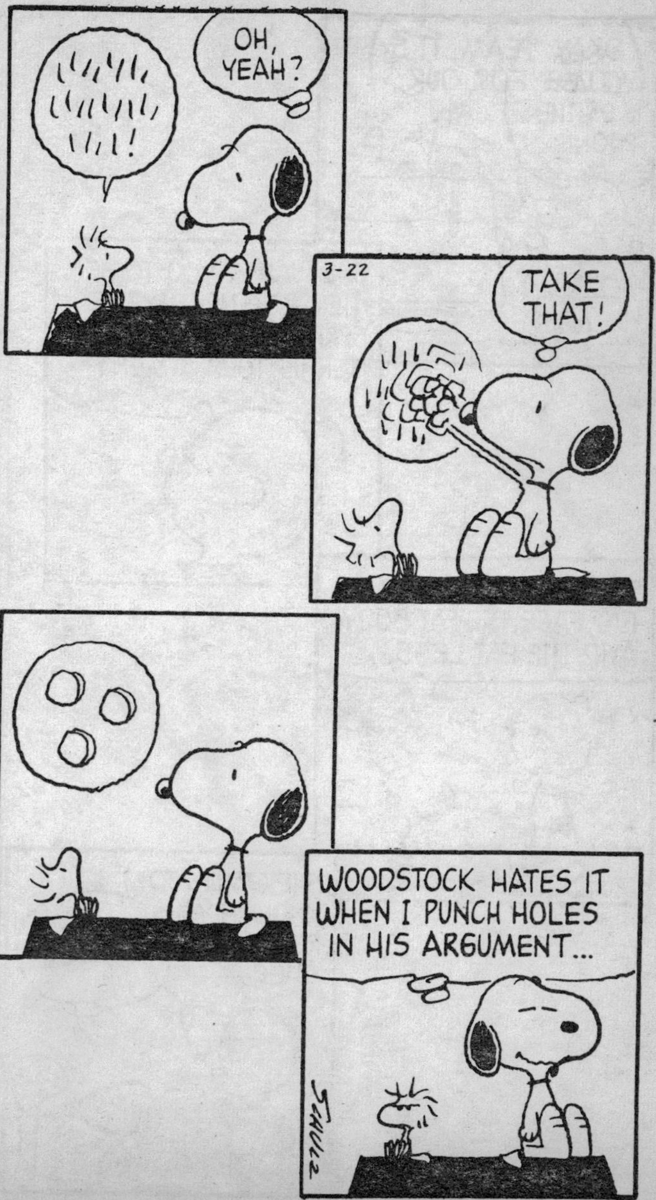
OH, YEAH?
3-22
TAKE THAT!
WOODSTOCK HATES IT WHEN I PUNCH HOLES IN HIS ARGUMENT...
SCHULZ

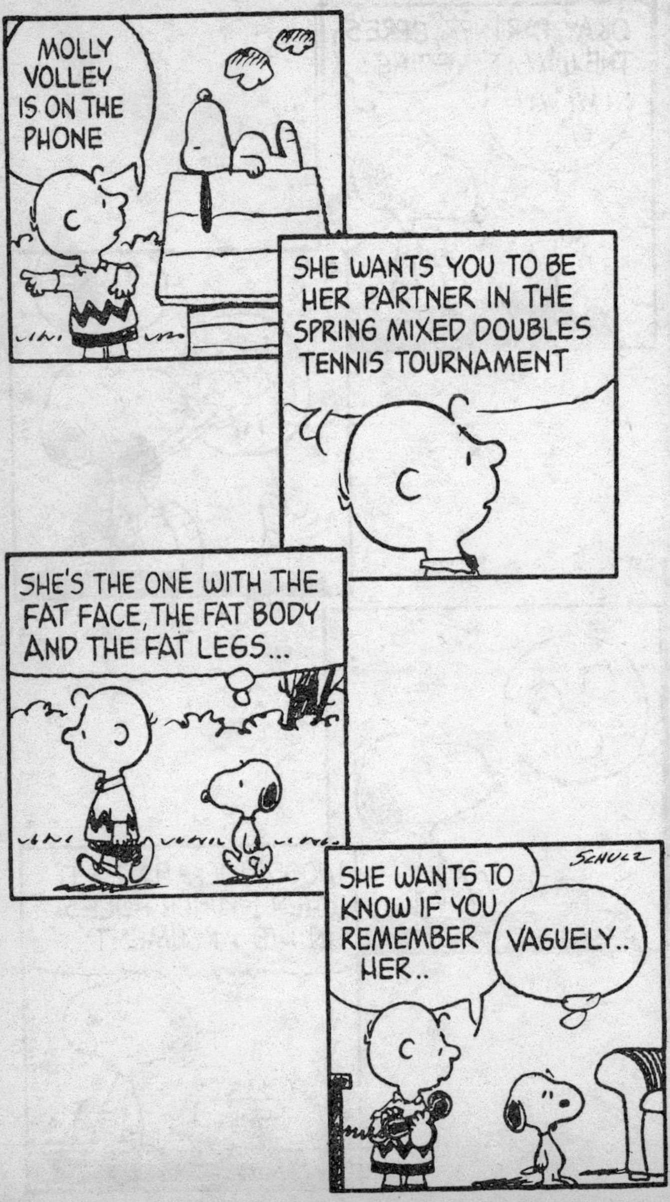
MOLLY VOLLEY IS ON THE PHONE
SHE WANTS YOU TO BE HER PARTNER IN THE SPRING MIXED DOUBLES TENNIS TOURNAMENT
SHE'S THE ONE WITH THE FAT FACE, THE FAT BODY AND THE FAT LEGS...
SCHULZ
SHE WANTS TO KNOW IF YOU REMEMBER HER..
VAGUELY..

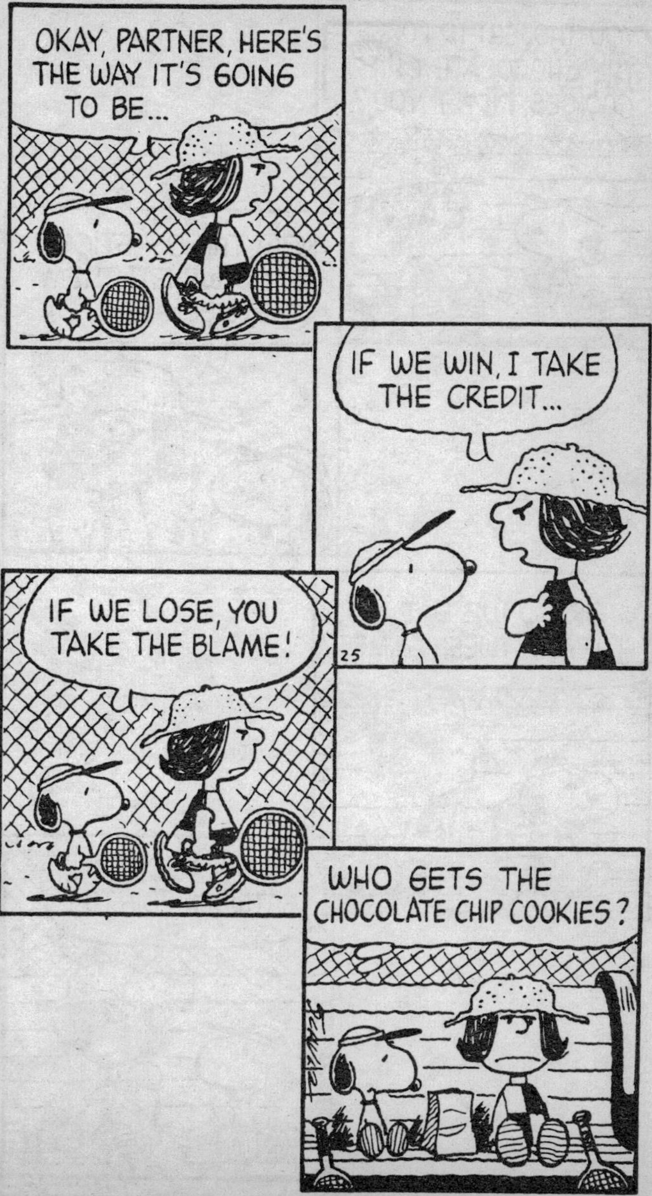
OKAY, PARTNER, HERE'S THE WAY IT'S GOING TO BE...
IF WE WIN, I TAKE THE CREDIT...
IF WE LOSE, YOU TAKE THE BLAME!
WHO GETS THE CHOCOLATE CHIP COOKIES?

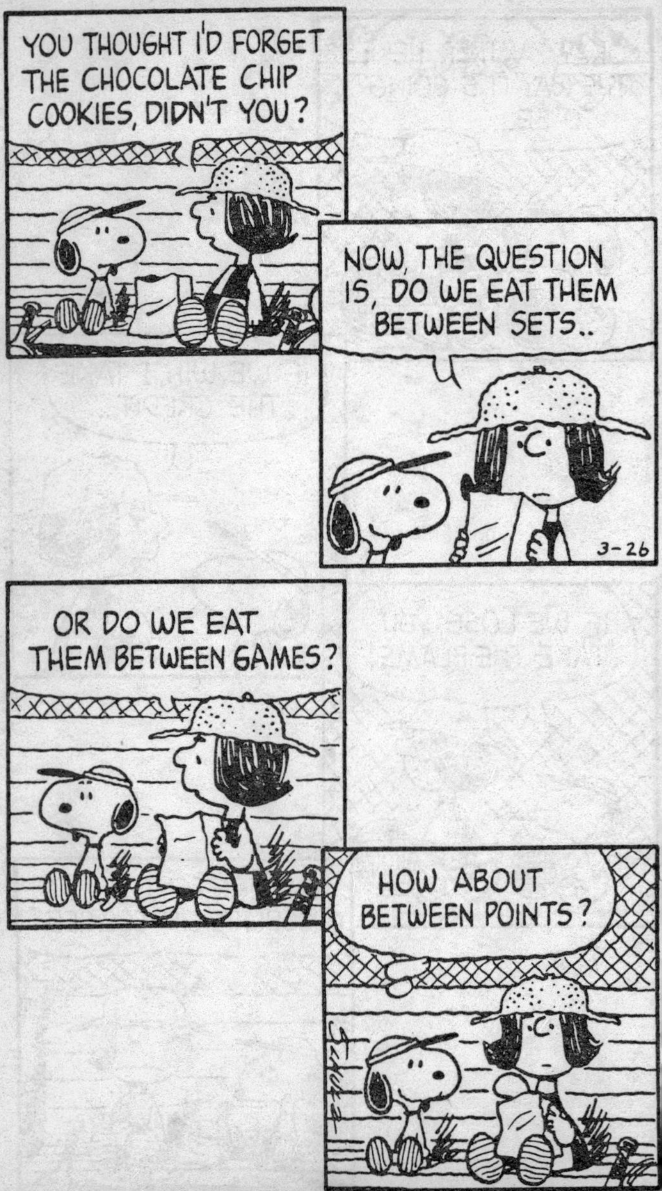
YOU THOUGHT I'D FORGET THE CHOCOLATE CHIP COOKIES, DIDN'T YOU?
NOW, THE QUESTION IS, DO WE EAT THEM BETWEEN SETS..
3-26
OR DO WE EAT THEM BETWEEN GAMES?
HOW ABOUT BETWEEN POINTS?

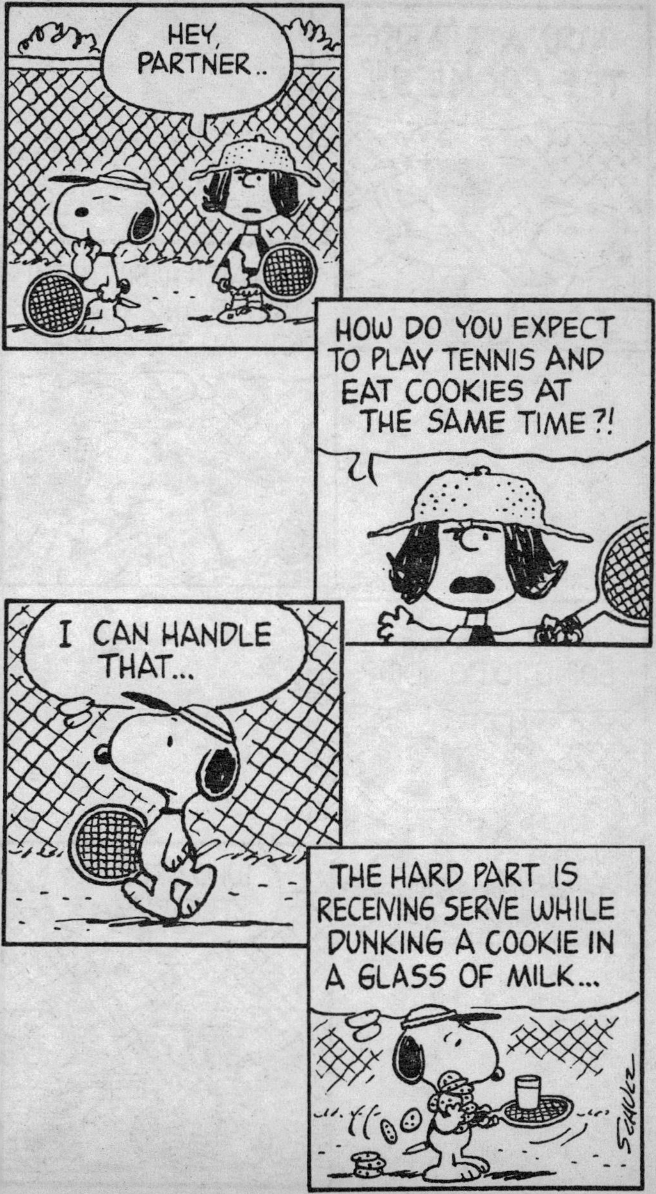
HEY, PARTNER..
HOW DO YOU EXPECT TO PLAY TENNIS AND EAT COOKIES AT THE SAME TIME?!
I CAN HANDLE THAT...
THE HARD PART IS RECEIVING SERVE WHILE DUNKING A COOKIE IN A GLASS OF MILK...
SCHULZ

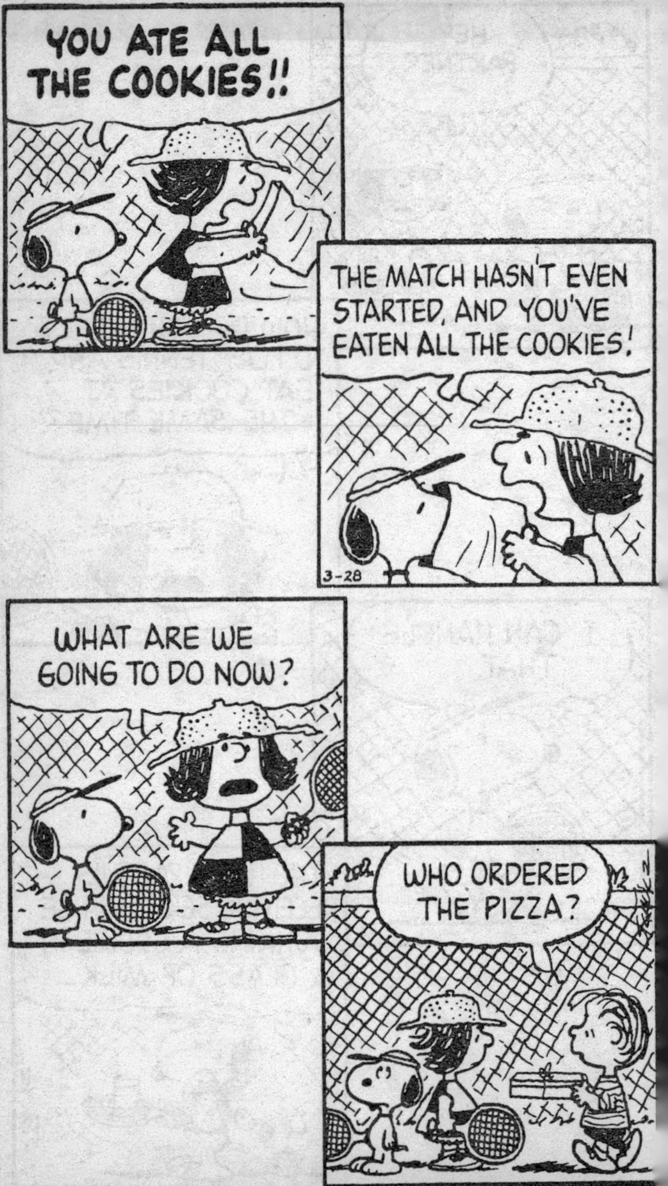
YOU ATE ALL THE COOKIES!!
THE MATCH HASN'T EVEN STARTED, AND YOU'VE EATEN ALL THE COOKIES!
3-28
WHAT ARE WE GOING TO DO NOW?
WHO ORDERED THE PIZZA?

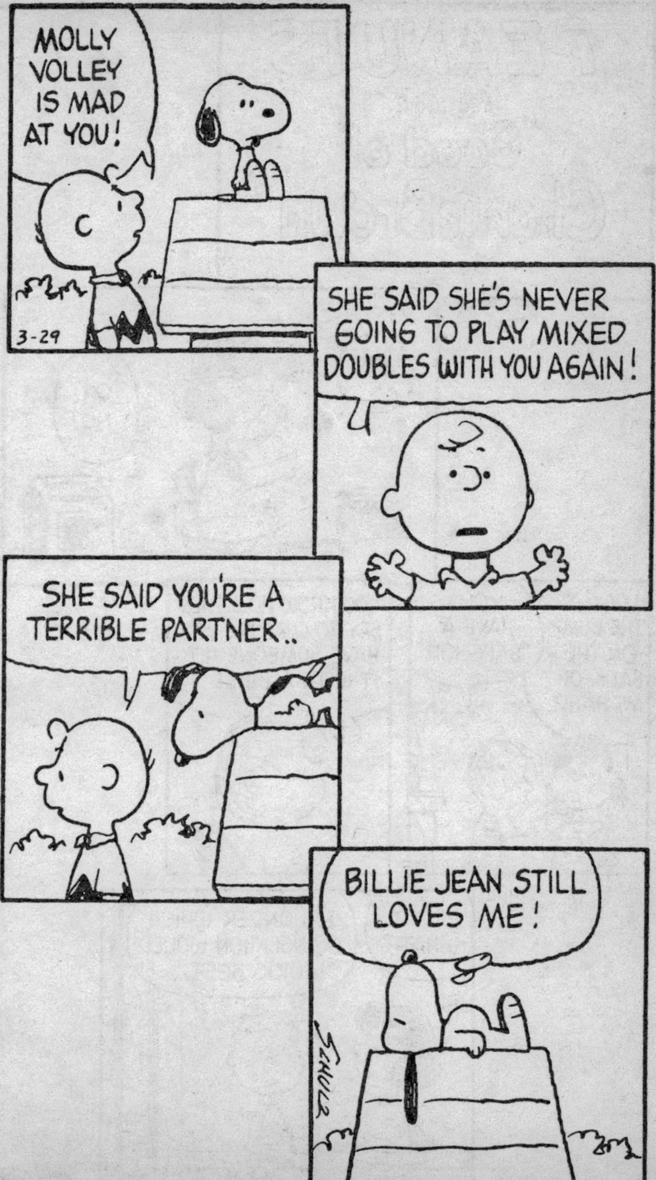
MOLLY VOLLEY IS MAD AT YOU!
3-29
SHE SAID SHE'S NEVER GOING TO PLAY MIXED DOUBLES WITH YOU AGAIN!
SHE SAID YOU'RE A TERRIBLE PARTNER..
BILLIE JEAN STILL LOVES ME!
SCHULZ

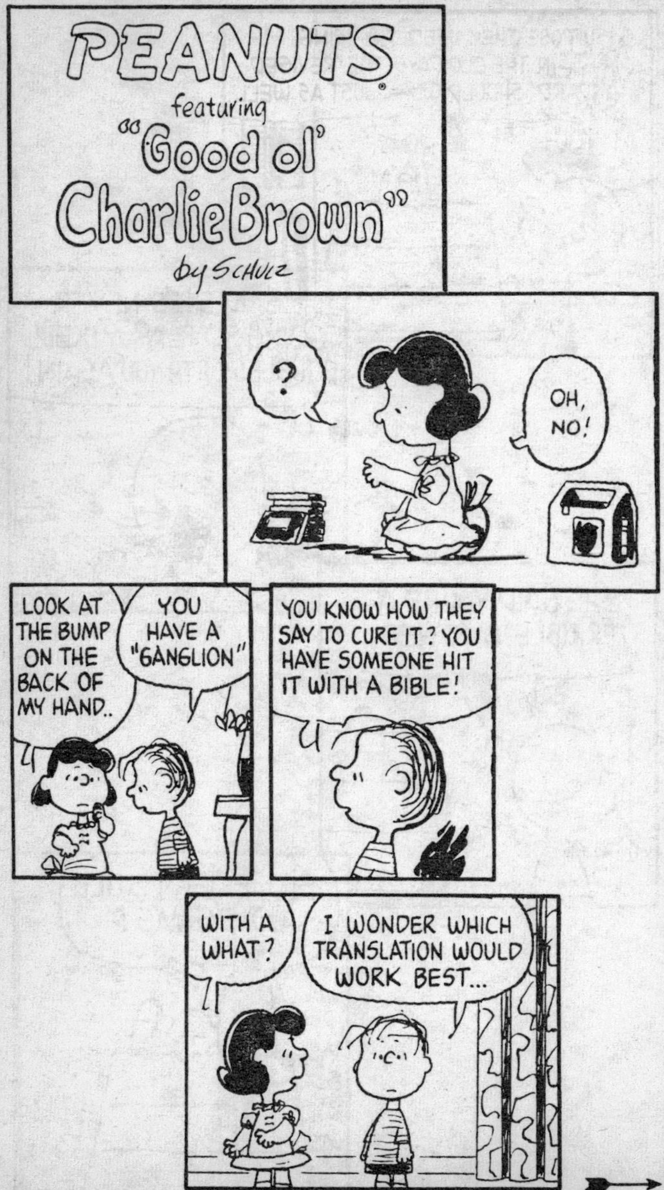
PEANUTS
featuring
"Good ol' Charlie Brown"
by SCHULZ
?
OH, NO!
LOOK AT THE BUMP ON THE BACK OF MY HAND..
YOU HAVE A "GANGLION"
YOU KNOW HOW THEY SAY TO CURE IT? YOU HAVE SOMEONE HIT IT WITH A BIBLE!
WITH A WHAT?
I WONDER WHICH TRANSLATION WOULD WORK BEST...

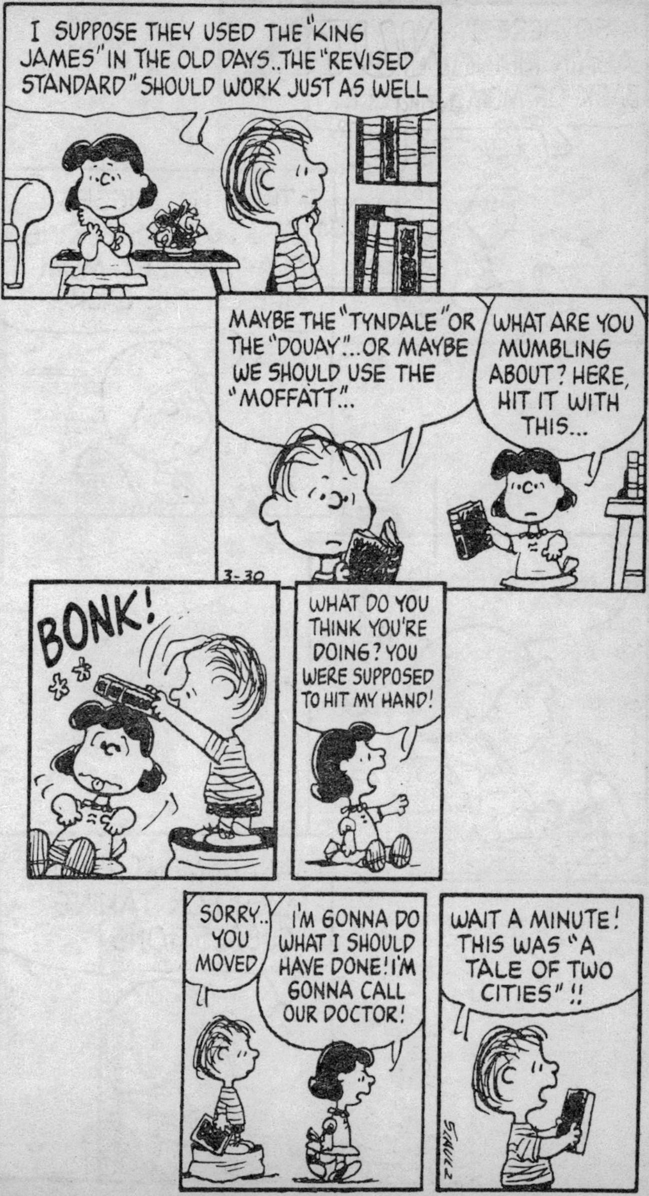
I SUPPOSE THEY USED THE "KING JAMES" IN THE OLD DAYS..THE "REVISED STANDARD" SHOULD WORK JUST AS WELL
MAYBE THE "TYNDALE" OR THE "DOUAY"...OR MAYBE WE SHOULD USE THE "MOFFATT"...
WHAT ARE YOU MUMBLING ABOUT? HERE, HIT IT WITH THIS...
3-30
BONK!
WHAT DO YOU THINK YOU'RE DOING? YOU WERE SUPPOSED TO HIT MY HAND!
SORRY.. YOU MOVED
I'M GONNA DO WHAT I SHOULD HAVE DONE! I'M GONNA CALL OUR DOCTOR!
WAIT A MINUTE! THIS WAS "A TALE OF TWO CITIES"!!
SCHULZ

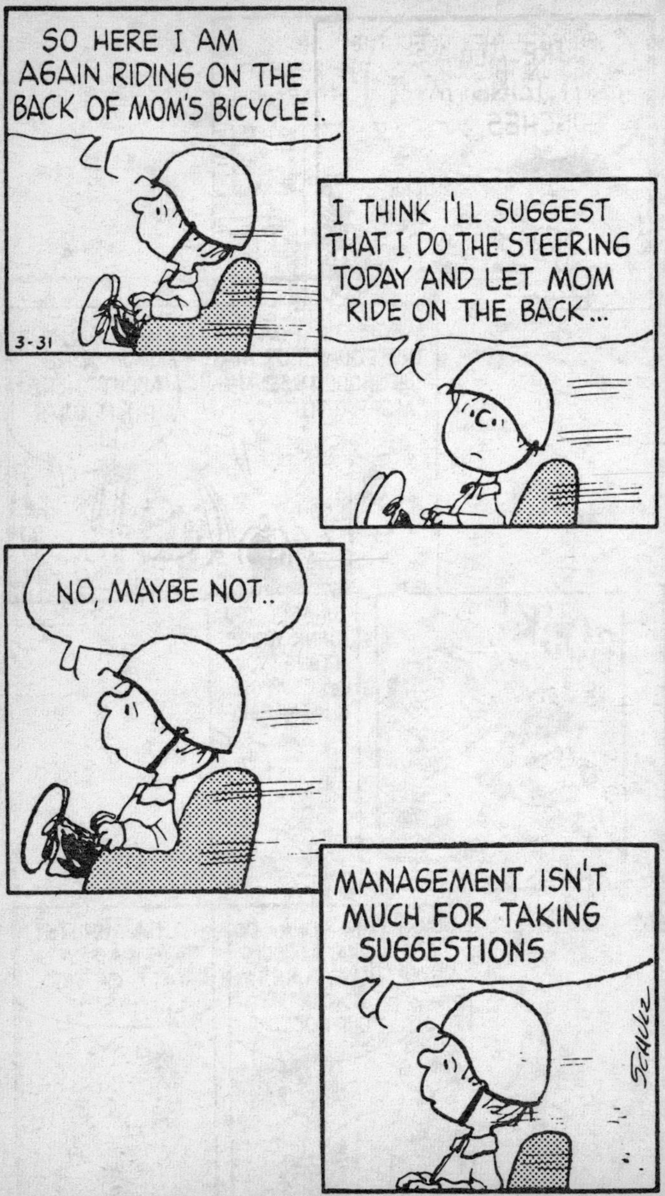
SO HERE I AM AGAIN RIDING ON THE BACK OF MOM'S BICYCLE..
3-31
I THINK I'LL SUGGEST THAT I DO THE STEERING TODAY AND LET MOM RIDE ON THE BACK...
NO, MAYBE NOT..
MANAGEMENT ISN'T MUCH FOR TAKING SUGGESTIONS
SCHULZ

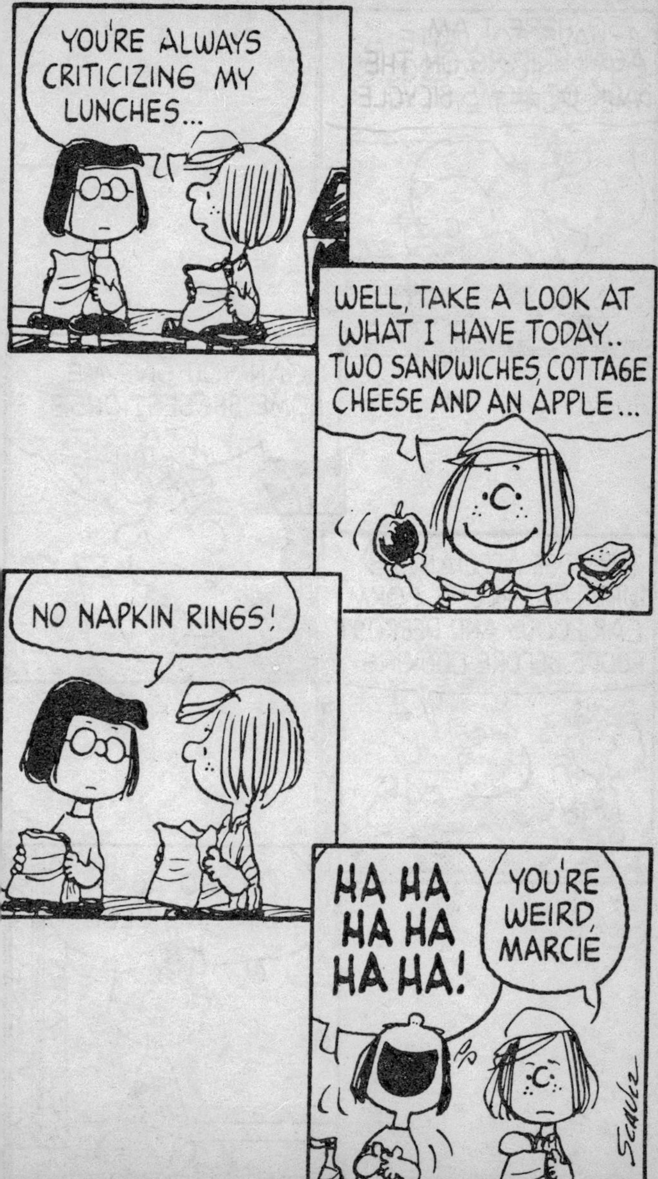
YOU'RE ALWAYS CRITICIZING MY LUNCHES...
WELL, TAKE A LOOK AT WHAT I HAVE TODAY.. TWO SANDWICHES, COTTAGE CHEESE AND AN APPLE...
NO NAPKIN RINGS!
HA HA HA HA HA HA!
YOU'RE WEIRD, MARCIE
SCHULZ

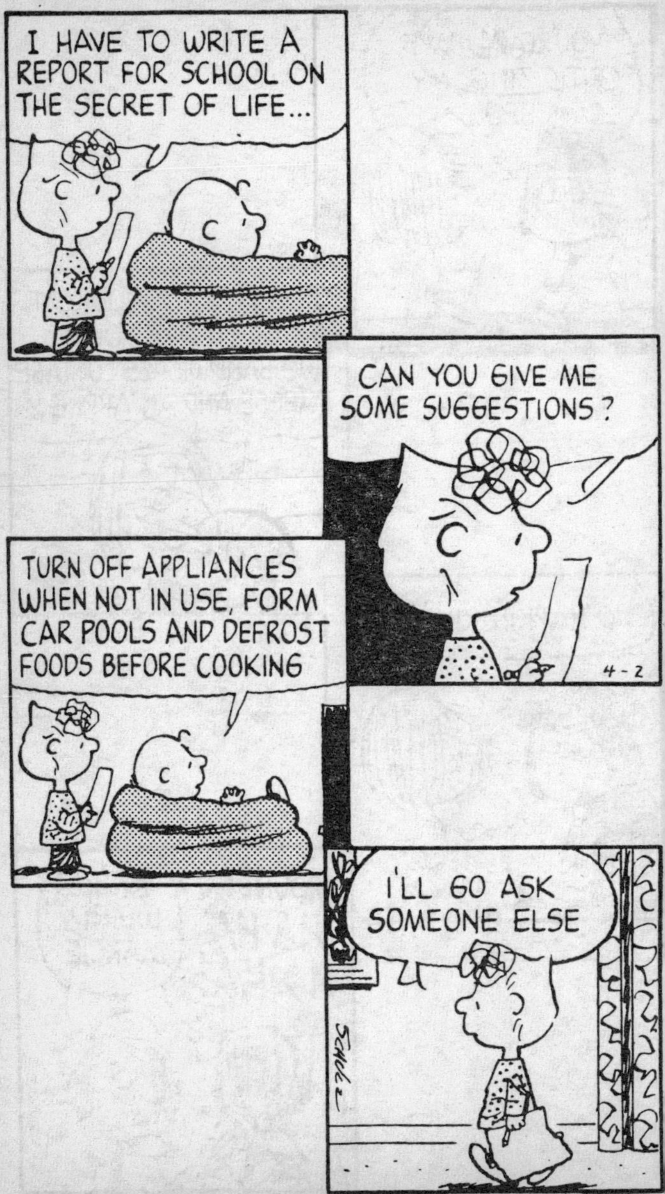
I HAVE TO WRITE A REPORT FOR SCHOOL ON THE SECRET OF LIFE...
CAN YOU GIVE ME SOME SUGGESTIONS?
4-2
TURN OFF APPLIANCES WHEN NOT IN USE, FORM CAR POOLS AND DEFROST FOODS BEFORE COOKING
I'LL GO ASK SOMEONE ELSE
SCHULZ

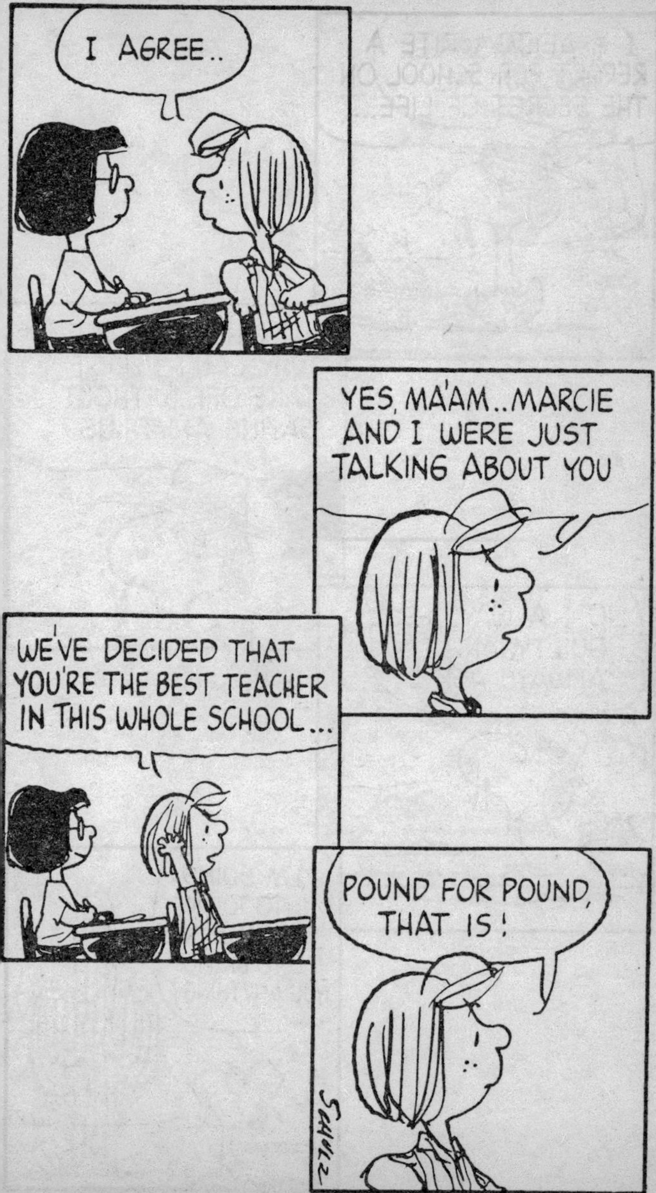
I AGREE..
YES, MA'AM..MARCIE AND I WERE JUST TALKING ABOUT YOU
WE'VE DECIDED THAT YOU'RE THE BEST TEACHER IN THIS WHOLE SCHOOL...
POUND FOR POUND, THAT IS!
SCHULZ

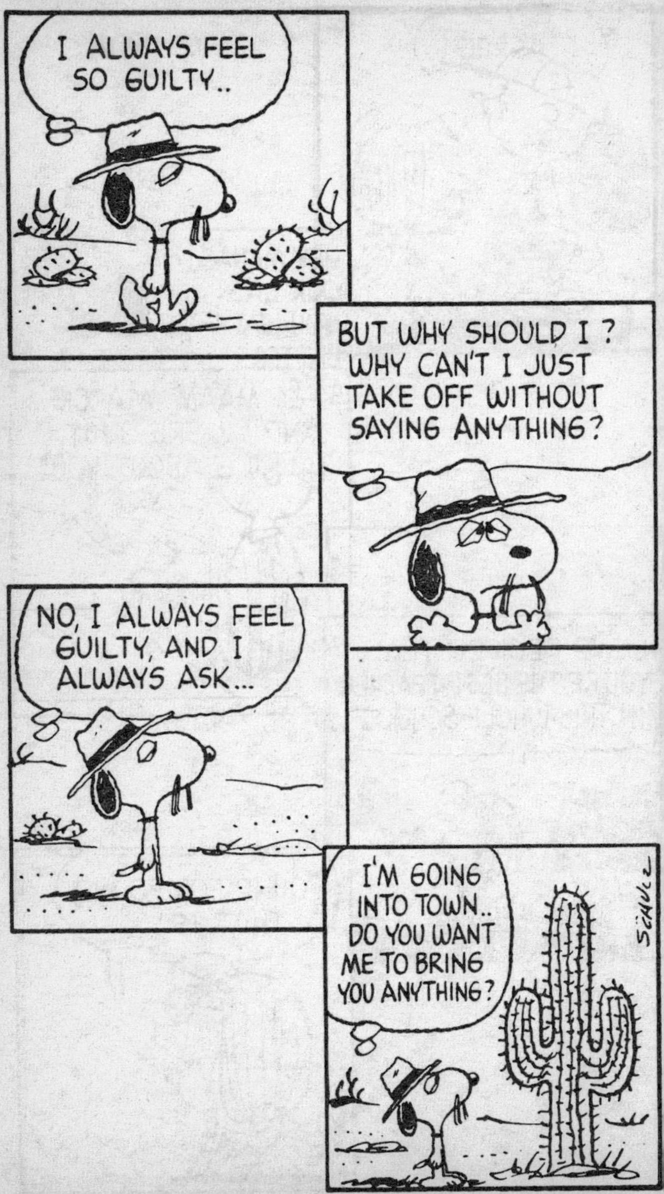
I ALWAYS FEEL SO GUILTY..
BUT WHY SHOULD I ? WHY CAN'T I JUST TAKE OFF WITHOUT SAYING ANYTHING?
NO, I ALWAYS FEEL GUILTY, AND I ALWAYS ASK...
I'M GOING INTO TOWN.. DO YOU WANT ME TO BRING YOU ANYTHING?
SCHULZ

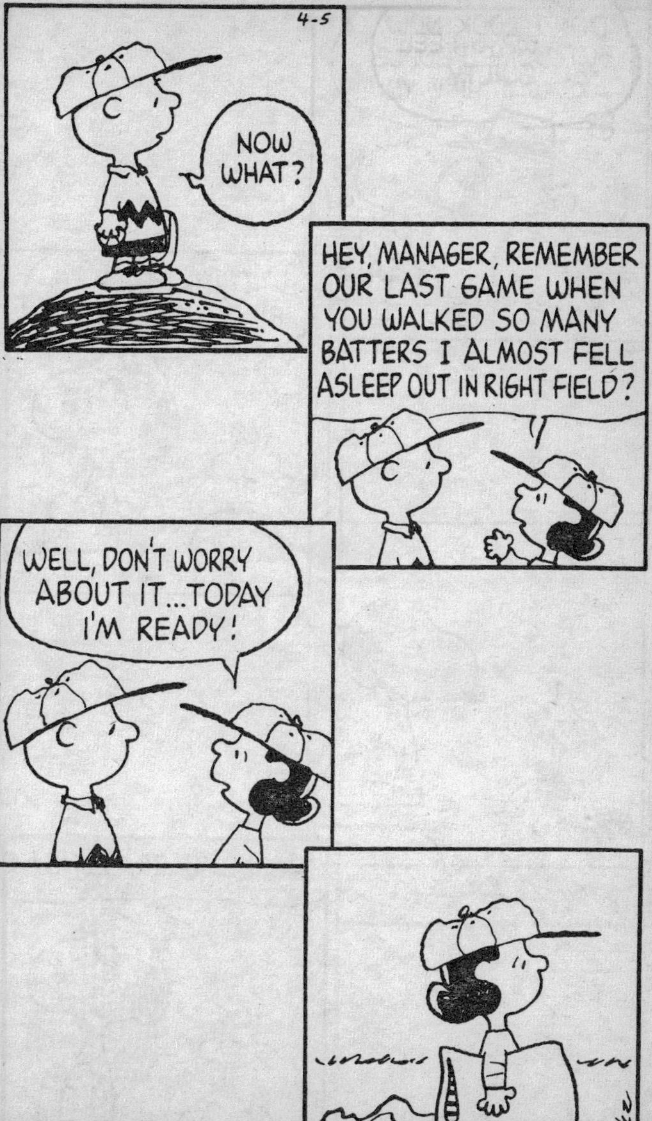
4-5
NOW WHAT?
HEY, MANAGER, REMEMBER OUR LAST GAME WHEN YOU WALKED SO MANY BATTERS I ALMOST FELL ASLEEP OUT IN RIGHT FIELD?
WELL, DON'T WORRY ABOUT IT...TODAY I'M READY!
SCHULZ

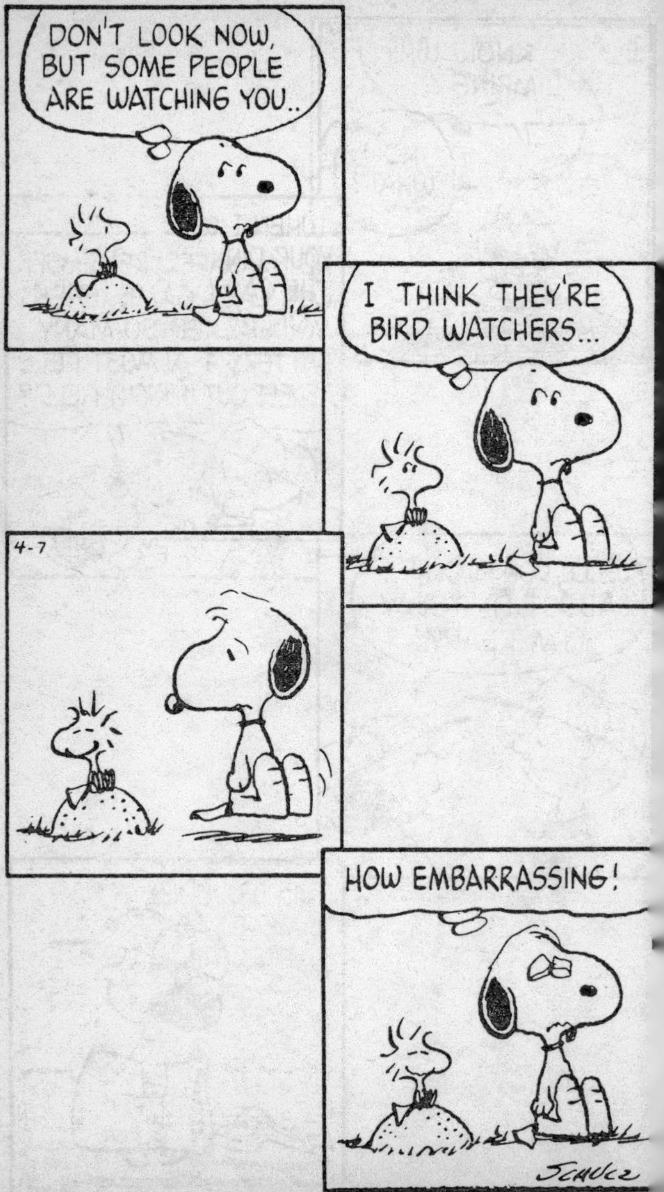
DON'T LOOK NOW, BUT SOME PEOPLE ARE WATCHING YOU..
I THINK THEY'RE BIRD WATCHERS...
4-7
HOW EMBARRASSING!

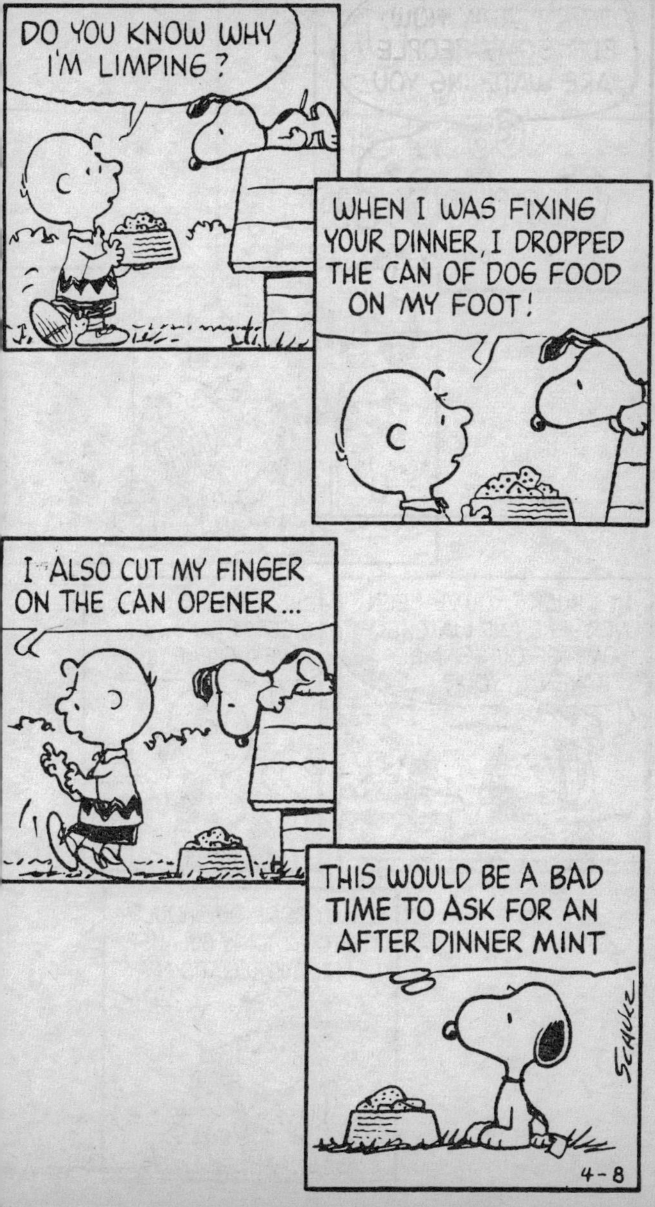
DO YOU KNOW WHY I'M LIMPING?
WHEN I WAS FIXING YOUR DINNER, I DROPPED THE CAN OF DOG FOOD ON MY FOOT!
I ALSO CUT MY FINGER ON THE CAN OPENER...
THIS WOULD BE A BAD TIME TO ASK FOR AN AFTER DINNER MINT
SCHULZ
4-8

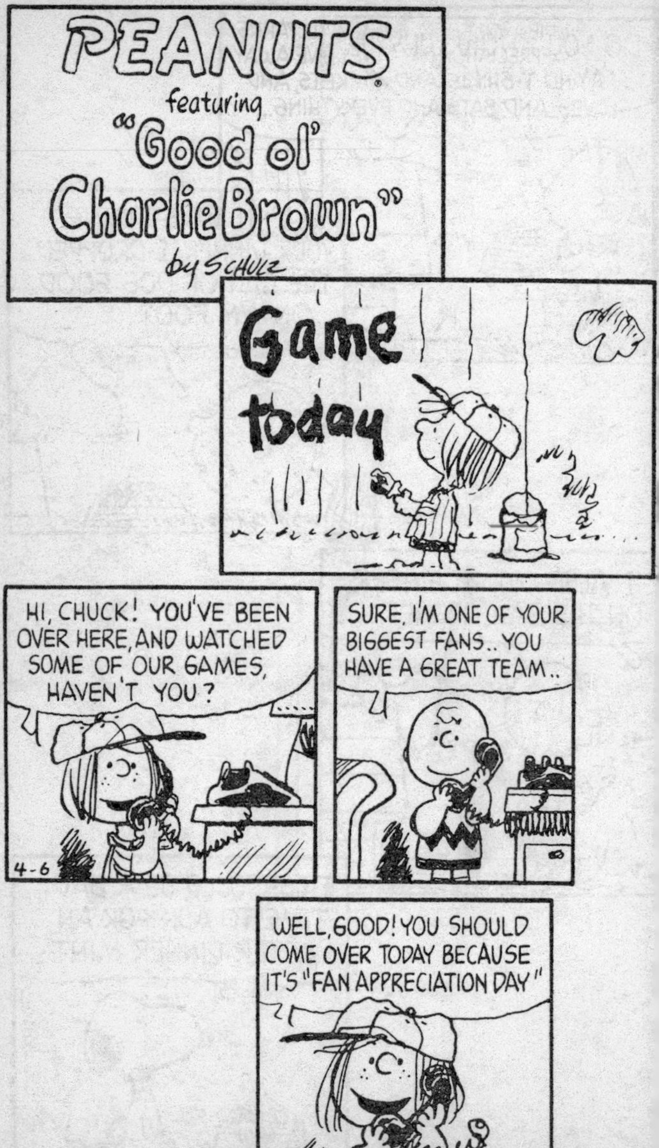
PEANUTS
featuring
"Good ol' Charlie Brown"
by SCHULZ
Game today
HI, CHUCK! YOU'VE BEEN OVER HERE, AND WATCHED SOME OF OUR GAMES, HAVEN'T YOU?
4-6
SURE, I'M ONE OF YOUR BIGGEST FANS.. YOU HAVE A GREAT TEAM..
WELL, GOOD! YOU SHOULD COME OVER TODAY BECAUSE IT'S "FAN APPRECIATION DAY"

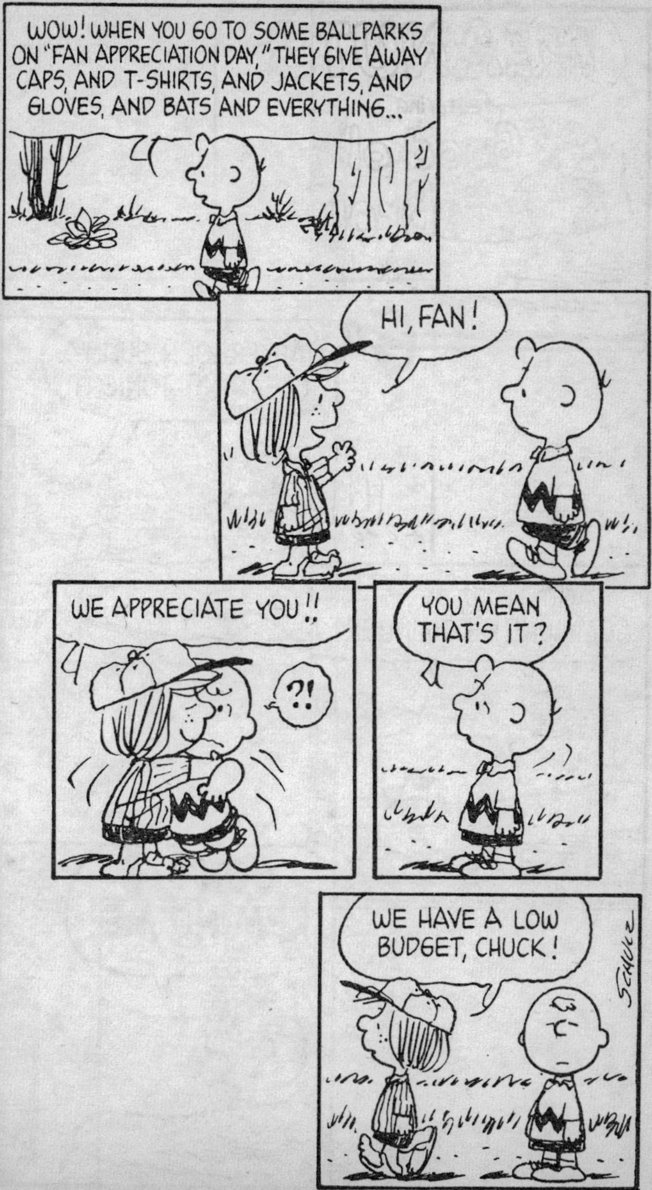
WOW! WHEN YOU GO TO SOME BALLPARKS ON "FAN APPRECIATION DAY," THEY GIVE AWAY CAPS, AND T-SHIRTS, AND JACKETS, AND GLOVES, AND BATS AND EVERYTHING...
HI, FAN!
WE APPRECIATE YOU!!
?!
YOU MEAN THAT'S IT?
WE HAVE A LOW BUDGET, CHUCK!
SCHULZ

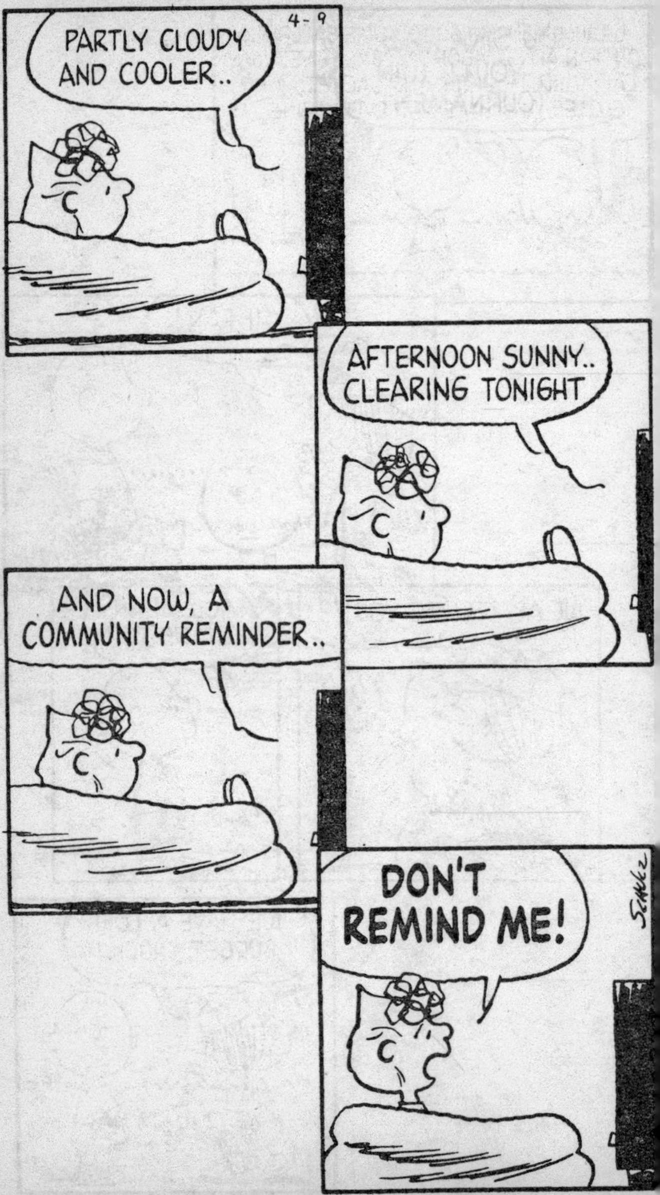
4-9
PARTLY CLOUDY AND COOLER..
AFTERNOON SUNNY.. CLEARING TONIGHT
AND NOW, A COMMUNITY REMINDER..
DON'T REMIND ME!
SCHULZ

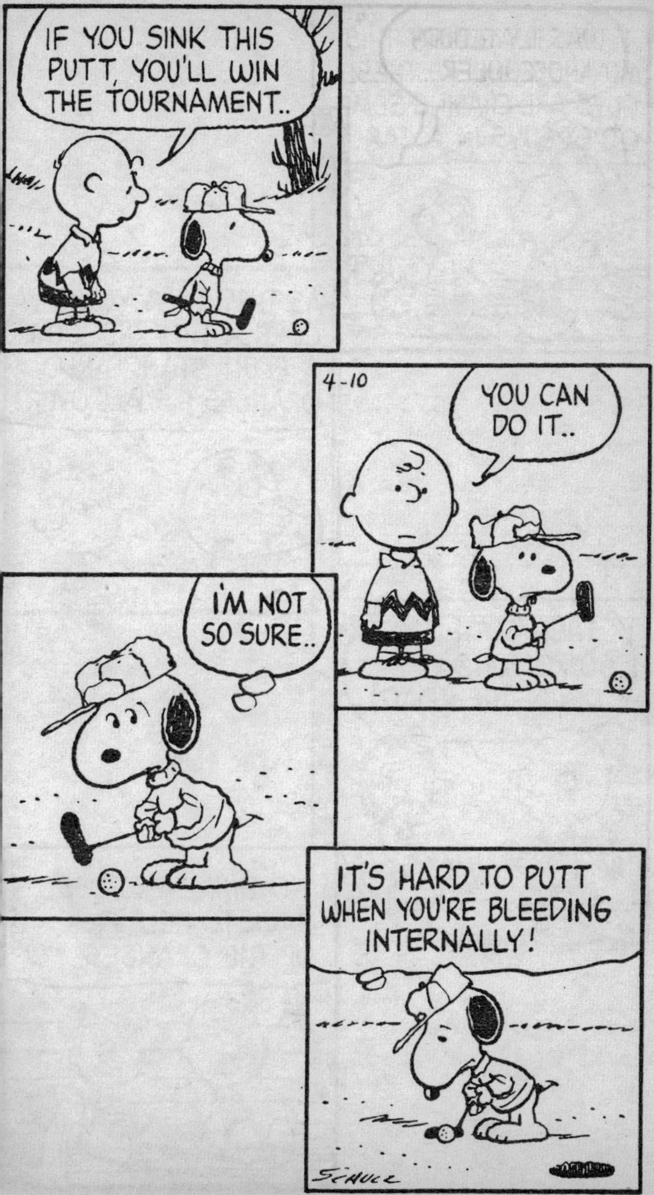
IF YOU SINK THIS PUTT, YOU'LL WIN THE TOURNAMENT..
4-10
YOU CAN DO IT..
I'M NOT SO SURE..
IT'S HARD TO PUTT WHEN YOU'RE BLEEDING INTERNALLY!

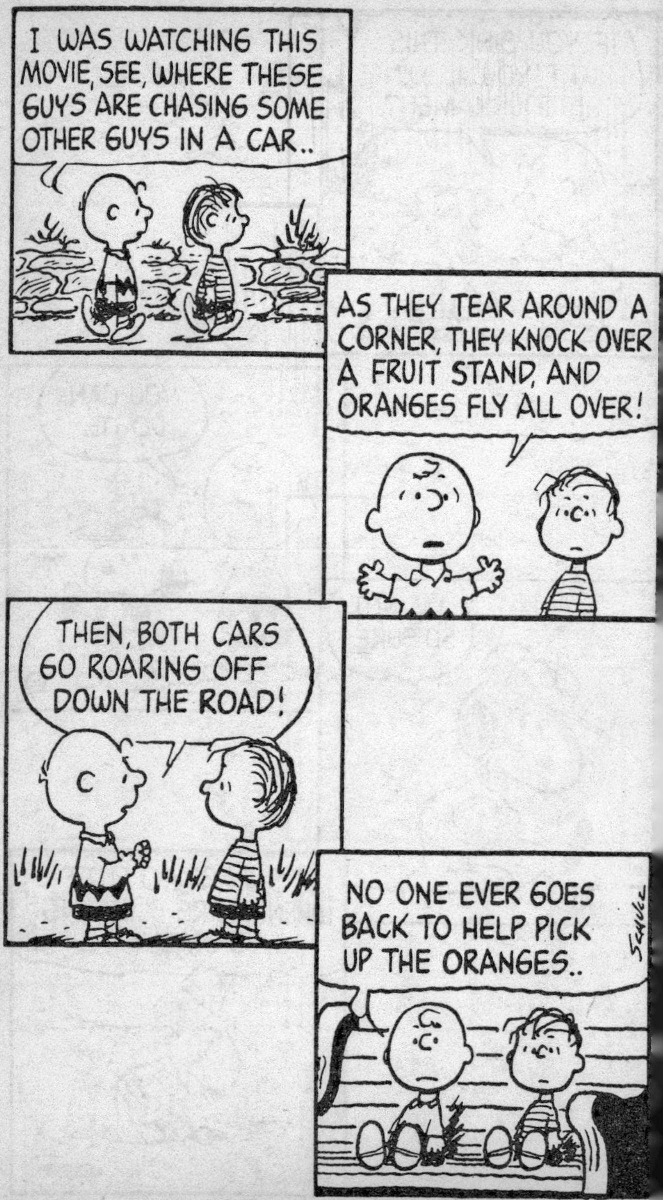
I WAS WATCHING THIS MOVIE, SEE, WHERE THESE GUYS ARE CHASING SOME OTHER GUYS IN A CAR..
AS THEY TEAR AROUND A CORNER, THEY KNOCK OVER A FRUIT STAND, AND ORANGES FLY ALL OVER!
THEN, BOTH CARS GO ROARING OFF DOWN THE ROAD!
NO ONE EVER GOES BACK TO HELP PICK UP THE ORANGES..
SCHULZ

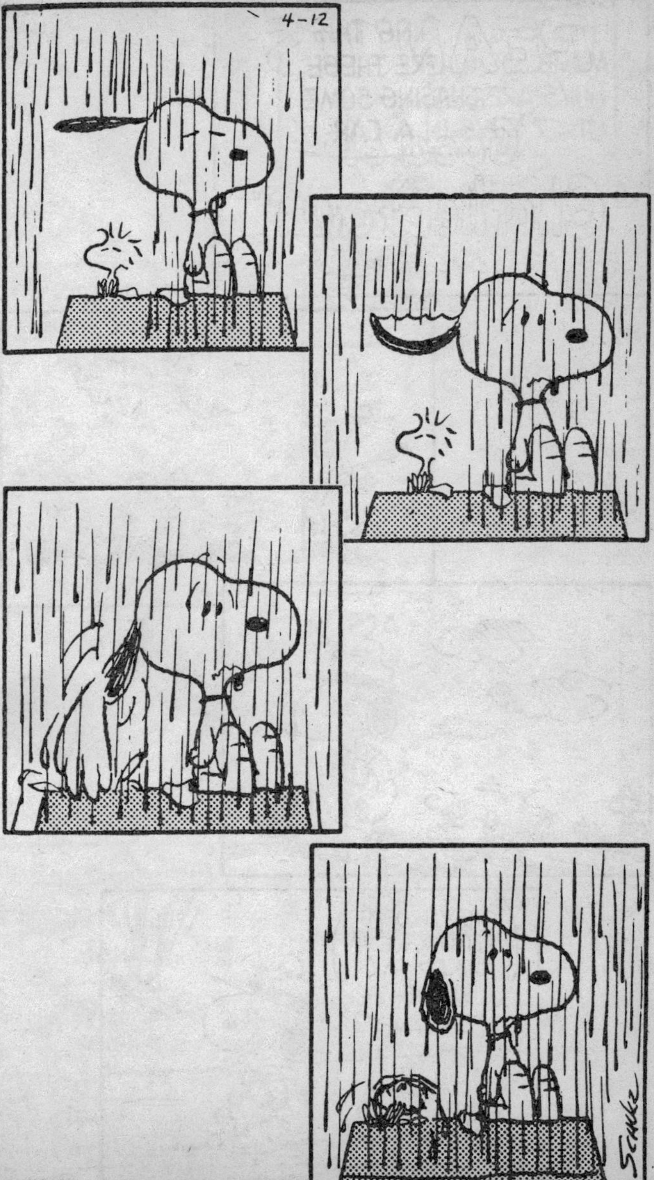
4-12
SCHULZ

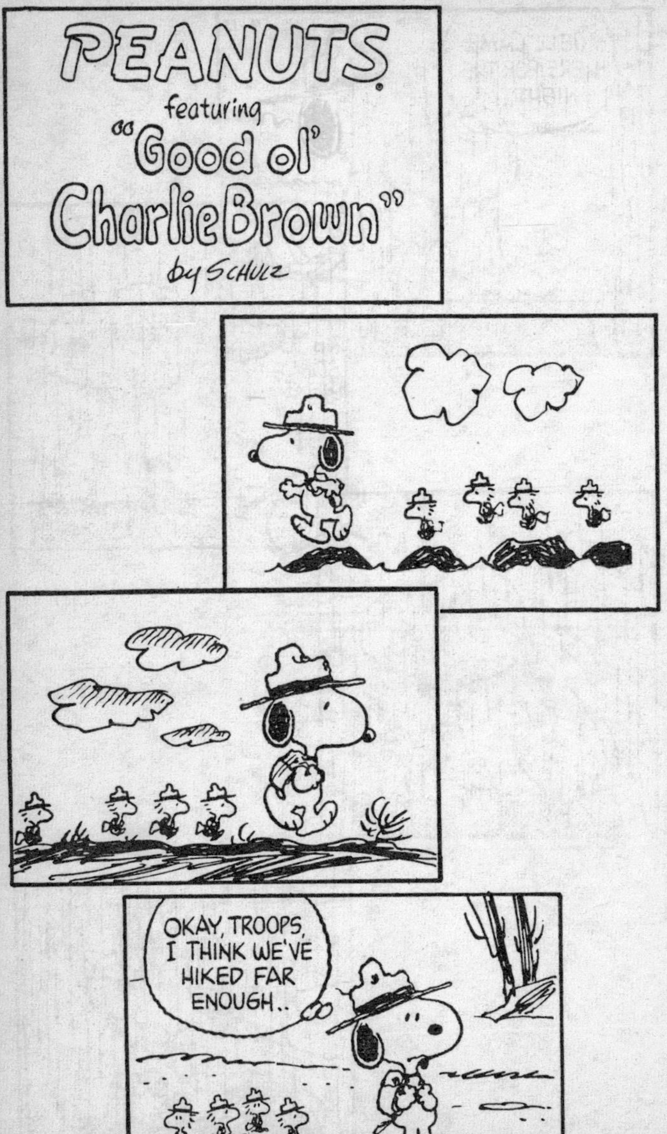
PEANUTS
featuring
"Good ol' Charlie Brown"
by SCHULZ
OKAY, TROOPS, I THINK WE'VE HIKED FAR ENOUGH..

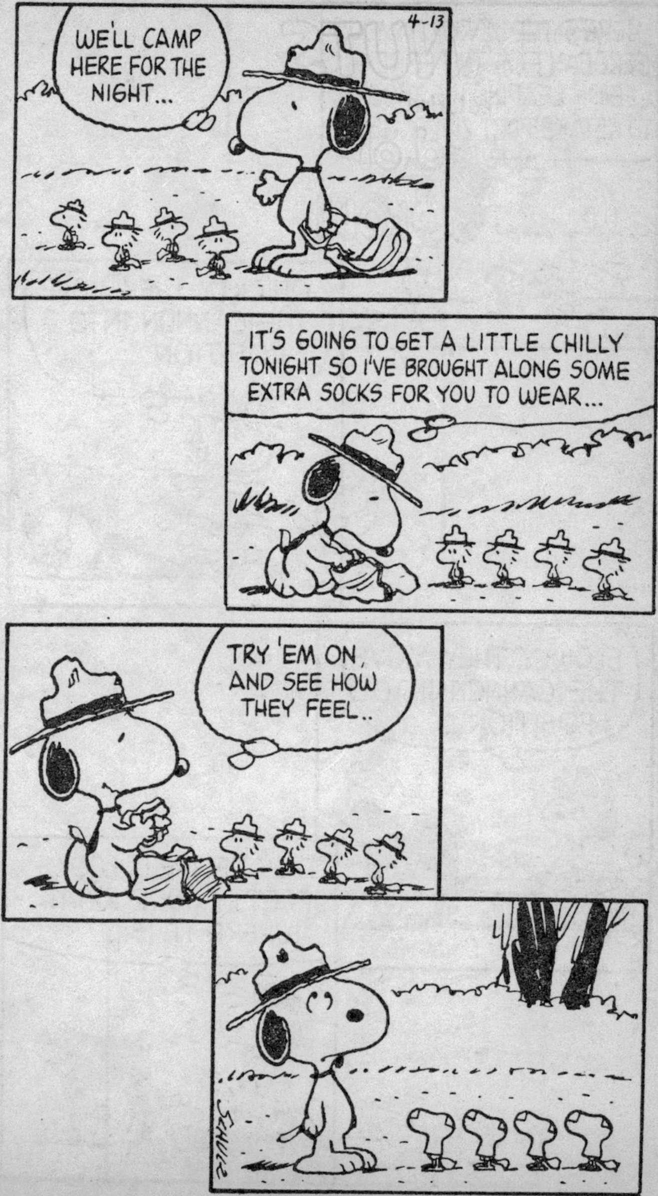

4-13
WE'LL CAMP HERE FOR THE NIGHT...
IT'S GOING TO GET A LITTLE CHILLY TONIGHT SO I'VE BROUGHT ALONG SOME EXTRA SOCKS FOR YOU TO WEAR...
TRY 'EM ON, AND SEE HOW THEY FEEL..
SCHULZ

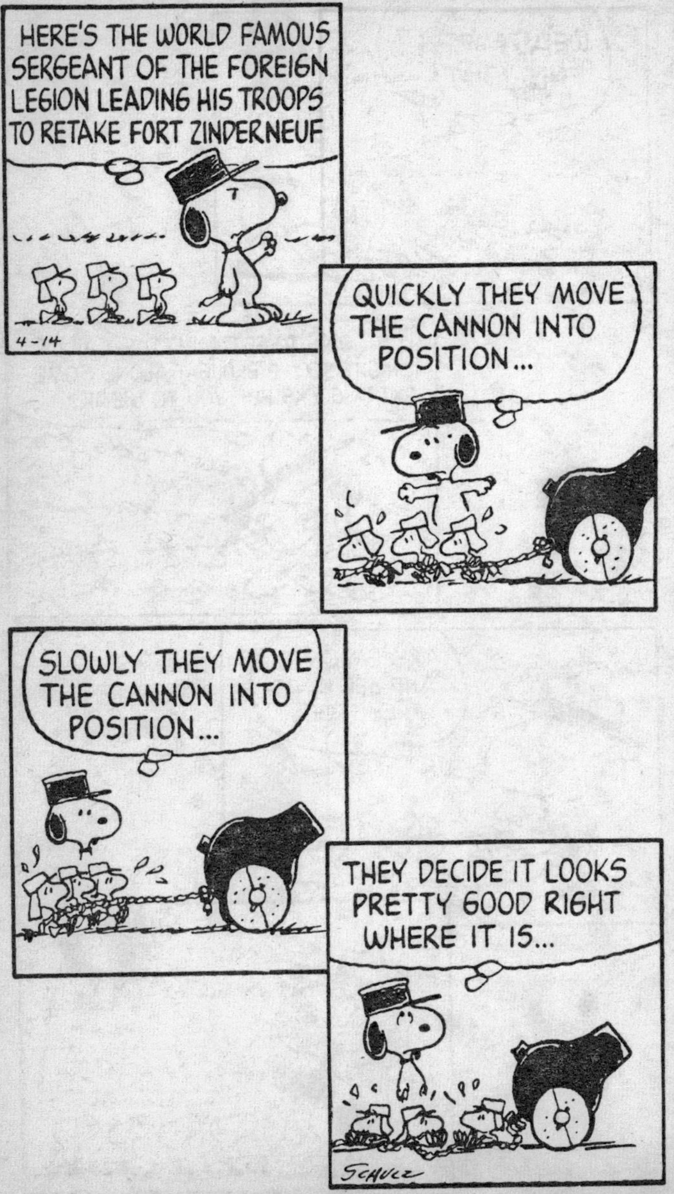
HERE'S THE WORLD FAMOUS SERGEANT OF THE FOREIGN LEGION LEADING HIS TROOPS TO RETAKE FORT ZINDERNEUF
4-14
QUICKLY THEY MOVE THE CANNON INTO POSITION...
SLOWLY THEY MOVE THE CANNON INTO POSITION...
THEY DECIDE IT LOOKS PRETTY GOOD RIGHT WHERE IT IS...
SCHULZ

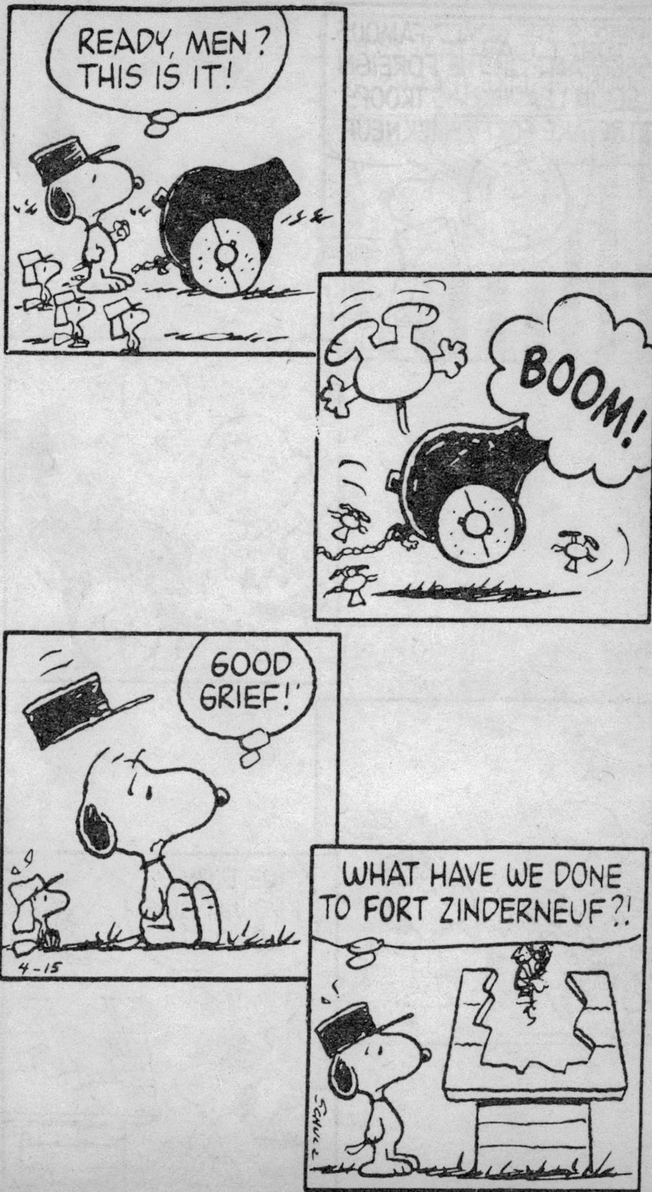
READY, MEN? THIS IS IT!
BOOM!
GOOD GRIEF!
4-15
WHAT HAVE WE DONE TO FORT ZINDERNEUF?!
SCHULZ

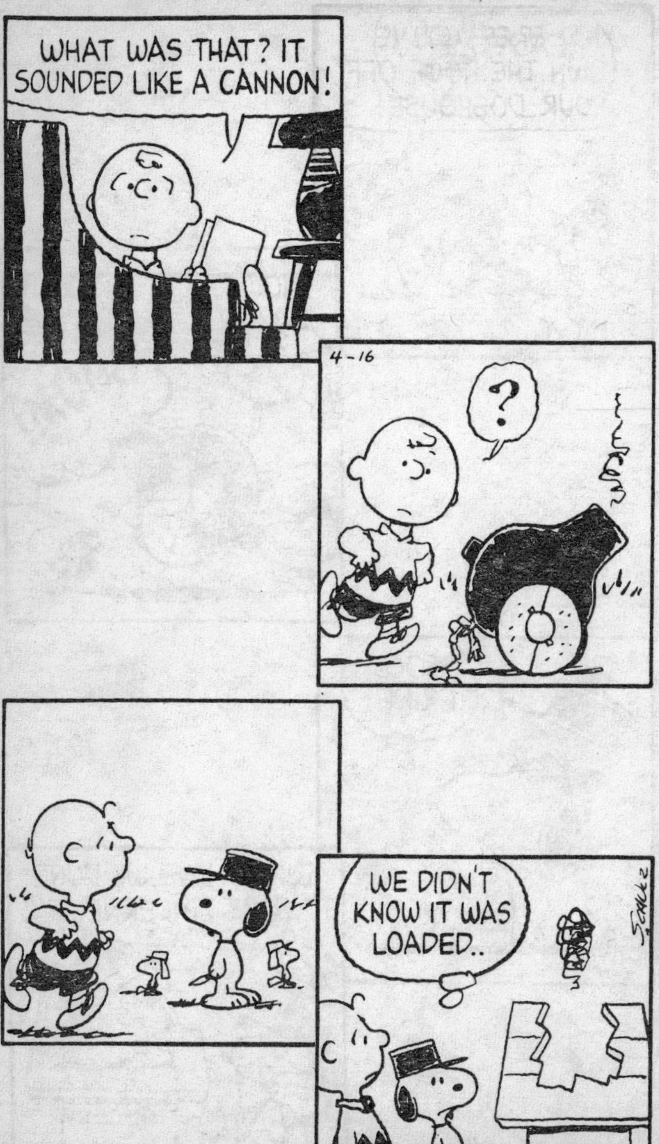
WHAT WAS THAT? IT SOUNDED LIKE A CANNON!
4-16
?
WE DIDN'T KNOW IT WAS LOADED..

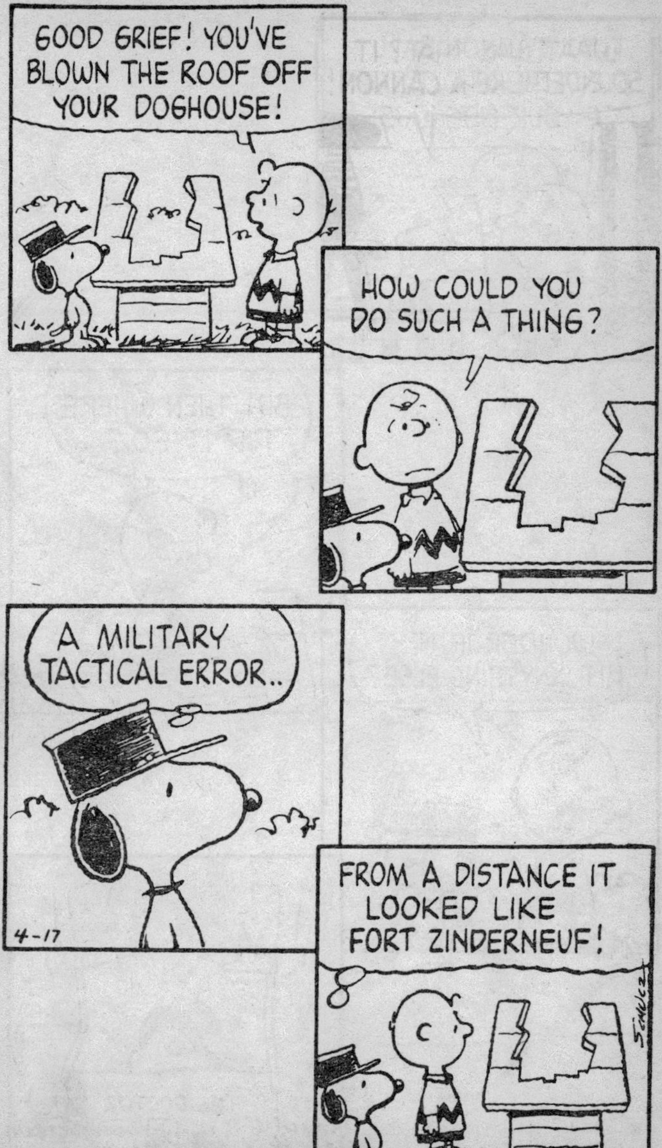
GOOD GRIEF! YOU'VE BLOWN THE ROOF OFF YOUR DOGHOUSE!
HOW COULD YOU DO SUCH A THING?
A MILITARY TACTICAL ERROR..
FROM A DISTANCE IT LOOKED LIKE FORT ZINDERNEUF!
4-17
SCHULZ

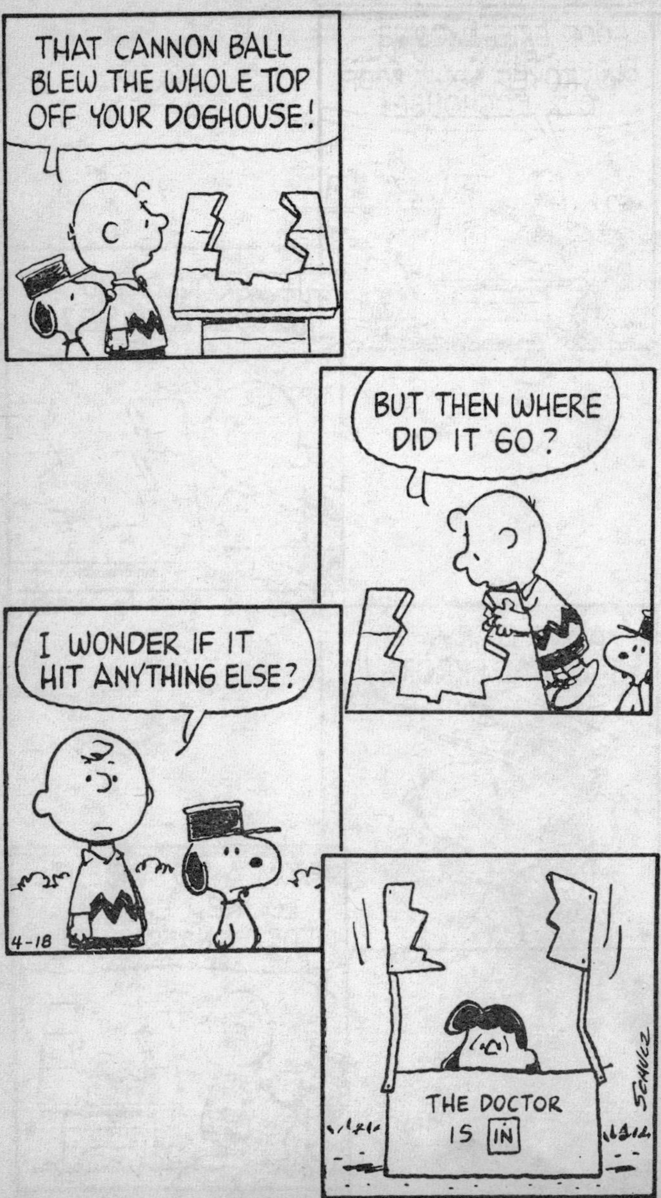
THAT CANNON BALL BLEW THE WHOLE TOP OFF YOUR DOGHOUSE!
BUT THEN WHERE DID IT GO?
I WONDER IF IT HIT ANYTHING ELSE?
4-18
THE DOCTOR IS IN
SCHULZ

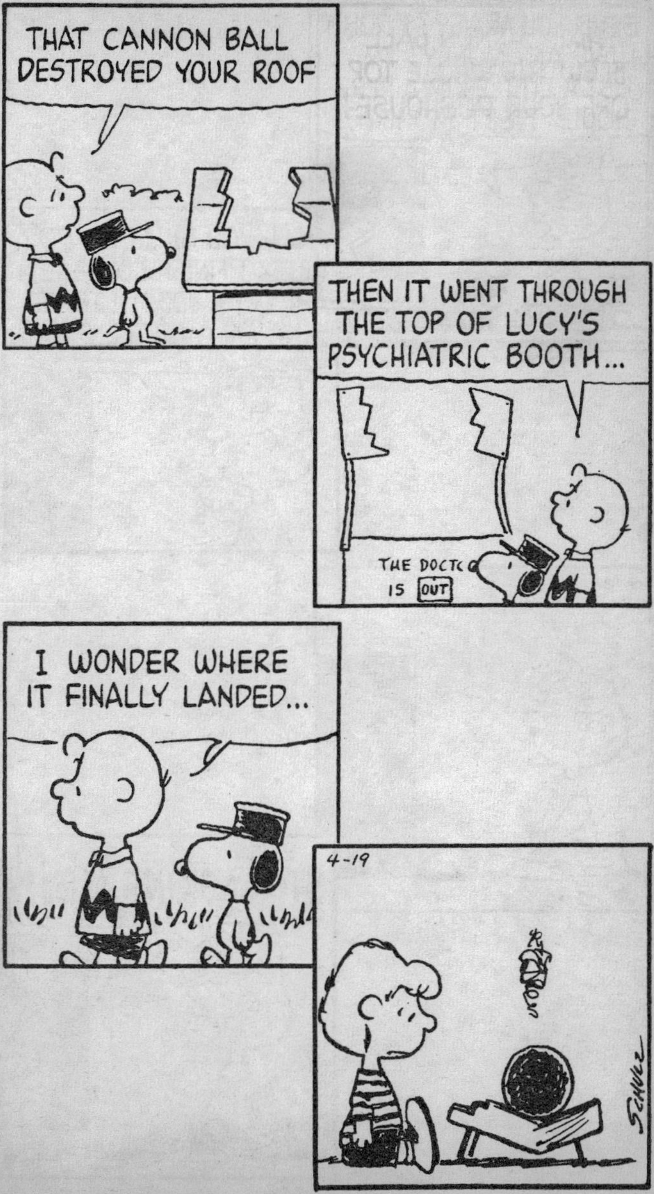
THAT CANNON BALL DESTROYED YOUR ROOF
THEN IT WENT THROUGH THE TOP OF LUCY'S PSYCHIATRIC BOOTH...
THE DOCT
IS OUT
I WONDER WHERE IT FINALLY LANDED...
4-19
SCHULZ

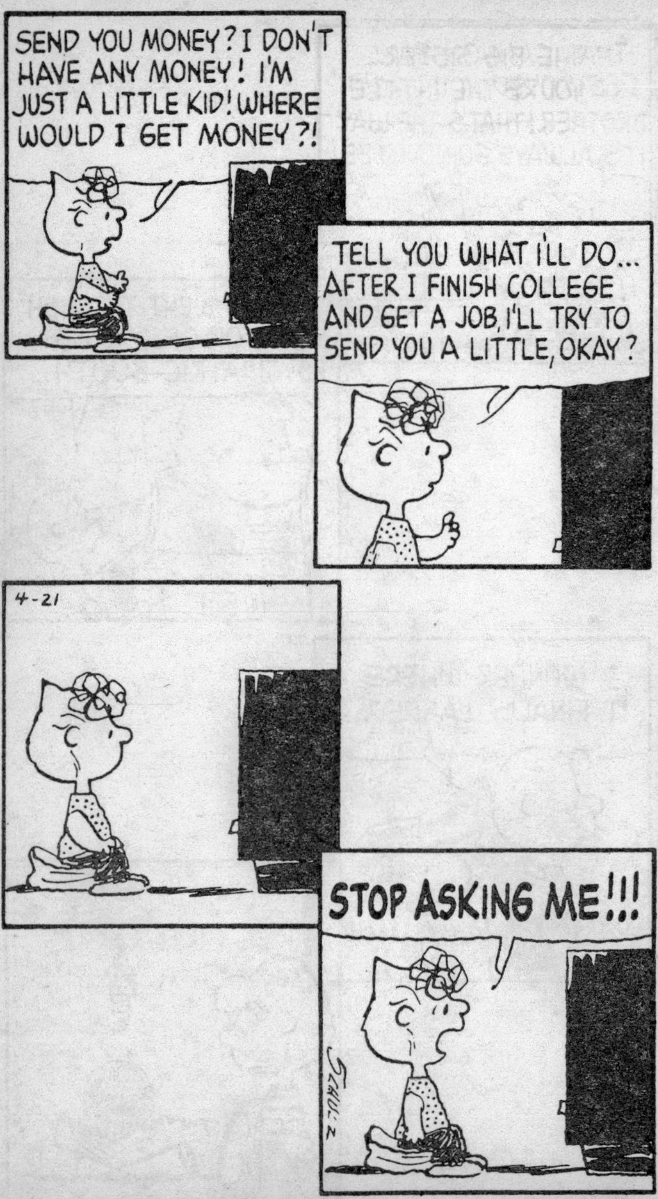
SEND YOU MONEY? I DON'T HAVE ANY MONEY! I'M JUST A LITTLE KID! WHERE WOULD I GET MONEY?!
TELL YOU WHAT I'LL DO... AFTER I FINISH COLLEGE AND GET A JOB, I'LL TRY TO SEND YOU A LITTLE, OKAY?
4-21
STOP ASKING ME!!!
SCHULZ

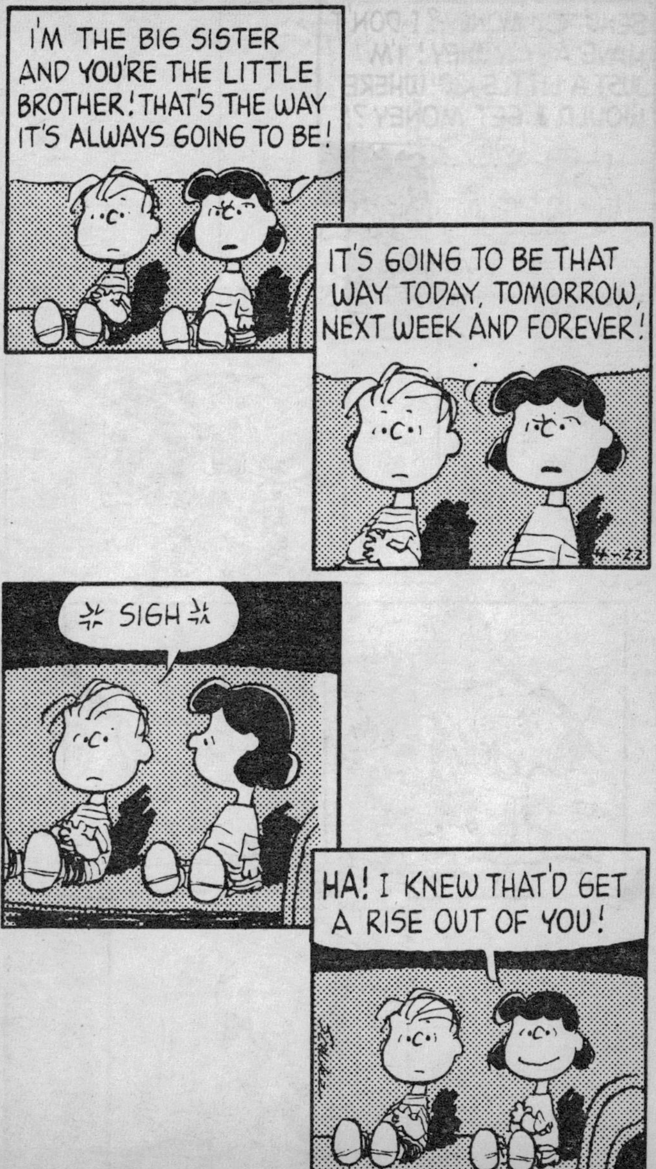
I'M THE BIG SISTER AND YOU'RE THE LITTLE BROTHER! THAT'S THE WAY IT'S ALWAYS GOING TO BE!
IT'S GOING TO BE THAT WAY TODAY, TOMORROW, NEXT WEEK AND FOREVER!
4-22
* SIGH *
HA! I KNEW THAT'D GET A RISE OUT OF YOU!

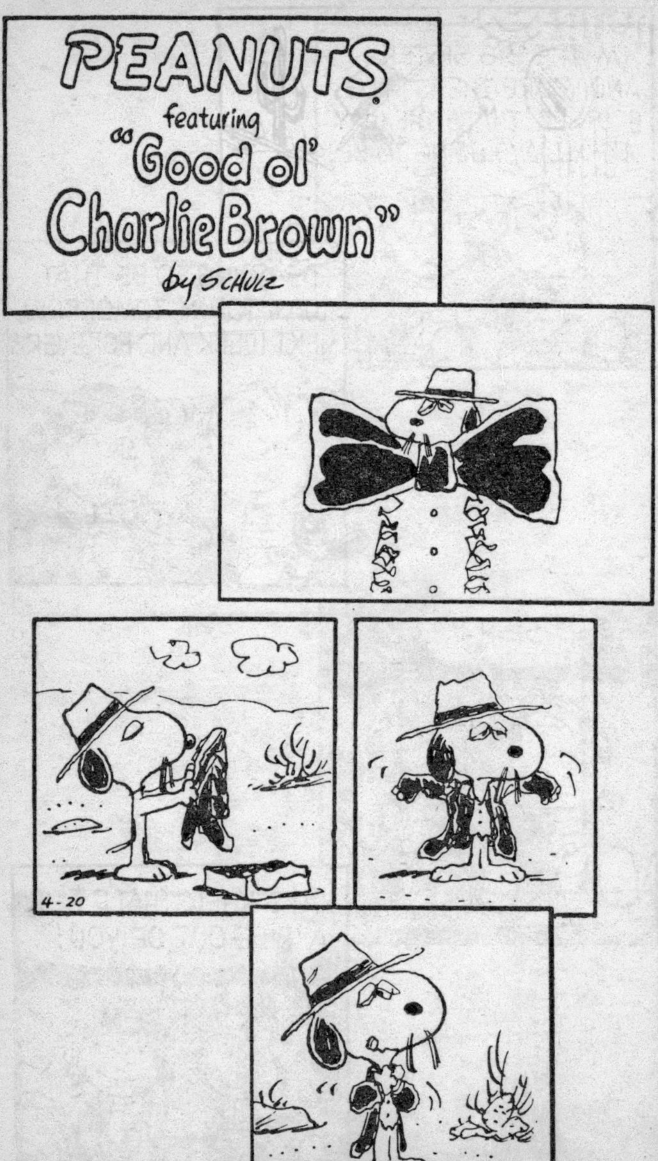

PEANUTS
featuring
"Good ol' Charlie Brown"
by SCHULZ
4-20

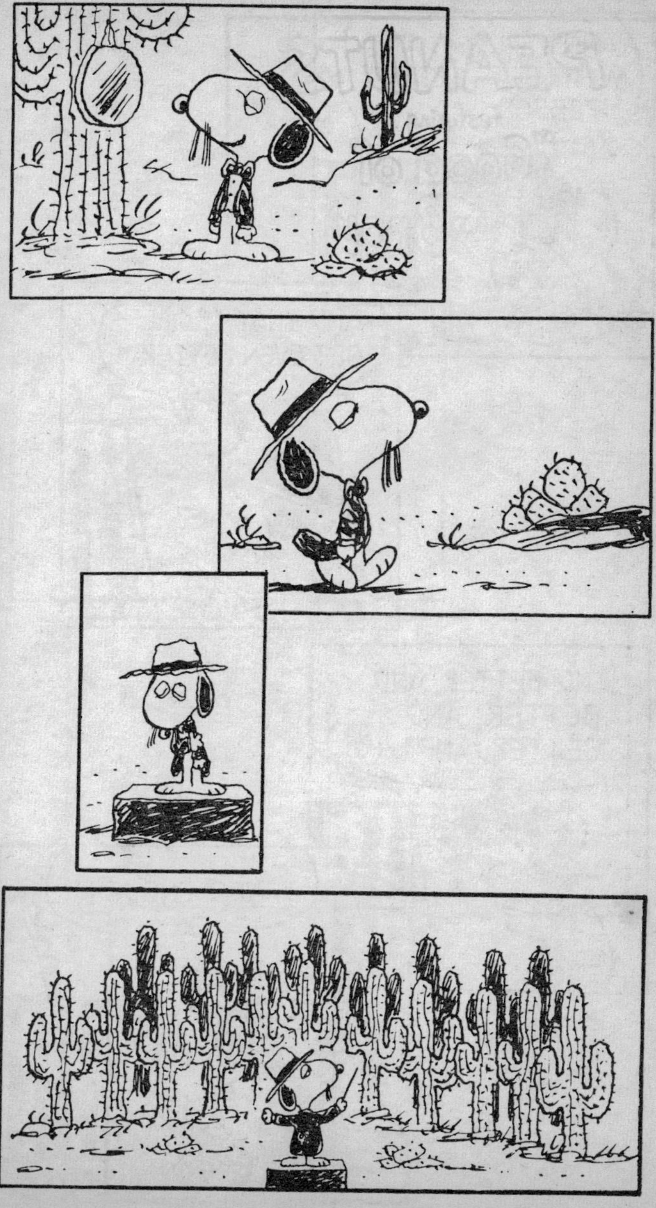

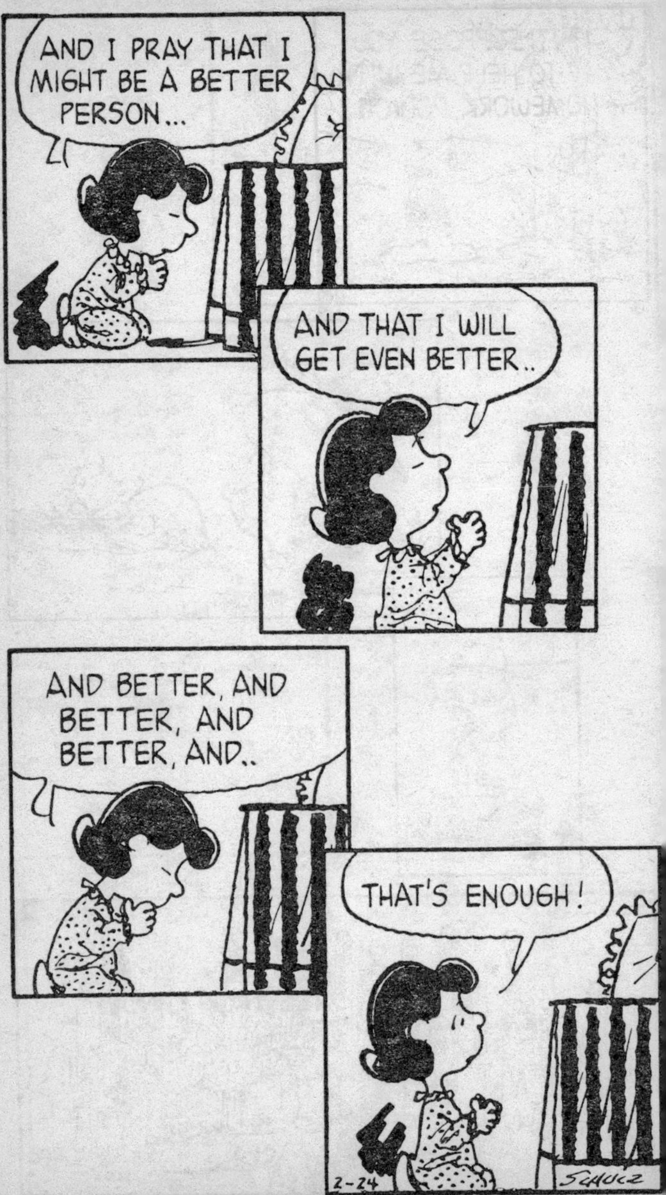
AND I PRAY THAT I MIGHT BE A BETTER PERSON...
AND THAT I WILL GET EVEN BETTER..
AND BETTER, AND BETTER, AND BETTER, AND..
THAT'S ENOUGH!
2-24
SCHULZ

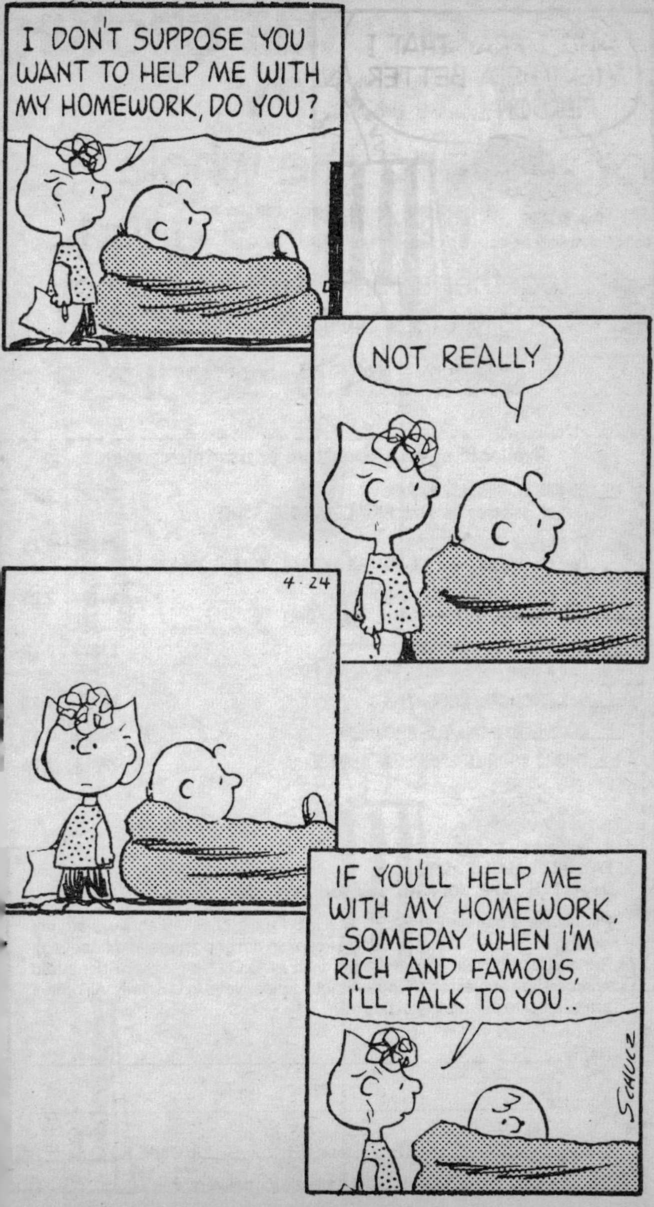
I DON'T SUPPOSE YOU WANT TO HELP ME WITH MY HOMEWORK, DO YOU?
NOT REALLY
4-24
IF YOU'LL HELP ME WITH MY HOMEWORK, SOMEDAY WHEN I'M RICH AND FAMOUS, I'LL TALK TO YOU..
SCHULZ

CHARLIE BROWN, SNOOPY and the whole PEANUTS® gang...

Copr. © 1952
United Feature Syndicate, Inc.

together again with another set of daily trials and tribulations by

CHARLES M. SCHULZ

Available at your bookstore or use this coupon.

___ GO FOR IT, CHARLIE BROWN (Vol III, selected from DR. BEAGLE AND MR. HYDE)	20793	2.25
___ IT'S CHOW TIME SNOOPY (Vol I, selected from DR. BEAGLE AND MR. HYDE)	21355	2.25
___ LOOK OUT BEHIND YOU, SNOOPY (Vol I from HERE COMES THE APRIL FOOL)	21196	2.25
___ DON'T BET ON IT SNOOPY (Vol II from HERE COMES THE APRIL FOOL)	21333	2.25
___ GET PHYSICAL, SNOOPY!	20789	2.25
___ LET'S PARTY, CHARLIE BROWN	20608	2.25
___ THIS IS YOUR LIFE, CHARLIE BROWN	23918	2.25

FAWCETT MAIL SALES
Dept. TAF, 201 E. 50th St., New York, N.Y. 10022

Please send me the FAWCETT BOOKS I have checked above. I am enclosing $..................(add 50¢ per copy to cover postage and handling). Send check or money order—no cash or C.O.D.'s please. Prices and numbers are subject to change without notice. Valid in U.S. only. All orders are subject to availability of books.

Name_____

Address_____

City_____State_____Zip Code_____

Allow at least 4 weeks for delivery.

TAF-3